JACOB'S WAR

Visit us at www.boldstrokesbooks.com

By the Author

Lake Effect Snow

Collision Course

Jacob's War

JACOB'S WAR

by

C.P. Rowlands

2012

JACOB'S WAR

© 2012 BY C.P. ROWLANDS. ALL RIGHTS RESERVED.

ISBN 10: 1-60282-740-0
ISBN 13: 978-1-60282-740-0

THIS TRADE PAPERBACK ORIGINAL IS PUBLISHED BY
BOLD STROKES BOOKS, INC.
P.O. BOX 249
VALLEY FALLS, NY 12185

FIRST EDITION: SEPTEMBER 2012

CREDITS

EDITOR: CINDY CRESAP
PRODUCTION DESIGN: SUSAN RAMUNDO
COVER DESIGN BY SHERI (GRAPHICARTIST2020@HOTMAIL.COM)

Acknowledgments

Twenty-three years ago, we bought this house and met a wonderful family several houses away. They were a traditional family with four little boys, mother, and father. The youngest was in diapers. They were true neighborhood kids and we loved them like our own children. Those little boys helped us year-round as they grew up—they even brought in the groceries, mowed our yard, and shoveled our walks in the winter. Today two of those little boys are in jail, due to drugs. Because of them, I wrote this book.

Thanks to all the usual suspects and new folks that were a huge help in the writing of this book: John, Rosy, Randy, Jan, Cabot, Nikki, Michelle, Sue, Linda, Lance, Bret, Shan, Chad, Ryan, Sherry, David, Jeanne, Judy, Angie, Boz, and Sharon. A special thank-you to my partner, Gloria, for putting up with me during the long and sometimes bizarre investigation of drugs and law enforcement.

Some of you read it for me and some of you provided professional insight and facts. And some of this story is yours. I've never seen anyone work as hard or as many hours as law enforcement, whether it's at a local, county, State, or Federal level. Any errors in the translation of law enforcement procedures and manufacture of drugs are mine, not yours.

As I say, in this book, drugs aren't particular and don't care about people. They don't care who you are, how much good you do, or what kind of life you lead. Drugs just want you to love them.

Thanks for accepting my book, Rad, and thank you, Cindy, for all your help, hard work, and advice on what I tried to write. As I say every time I have the chance, I am proud to be a Bold Strokes author.

Dedication

To the hardest working street cop I've ever known:
Field Sgt. Jennifer Boswell

CHAPTER ONE

February 28
Late in the afternoon

Katie Blackburn tugged on her winter boots while keeping an eye on the latest weather forecast on the computer. "Be careful, people," the announcer said. "We've got fourteen inches of snow and more on the way."

"No kidding," Katie muttered as the wind slapped her office windows hard.

"Winds are gusting past fifty miles per hour. Most Milwaukee businesses are closed and—"

"Not this business. Yet." Katie turned the computer off.

"Ms. Blackburn?" The night security guard leaned into the reception area of her office. "Are you going home soon?"

"Just leaving, John," Katie said as she zipped up her long coat. "Has everyone else gone?" There were five other companies in the Howell Avenue Business Center and, as usual, she was the last to leave.

"There was a white pickup parked beside your car about twenty minutes ago when I started my rounds on the top floor. By the time I got down here, it had gone. Were you expecting anyone?"

"No, no one. A white pickup?" Katie turned off her desk light and walked into the front room. "I'm headed for Mom's monthly poker party. Wish me luck." She grinned at him and shifted the load she carried in her arms. John had been here when she bought this space for her advertising agency. Since then, they had closed this place together many times.

"It was a big truck, four doors, with an odd electric blue hood ornament. I've never seen it before." He took one of her bags while she locked her door. "I'll walk you out."

Katie pulled her hood up and tightened her scarf around her neck. As she expected, the wind hit them like a hammer when they stepped outside. It rocked her silver Chevy SUV Explorer as she wrestled with the door. John hung on to the vehicle's frame and shielded her from the wind while she put her weekend work and bags on the backseat—

"What the hell?" With a startled gasp, she jerked back into John.

There was a body on the floor of her car.

He leaned past her. "God, it's a woman. She's alive, but look at the blood."

"Call the police, now." Katie slammed the door and got in the front seat behind the wheel. "Urgent Care is only a half block away. I'll meet them there."

"No, Ms. Blackburn. Wait…" The wind took his words. John stepped away as Katie backed the SUV out and headed for the clinic.

❖

"God almighty." Allison Jacob gripped the steering wheel as a powerful gust shook her car. She squinted at the Howell Avenue police station, which was only a smudge in the near darkness. The big engine rumbled, missed a few beats, then caught again as deep snow grabbed the car's wheels. Her eyes were riveted on what she hoped was the station's driveway.

"Shit." She'd hit the curb and landed on the sidewalk. AJ shifted the car into reverse and blasted backward through a snowdrift and into the street with a breathtaking thump. She shifted the car into first, but before she could move, red and blue lights lit up beside her. She powered down her window.

"Did I see your car on the sidewalk?" Bill Whiteaker, Chief of the Milwaukee Special Investigation Section, leaned out into the storm to taunt her.

"I missed the driveway."

The chief and his driver both laughed. "Get a real car and sell that hunk of metal," Bill said.

AJ revved the engine and the big growl made them all smile. "The last time you said that about this car, it cost you, big time. I took you with miles to spare."

"That was before we got these new ones." Bill thumped the side of the new police car. The snow fell off the cruiser door like a waterfall.

"You think?" AJ teased him. "You're going to get your suit all snowy. Sir."

"Ah hell, come on, I'll buy you a burger for dinner. I haven't seen you all day."

AJ followed them into the station's parking lot, zipped up her coat, and snapped on matching earmuffs. Together, they pushed through the snow and fought the storm to the Copper Penny, the bar across the street. Bill and his driver, a rookie named Talley, held the door against the wind as AJ ducked under their arms into the warmth. The bar smelled like hamburgers and beer.

"Jacob," one of the off-duty uniforms at the bar yelled at her. "Shut the door. There's more snow inside than in the parking lot." The other two cops beside him laughed until they saw the chief behind her and went back to their food. AJ grinned at their reflections in the bar mirror as she passed behind them, discreetly checking out the bar. Nice little crowd, she thought, considering the weather. People were catching a quick burger before they tried their luck against the blizzard.

A red-haired woman in jeans and a white button-down shirt danced by herself in the middle of the room, singing at the top of her lungs. She held on to a bottle of beer like it was God.

AJ found a chair at the back of the bar. It was away from the noise and the rest of the customers. She sank into a chair with a tired sigh. The music was old. Ella Fitzgerald? The redhead didn't have a bad voice, but she looked tanked.

Bill sent Talley to the bar with their order. "Where were you all day?" he said.

"On National Avenue. I teamed up with one of your cops, Bonnie Logan. Man, she's good. Some boys were mixing it up, a hit and slip. By the time we got them processed and I left Central, the storm was in full swing."

Bill shook his finger at her. "They warned me about you. You've been running on next to no sleep since you got here, and I'm under strict orders to see that you eat at least once a day." Bill turned her face toward the light. "How'd you get the mouse on your cheek?"

"I was leaning into a van that had Clorox, batteries, and other stuff, trying to decide if they cooked meth in the vehicle. It sure smelled like it. A woman shoved me into the metal frame." She touched her face as if she were just aware of the bruise. "It's always tough in those neighborhoods. This is your city. You know how it goes."

"Yeah, I do," Bill said as the food arrived. "Jock has been trying to reach you."

"Mr. DEA?" AJ grabbed some fries.

"They caught a vanload of ephedrine coming up from Chicago early this morning. Jock said you weren't answering your phone."

"He called?" AJ fumbled with the phone clipped to her belt. "There aren't any messages. Did Jock and the boys follow the van?"

"No, they impounded it. A trooper stopped the vehicle because a headlight was out. One thing led to another, and someone called your drug unit."

"Damn. If State turned it over to Jock, he should have released the van and tailed it." AJ took a big, satisfying bite of the hamburger. "You know what's wrong with him, don't you? When Charles Ryan formed this task force with you and the DEA, Jock thought the job was his. My job. He didn't want to work with my ATF group or you. I made him a team leader, but he's still ticked.

The door jerked open and Jock strode inside.

"Where have you been?" He leaned toward her.

"Working," AJ said after she swallowed the food. He looked tired and clearly angry.

Jock moved closer. He turned his back to the room. "You look like crap."

"Good to see you too." She smiled calmly at him. "What's up?" Nothing short of a heart attack was going to keep her away from this food.

"Did Bill tell you that we picked up some green on the interstate today?"

"He was just giving me the information."

"That and two barrels of Oxys. Everything's across the street in the evidence locker. Oh, and thirty-some throwaways. Your guys are going over those guns right now. They're processing the driver downtown at intake."

"Oxys? Shit." AJ frowned. "Jock, you should have released the van and followed it. Remember, we're supposed to be flying under the radar. You should have waited until someone took delivery. You blew the opportunity to take down a meth lab or a distributor. That way you get the drugs and the people who are using them, the whole enchilada." AJ took another bite.

"Jesus, AJ. Release and follow them?"

"Your job—our job—is to find out where it came from, who takes delivery." She ignored the dragon breath Jock spewed into her face. "Want a burger with us?"

"No." He straightened and unzipped his jacket. "I ran into Michael's girl gang twice this week but found nothing except a little paraphernalia on one of them."

Bill's head came up. "It wasn't on the daily log."

AJ set her burger down. "Jock, everything's important, even paraphernalia." She held his gaze. "Log it all in so I know what you're up to. It's not rocket science."

He leaned closer, his fingers curled around the edge of her table. "I'm too busy for the daily chatter." Jock had a snarky expression on his face. "We can't let a load of illegal drugs go, or follow them. And I don't care if you are Charles Ryan's golden girl or that our supervisor has this little *magic plan* for us. It's crap."

Light spit from his sarcastic, angry words fell across her face, but AJ stayed neutral. "It's not crap. It's your job. And make sure you keep up with the daily feed from everyone." She took another bite of the burger.

"Meet us over at the station." Bill stood.

Jock started to say something but clamped his mouth tight, zipped his jacket, and left. The door blew shut with a loud bang behind him.

AJ finally let her anger show. "Damn it. Two years with that jerk. If he doesn't get his act together and soon, I'm sending him home. Our entire team logs everything in daily except him and—" An anguished cry interrupted her.

The dancing woman clutched at her chest, then fell awkwardly to the floor. She hit a metal bar stool, splattering blood everywhere. Instinctively, AJ moved to the floor beside the woman. She bent to see if there was breath, but there was nothing. "Call the bus," she yelled, pinched the woman's nose, and blew a first breath into the woman's mouth. "Come on, people."

When she yelled, everyone jolted into action. One of the off-duty cops held a clean bar towel to the woman's head while AJ kept breaths and compressions going. When the paramedics arrived, she shoved out of their way but gripped the woman's hand as long as the medics allowed it. The woman had been pretty, once upon a time.

Bill handed her a wet bar towel. "Wipe your face. You'll want to check that woman's blood."

AJ pushed back a gag. She hated the smell of blood. "Did you see her color? I'd bet it was a heart attack." She scrubbed the towel across her face one more time.

"I've known her for a long time. She's a heavy drinker," the bartender said as he ran water in one of his sinks. "Here, wash your hands."

"Could I have her name?"

The bartender wrote it on a bar napkin and handed it to her.

"Lu Wright?" AJ read out loud and he nodded. "Thanks. I'll follow up."

"Good work," one of the cops said to her as he put on his jacket and started for the door.

She went back to her chair and hid her shaking legs under the table, unsure that the woman would even make it to the hospital. "It's cold," she said, examining the rest of the burger. "Well, at least I got some food tonight. Let's go back and take a look at what Jock has in evidence." She looked down at her bloodied shirt. "I'd better change clothes too."

CHAPTER TWO

B eyond angry, Katie walked into the Howell Avenue police station. The police had impounded her car, and neither she nor the policeman had spoken a word on the trip to the station.

This is what she got for being a good citizen. She'd gotten the woman there, alive, but not one person had mentioned that minor fact.

She stomped the snow off her boots onto the floor mat and sulked at the station's front desk, waiting for God knew what. "As if this isn't bad enough," she said under her breath and stared at the storm outside. The lobby was familiar but much smaller than she remembered from the business call she'd made here years ago. It had been an insurance company.

"Oh damn. Mom's party." She rummaged in her coat for her phone and hit speed dial. "Mom, I'm at the police station and—" She took a deep breath while she waited for her mother to calm down. "When I left work there was a woman in the back of my car, on the floor and—no, she wasn't dead, but badly injured."

The policeman who'd driven her here asked her to wait a minute and then went up the stairs.

"What, Mom? No, don't you dare come down here. Do you have any idea what it's like outside? At any rate, they impounded my car so I'm going to be late." She listened for a minute. "I imagine they want what little information I have, which is nothing. I just want my car back. I've got to hang up. I'll be there as soon as I can."

She hung up with a "Holy shit, what's next?" and began to pace to get rid of the weird shakiness running through her.

As if the night wasn't strange enough, her best friend Bonnie, a Milwaukee cop, had been at Urgent Care, finishing up another unrelated call. Bonnie had recognized the victim they took out of Katie's car and yelled—really yelled—at her for not waiting for the police at her office. "Katie, I know this woman. She hangs out with people that have been known to kill," had been her exact words.

Hard boot heels echoed on the marble floor above her, and a blur of brown descended the stairs. A blonde in a dun colored duster held out her hand.

"Ms. Blackburn? I'm Allison Jacob. Thanks for hanging in there for us on such a bad night." Her voice was pleasant and friendly.

"Did I have a choice?" Katie shot back but found herself staring. The person in front of her was knock-me-down cute. Something inside of Katie caught. For some reason, she was on full alert.

"Because of the storm, we're bringing your car here for the night. This would be the time to get what's important to you. I'll let you know when they get here."

Katie felt herself settle a bit in front of Allison Jacob's smile and even forgot her anger for a moment. "The only thing I have with me is my phone. All my personal things, my work, my computer, everything, is in the backseat of that car."

"We'll get it all, I promise. Follow me please."

Like Allison Jacob, the upstairs office was not standard by a long shot. Too many green plants, family photos, and warm colors, plus the biggest desk Katie had ever seen in a police station. Allison hung her long leather duster on a clothes tree, then held out her hand.

"Your coat?"

Katie handed over her coat and took a more thorough look at the woman in front of her. The tan blazer fit her slightly-squared but feminine shoulders beautifully.

"Please. Have a seat," Allison said. She gestured at a chair. "How about some coffee? I was on my way out when Bonnie Logan called from the clinic. You transported a woman there?"

"There was a woman on the floor in the backseat of my car when I left my office. I thought she was dead." Katie's foot was tapping on the floor and she put a hand on her knee, trying to calm down.

Allison picked up her phone. "Bill, would you bring us some coffee?" She turned her head away from Katie but not far enough to hide the grin on her face. "No, Bill. The fresh coffee that I made. And the file we were just looking at, please?"

Katie made herself look away. Allison Jacob was a treat and that genuine smile lifted her mood. Was this the new, modern policewoman? She guessed that they were about the same age. Allison's layered dark blond hair tapered over the ears to her collar, framing high cheek bones…with a bruise? Maybe she was a hands-on cop?

"AJ, open the door," a deep male voice said. "I've got my hands full."

Allison leaned to look around Katie, but Katie was up quickly and opened the door.

An older man glanced briefly at Katie, then at Allison, as he juggled a carafe and cups. He thanked her as he went by.

"Bill, this is the woman that Bonnie called us about, Katie Blackburn. Ms. Blackburn, this is Chief William Whiteaker." He set the coffee on the desk. "Thanks," Allison said and carefully extracted the folder from under his arm.

The chief's glasses caught the lights as he shook hands with Katie and smiled. Another genuine smile, Katie noticed. He was tall, with a little paunch, a full head of white hair, and expensive suit. She'd grown up in police stations, tagging after her father. The chief definitely felt like police, but she wasn't sure about Allison Jacob. AJ? Was that what he'd called her?

"Wait, where are the photos?" Allison said.

He snapped his fingers. "The other file." His voice trailed him out the door.

Katie leaned back in the chair, gripped the coffee cup, and watched Allison Jacob shuffle papers. The anger and frustration popped up inside her again, and she took a deep breath and looked around the unusual office. When she turned back, her gaze connected with Allison's dark, amused eyes.

Allison gestured at the office with a wry expression. "This is Bill's office. He lets me use it when I need to talk to someone. Mine's on the first floor. It's about the size of a broom closet." She looked down at the papers on her desk, then continued. "Correct me if I don't have the right information. Katie L. Blackburn, owner of Blue Ridge, Inc. Your business is just down the road?" She tapped a pen on the paper. "What does Blue Ridge do, please?"

"We're a public relations and advertising firm. Doubled in size over the last eight years." Katie held Allison's gaze. She didn't add that "doubled" meant six employees, not three.

"Your father was a city policeman for twenty-one years until he was injured in the line of duty. You worked for him at Diamond Security?"

"To get through college and two years after I graduated, but it wasn't enough to keep me interested." She took a drink of coffee. "Not enough money in it," she said after a beat.

"You can handle a weapon?"

"I'm not big on guns, but I can manage."

"Ha," Allison said with a light laugh that made Katie smile too. "You outshot a few people who work in this office. Look at this."

Katie took the paper and scanned the information. Last month, she and her youngest brother had taken afternoon target practice at the shooting range where cops traditionally practiced and qualified. How had they gotten this information?

"I got lucky?" Katie smirked but caught herself. *Good Lord, I'm flirting.*

"Actually, Bonnie Logan had quite a bit to say about you when she called me." Allison looked up with a quirky grin. "She told me that you were a good shot. You're friends?"

"Since high school. We worked together at Diamond Security for Dad while we went to college."

Bill Whiteaker stepped back into the room and put some photos on the desk. "I'm on my way home. Anything else?"

"No, that's all. Thanks for the burger." Allison smiled at him.

He smiled again at Katie and was gone before she could say good-bye.

"Do you own a gun?" Allison turned back to Katie.

"Not any longer. I gave it to my brother that day, the afternoon we were at the shooting range. It belonged to our father and he wanted it." Katie leaned forward with her elbows on the desk, irritated. "Why is it important whether or not I have a gun? I'm not a suspect. I'm just someone who understands that every minute counts with a severe injury. All I could think of was getting her to a doctor as soon as possible."

"The gun is still registered to you. Apparently, your brother hasn't done his paperwork. Bonnie gave me a lot of information about you, Ms. Blackburn. I only need to know what connection you might have to the victim. And you have to be wondering why someone chose your car."

"You bet I am," Katie snapped. "Got my weekend off to quite a start."

Allison held up one of the photos. "Do you know, or have you seen, this woman?"

Katie pulled in a quick breath. Was it Lu? No. She exhaled as she looked at the picture. A young woman in a white knit cap that matched her platinum hair looked at the camera with a cocky grin. It was a grainy black-and-white photo, and Katie knew immediately that it was a surveillance shot. The woman obviously knew that she was smiling at a store camera.

"No." Katie shook her head. And what on earth had made her think it might be Lu?

"Look again for me, please."

The woman in the photo leaned against a shopping cart that contained two boxes of diapers. She was tall. The coat was bulky, so Katie couldn't tell about the upper body, but the jeans fit slender, long legs. Katie thought the woman might be as tall as five eight or more. "I don't know her."

Allison nodded, took the photo back, and handed her another.

It was a young man, maybe mid-twenties or older with dark eyes and blond hair. A little handsome, Katie thought. Sensuous mouth and clean-shaven. It looked like a posed shot, not quite portrait quality, but it could be included in a résumé. He was somber, unsmiling.

"No. Not him either." She handed the photo back.

Allison regarded her thoughtfully. "That's the woman who was in your car tonight. The man is her live-in, possibly the father of her child. We're uncertain of their relationship."

"Who are they? I mean, do they have names?"

"She's called Seraph on the streets and he's Michael."

"Seraph? As in an angel?" Katie considered the names. "And Michael. Archangel?"

"I suppose," Allison said as the phone buzzed. "Jacob," Allison said into the receiver. "Okay. Thanks." She took a deep breath and replaced the receiver quietly. "Your car's here. There'll be a box at the front desk for you, so you can pack up what you need to carry. We'll give you a ride home." A line appeared between her eyebrows as she frowned. "And you've never seen that woman before or have any knowledge of her?"

"No," Katie said. "But Bonnie really went off on me for being in the car with her. She said she hangs around with people who… kill?"

"Bonnie is right," Allison said. "Do you have any idea how she got into your car?"

"No idea. I always lock it, but it's possible I forgot." Katie concentrated. She'd asked herself the same question more than once tonight.

"According to the clinic and Bonnie, that woman, Seraph, was wrapped carefully in an old blue blanket. It's apparent she was placed there, just didn't stumble inside. But how, if it was locked? Who else has a key to your car?"

"It was my dad's car, so my mother still has a set of keys. There's an extra key at my house." Katie mentally ticked it off in her mind and realized she hadn't seen the key at her house in quite a while.

For the first time, Allison's posture tensed and she straightened in the chair. "Seraph is an important part of an ongoing investigation.

It looks like your SUV was just a dump site, but that's odd too. Is there someone around that might want to harm you?"

"No, absolutely not. Am I in danger?"

Allison shook her head. "Probably not you, personally, but your car could be if they look for that woman. It's also possible they thought Seraph was dead."

"It was my father's car, and I admit to being attached to it. My uncle owns the dealership where my Dad bought it. I'll get a car from him until I get mine back. Let me call someone. Maybe you won't have to have someone drive me home." Katie held up a finger as in wait-a-minute while she dialed her oldest sister at their mother's. Allison unfolded from the chair and walked to the window while Katie spoke with her sister.

"My sister will come and get me."

"The weather bureau said the storm's winding down. That's good news."

"Take care of my car," Katie said and stood. Still uneasy, her anger lingered.

"We will, I promise. Thank you very much, Ms. Blackburn." Allison handed Katie her coat. "We'll need another conversation after we finish with your car."

"I'm not going anywhere. And it's Katie. Please." Katie bent to zip her coat. "Who do I call if something else…"

Allison took a card from a leather case in her pocket. "This is all you need. Anytime, day or night, Ms. Blackburn—Katie—and I mean anytime. We'll be in touch." She handed another card to Katie. "Here, take one of the chief's, just in case. And everyone calls me AJ."

Katie shoved the cards into her coat pocket, shook hands, and went down the stairs to the front desk. Allison's hand in hers had been warm and firm. The sound of a boot on a marble floor sounded and she looked up. AJ leaned on the railing of the floor above her and held her hand up as if to say good-bye. Katie nodded.

The policeman at the desk held up a box. Katie followed him to the underground garage and he logged in every single item she took from the backseat. Finally, they were done and she went out into the storm again. The bronze lights from the Copper Penny shone through the blowing snow as Katie ran across the deserted street to the bar. There was only one car in the parking lot. It was a late model dark sedan with the motor running. Katie looked at it when she reached for the door. The car appeared to be empty, but the blowing snow obscured her vision.

Chapter Three

A cloud of snow swept across the blue sedan in the Copper Penny parking lot. Michael sat with Ariel and watched the woman with a box in her arms leave the police station and run toward them. Her face was obscured by a hood as she struggled with the door in the wind.

"Son of a—" Michael slammed the palm of his hand against the steering wheel. "The girls screwed up. I can feel it." He saw Ariel straighten at his sharp, angry words, then edge away. "This whole mess is Seraph's fault. She started the fight today. Yelling at me about her kid and leaving the business. Leaving Milwaukee."

He took a deep swig of the energy drink he always carried. "Seraph's fingerprints are on record. Drugs, prostitution, you name it, she did it. What a fucking screwup." Michael turned to Ariel. "How did you know the body would be at the Business Center?" Her eyes seemed darker than usual and wild; she tucked a loose strand of blond hair behind her ear.

"Michael, stop. It's under control. After you left, I did exactly what you told me to do and called Elena. She and two of the girls were at your house right away. Elena called Lu Wright, and Lu suggested her old girlfriend's car at the Business Center. They put Seraph's body in Elena's pickup, met Lu, and got the key to that woman's vehicle." Ariel raised her eyebrows at him. "They'll never trace anything back to you."

Michael took a deep breath and thought about Ariel's words. There were only two women he trusted. Now, with Seraph gone, there was only Ariel. Elena had been avoiding him ever since he and Seraph had started fighting. She'd only come for Seraph because Ariel had called her. And Lu Wright? He'd known Lu for a long time, but she'd always been Elena's.

He scrubbed his face with his hands and let his head tip back against the seat. Lately, his mind was like an interstate highway with too many exits. Focus, he said to himself. You can do this. What he did at work every day was a thousand times more complicated.

Another problem was the farmhouse. The last shipments of meth from there had been marginal. They'd set that operation up too fast. Things were moving so quickly; business was so good that they could barely keep up. And he wasn't the only source in Milwaukee. The new load of pure ephedrine from Mexico should be in today or tomorrow. He needed to hurry. A bad economy was good news for him. His meth was selling like crazy and the money was piling up.

"Would you go down to the farmhouse to work with Owen? That kid's doing something wrong." He kept his voice casual. He needed Ariel's sure touch with the product. She was the best cooker he had, the only one he trusted with the high-end meth for his own personal contacts in Milwaukee. In the last three months, his business sales had outsold the street action, and once again, he and Elena had tangled, hard. Then Seraph had stepped into the middle of it all and—

"I'll go," Ariel said, her eyes still focused on the door to the bar. "How long?"

"A week at most," Michael said, staring out into the blowing snow. "See what's wrong with him. I'll break you in on the computer when you get back and show you what Seraph did. Until then, I'll handle the money from my office." He smiled at her. He liked her more than he'd told her. She was quiet and smart, but best of all, a non-user, just like him.

Damn, it had been such a sweet little operation. Seraph had organized and maintained the business. Elena, smart and tough, ran the streets with her girl gang, the angels. Ariel had managed the production. All he had to do was handle the money, watch it grow. He didn't need drugs. The money was his addiction. Most of them skimmed product occasionally—Seraph sure as hell had, right in front of him—but Ariel was all-business, focused on the job, the money, just like Seraph had been when she first came to him. If Seraph had just stayed clean.

"We won't have a problem with the cops." Ariel pointed her chin across the street at the brick building.

"I don't know. Just as we've gotten quicker and smarter, so have they. It's not as safe as it was, say, a year ago. If you stay in the suburbs or the country, you're still okay, but not in Milwaukee. Except, of course, what you're doing in my garage."

"Why are we following that woman? Lu's old girlfriend?"

"Because now we know she came to the cops. And I want to know where Seraph's body ended up."

"You told me that you don't kill people on this job. That's part of why I agreed to work for you. I know about Elena, but anything goes on the streets." They stared at each other for a moment.

"I haven't *ever* killed anyone—until today. Seraph was my first and, believe me, that was an accident." He sighed. "I didn't lie to you, Ariel. I don't use and I don't kill."

He hadn't lied. Elena and the angels had killed people. In fact, the only person he'd ever known that loved to kill *was* Elena, but today was something else altogether. What really scared him was that he couldn't remember what happened when he and Seraph had argued. All he could recall were some of the words she had screamed at him, his heart thumping wildly in his chest, almost drowning in his own sweat and then, standing over her with a bloody baseball bat.

Did I really kill her? I swear to God, it was an accident.

"Stupid," he muttered and took another long drink of the energy mix. How in the hell had he gone from a farm in Kansas to dealing drugs in Milwaukee? He didn't even like drugs. All he wanted was the money. He had been the family's Golden Boy. The one who always succeeded, the dependable son. Seraph was his cousin, and close like a little sister. He should have just given her what she wanted. Had he been angry enough to kill her? God, they'd grown up together, were family. Sure, they'd argued before—but murder?

There was a day he remembered, Seraph's hair the color of wheat, when she ran across the field to see him. He'd stopped the tractor so she could tell him that a boy had finally kissed her. He'd given her a brotherly hug and they'd talked a while before he had to start the tractor again and get back to work. That night, he'd backed the boy into a corner and threatened him with certain death if he harmed Seraph. Now he was the one who'd done the harm.

He felt sick. Maybe he should see a doctor? No, not maybe. He definitely wasn't himself and hadn't been for a while. Michael looked out into the blowing snow, trying to understand what was happening to him. Hell, he was just a banker.

Chapter Four

The wind shoved Katie's hood back as she struggled with the door to the bar. Snow peppered her face, and she literally blew inside. The bartender, mop in hand, paused mid-movement as Katie hung her coat over a chair, tossed the box on a table, and took the end stool. Already in motion, the bartender held up the square bottle with a shot glass.

"The usual?" he said. "How've you been?"

"A crazy day. I'm waiting for a ride," she said, then remembered she'd forgotten the wine for her mom's party. "What do you have in the way of wines? Anything red and sweet?"

The bottle sang faintly against her shot glass. She could smell the whiskey. He leaned down, checked his wine stock under the bar, and held up a long-necked bottle that shimmered ruby red in the bar lights.

"That'll do," she said and shoved money onto the bar. "Keep the change." She wrapped her arms about her with a little shiver. There'd been a car, idling in the parking lot, but she was his only customer.

Agitated again, Katie spat out, "Damn," and stared into the dark, amber liquor. A woman in her car? How crazy was this? Confused that someone would do this to her, she remembered Bonnie's face. Something else besides anger had been in Bonnie's eyes. Alarm?

She tapped the shot glass with her fingers, mulling over the photos she'd seen at the police station. The woman, Seraph, was pretty in a chic, thin way, but something was off with that smile. Then her mind connected the dots. The woman was high. Fine, she was high, but who was she? AJ had said "a suspect in an ongoing investigation" which told her nothing.

Allison Jacob—AJ—had certainly been an experience. She'd been furious when she'd walked into the police station. Maybe AJ had noticed and tried to calm her with smiles, even a little teasing about the gun business that they both knew wasn't relevant. That had come from Bonnie, and who knew what Bonnie had said to AJ? Katie smiled a little, speculating on that conversation. Anyway, she wasn't a suspect, but why had they dumped that woman—Seraph?—in her car?

"How long has that police station been across the street?" she said to the bartender.

"About five months." He wiped his hands on the apron tied around his good-sized belly. "They moved in at the end of last September. Today's the last day of February? Right, that makes it five months. One day the building was vacant, and the next, it was crawling with cops."

Katie smiled. "Can't hurt your business."

He ran his hands through his neat gray hair. "I like having them there. The neighborhood's been quieter for sure. You're right; they haven't hurt the bar."

"Do they ever come over here?"

"Yeah, but it's a mix of uniforms and suits. Not your usual cop trade. And quiet."

Katie nodded, then went back to staring at the whiskey and checked her watch. Her sister would probably be here in fifteen minutes. The bartender finished mopping the floor and disappeared to put the bucket away. Another Miles Davis song began. For the second time that night, she thought of Lu Wright.

This music was why Lu had started coming here in the first place, all those years ago. How long had it been since she'd seen her? Three? No, four months. Lu had called and they'd sat right here in the same chairs.

She'd gone to Lu's apartment that night and put her to bed. Lu's place was a mess, so Katie had done the dishes, picked up the place, and made sure there was food in the refrigerator. By the time she'd gotten back to check the bedroom, Lu had wet herself. She'd stood her in the shower, cleaned her up, and put her to sleep on the couch. That had been a long night. She'd left for her own place just as the sun was coming up, and she hadn't taken her calls or seen her since.

Katie tried to think of something else. Anything else other than Lu Wright. She remembered the business cards in her coat and placed them on the bar. "William Whiteaker" the card read and "Chief—Special Investigation Section" under his name. His cell, office, and e-mail information followed.

"Allison Jacob" was printed in script on the other card. *Script?* The print was dark green, not black, with her e-mail and a telephone number, but no title—or job description. What was she? Not your regular cop. Maybe a detective? I forgot to ask, Katie thought, frowning down at her drink. What else did I forget?

Mentally, she started at the top and cruised her memory of Allison Jacob down to the brown leather boots. That turned-out leather duster coat was unusual, and she'd noticed carefully manicured nails. The brown tee under Allison's tan blazer matched those thick lashed, brandy-brown eyes, the same color as the liquid in Katie's shot glass. She was a puzzle but an eye-stopper. That *presence* that she had was certainly special. *Cute enough to make me flirt.* Katie smiled wryly to herself.

The bartender walked down the boards, close to her. "We had quite a scene with Lu today."

"Lu?" Katie held her breath.

"I had to call rescue about dinner time. She passed out, stopped breathing, and her color was odd. Really gray. One of those cops from across the street, a woman, gave her CPR until the rescue folks came. A really nice looking woman, but doesn't talk like a cop. Well, except for today. I swear, that woman changed into another person right in front of me. The entire bar snapped to attention." He moved and put his foot up on the ice chest. "I'm pretty sure she saved Lu's life, so I don't care what she talks like. She comes in with an older man now and then, but she's never in a uniform. Oh, and once in a while she comes in with that cop that you know. The tall woman with the braid."

"Bonnie?" Katie said and he nodded. She looked down at the cards on the bar in front of her. It had to be AJ. She could call Bonnie and ask. Being friends for over twenty years had its perks.

The music stopped and the bartender turned to the sound system. Katie leaned back, thinking about what he'd just told her. If Lu was in the hospital, she'd be getting a call. She had Lu's legal and medical power of attorney, and they'd have to contact her.

All those years with Lu. God, how she'd tried to stay away. She'd even worked in California for six months, made friends, and had a few lovers. She remembered the confidence she'd brought back here to Wisconsin. She'd been home three weeks, run into Lu in the grocery store, and everything had just drained away the minute Lu's hand fell on her shoulder.

Katie looked down at the shot waiting for her. Who was she kidding? Lu had her from the moment they'd met. That exciting, smart personality with a little hint of danger, and her long, red, silky hair and bright, blue eyes.

The therapist that Katie had seen for about eight months had said that she was just unprepared for Lu. Katie's childhood had been so secure and average that it had been the *difference* that had turned her head. Lu was unlike anyone she'd ever known. The closest her family had come to *different* was Uncle Henry. He'd smoked cigars, never married, and stuttered. Her mother had taken care of him until he died, just as quietly as he'd lived.

Lu's red hair had darkened over the years, but it was still long, and sometimes her eyes were bright. When Katie had started her business, she had put Lu on the company insurance. Jobs slipped through Lu's fingers like water, and even though they were already fighting and staying away from each other, Katie knew no one else would take care of her.

"Oh," she said under her breath, remembering the strange sensation when she'd turned to Allison Jacob for the first time tonight. Those quiet and *alert* feelings were similar to something she'd once felt with Lu.

Another Miles Davis tune began as she lifted the shot glass. Her sister opened the bar door as she set the empty glass back on the bar.

CHAPTER FIVE

AJ waited at the window until she saw Katie safely enter the Copper Penny. Damn it. It wasn't an accident that Seraph had ended up in Katie's car. Someone who knew Katie had chosen the silver SUV. Bonnie had said the car wasn't broken into. A remote or a key had been used. Katie had been adamant that she knew no one who would do this. She believed Katie, but she'd also told Katie the truth. Somebody probably would track her car—but what she hadn't said was that they'd probably track Katie too.

AJ walked to the war room to see what the task force had added to the operation today. She picked up a marker and added Katie's name beside Seraph's, then went over the photos Bonnie had sent from the clinic on her phone. Seraph had been wrapped carefully. Someone had taken time. Since she lived with Michael, it could have been him. Or one of his gang members, the angels. She took another look at the photos. That blanket? It was a woman's touch.

AJ studied the photos hung on the corkboard in front of her. They had over twenty of Michael's street gang girls identified. Her group had spent over three months sifting through the street drugs in Milwaukee, shadowing Bill's police, looking for drug action in upper level businesses or professionals. The locals would handle the street-level dealers. They wanted someone at the top with deep ties to the Midwest. Someone who could afford the time and money to move drugs efficiently from state to state.

For years, the government had chased drugs up from the southern borders only to lose them in cities or the back woods. It cost huge amounts of money and time with very little success. Finally, her supervisor in Washington D.C., Charles Ryan, had wrangled a "test run," a new way to track and handle the problem. He had a group in Iowa, a bigger one in Missouri, and her little pack of people here. The task force that she and Bill Whiteaker led was a combination of his Milwaukee city police, and equal parts ATF and DEA, all operating under the Justice Department.

Charles had chosen a local banker as their target, and for three weeks, they'd quietly investigated John Michael Cray, Assistant Vice-President at Bennings International.

Charles had also chosen the federal people that became her team, including Jock. No one could sniff out drugs like Jock, but he was unable to wrap his mind around the shadowing of drugs primarily for information. After Jock had left tonight, she and Bill had called Charles. If they shifted Jock back into the local DEA, he'd be more effective working directly with street-level dealers and users. Charles was receptive and promised to get back to them in the next few days. They had both written an assessment of Jock's few months in the task force, and sent it off to Charles when Bonnie Logan had called her about Katie Blackburn.

Actually, she'd like to move Bonnie into Jock's position, but Bonnie needed more training. Maybe when they were done with Michael and all the levels of his operation? So far, they'd identified the street and parts of the corporate connections, but both she and Bill had a feeling there was more. They both felt Michael worked with others at similar business positions. Charles hoped it was in different states.

She stepped closer and looked at a photo of Michael, one that she had taken as she stopped at the main office of his bank. Dressed in a business suit, she'd gone in for her first look at the facility and gotten the shot just as he'd left his office and was standing at the elevator. He was tall and his suit was expensive, but he looked like a farm boy with blond hair and brown eyes. She'd picked up some investment booklets while he talked with people. Hands in his pockets, he'd leaned against the wall, talking with the others, open and friendly. What had struck her most was his smile. He did that. A lot.

With a tired sigh, she turned out the lights and went for her coat in Bill's office. One more stop and she was done.

The wind grabbed at her as she stepped outside. Her car started immediately and she grinned. It always started. Despite its slightly battered appearance, she loved this wrecked, unmarked cop car she'd found in New Mexico. Some friends of hers had left the exterior alone, aligned it, and dropped a 2008 Dodge Charger cop engine in it with heavy-duty brakes, a 340 hp Hemi V8 that went from zero to sixty in seconds. Six on the floor, it always started in the winter, and, dear God, it was fast, all beautiful screaming speed.

A city snow plow went by. She sped up and followed it all the way to the clinic. The snow had ended, but the winds hadn't, and blowback from the plow splattered across her windshield, her mind working on Seraph with each swipe of the wiper. After Bonnie had called, she'd spoken with Seraph's doctor. He hadn't been hopeful that she'd get anything out of the injured woman, but she needed to see for herself. Seraph might be the break that would get them further inside Michael's organization, and AJ wasn't going to pass up a single opportunity.

Inside the clinic, she pushed through the heavy doors with a little grunt and shifted her bag to the other hand. Two cops, one considerably older than the other, sat on either side of Seraph's room. Both stood and asked for her identification.

Seraph was on her side, facing the door, eyes closed and surrounded by IVs and monitors. AJ took a good look at her, spoke her name, but Seraph didn't respond. AJ repeated her name several times. Just as AJ was about to go, Seraph moved.

"Where's my baby?" Seraph's voice was barely a whisper.

"I don't know," AJ said and leaned over to get a look at the injury. Seraph had a lot of stitches and the doctor had confirmed a concussion. Surprised to hear her speak, even if it was only a whisper, AJ held her ID in front of Seraph's eyes. "Allison Jacob," she said.

"You're a social worker? No…" Seraph tried to focus on the identification, her green eyes pale. "Christ—everything's blurry. What does that say?"

"It says ATF and I'll help you, if you let me."AJ moved a chair close to the bed and held up the small recorder. "I'm going to record this. Can you tell me how you ended up in the backseat of that car today?"

"I can't," Seraph whispered.

"Yes, you can. We can offer you protection."

"The last thing I remember is seeing Michael come at me with a baseball bat." She closed her eyes, and AJ thought she'd lost her. Suddenly, her eyes opened again. "Wait…the car in the snow. The girls thought I was dead…but Elena knew better." Seraph shifted restlessly.

"Elena?" AJ said.

"Angels…Elena kills…" Seraph's voice trailed off.

"Elena kills? Elena is an angel, one of Michael's gang?" Seraph didn't answer so AJ tried a different tack. "Tell me where your daughter is. We'll pick her up."

"Michael took her away."

"Michael's the father?"

"No…my cousin." Once again, AJ had to lean close to hear her. "I lost my job…on the streets with Meredith…needed a place to stay." Seraph took a deep breath. "Too dangerous for my little girl… he knocked me out with one punch." Seraph faded, but AJ waited. It was more than she'd hoped for. "When I came to, Meredith was gone. He'd taken her to a friend of his…if I didn't do what he said, the woman would put her up for adoption."

AJ scrunched the chair as close to the bed as possible. "How old is Meredith?"

"Three…in August."

"Where's her father?"

"Don't know." Seraph went quiet for a long moment. She mumbled but then said clearly, "Michael…something's wrong with him. Changed…angry all the time." She drifted. "I think he's on meth too. Am I going to jail?"

"I don't know," AJ said. "We need everything you can tell us about Michael and the operation, but first, you'll have to detox and take care of that concussion. If we help each other, Seraph, you can get through this and we can find your little girl."

"Anything for Meredith. Afraid of Michael…for the first time." Seraph coughed and put her hands to her head. "Guards…at the door? I ran the business for him…he'll look for me."

"We'll protect you, but I need your full cooperation to make this work. You ran the business? Michael's business?"

Seraph touched her silver-blond hair carefully. "He saved me… from the streets. He put me in charge…I kept track of his drugs."

AJ pushed more questions about Michael's operation slowly and tried to keep Seraph talking, but she finally drifted off into a deep silence. There was a black mark on Seraph's hand, a tattoo, and she bent to get a better look. It was a small black angel. AJ pressed the button for the nurse. When the nurse came, she left.

Seraph had denied nothing during the interview, something that rarely happened in her experience. My God, was it really possible that Seraph ran the business end of Michael's operation? And someone named Elena led the angels on the streets? Why had that name, Elena, never come up? They had thought Michael was in charge, the person who made the decisions and tracked the money. Now she was unsure. And it was obvious that Seraph was shocked by what he'd done to her. She had said *something was wrong with him* more than once.

"What the hell?" AJ said to herself. Seraph could have been confused, disoriented. But what if she was telling the truth?

AJ climbed the stairs to her small apartment over the garage. It took her about two minutes to strip down to skin in the bathroom, turn the shower on, and step into lukewarm water. Finally, it warmed up and she stopped shivering. She reached for the soap.

Later, wrapped in a warm robe, she sat on the floor in front of the laptop on the coffee table. *Always the damned reports.* "Damned data," she said. There was so much information every single day. This task force was her first command, and it was daunting. Normally, she was undercover, calling her own shots, invisible with just her wire and her wits. Now, everyone could not only see her, but they depended on her. If she screwed up, they all fell with her. She'd always been good under pressure, but this was different and it unnerved her.

With her eyes closed, she let her head drop back onto the couch. What was she thinking? This was as close to undercover as she would get without actually being undercover. The whole idea of the task force was to stay in the background and certainly why Charles had put her in charge. Not being seen was something she excelled at.

She sat up and went to work, beginning with a verification of the captured drugs and guns that Jock had entered into evidence at the station.

Next, she described her visit to Seraph at the clinic and inserted the flash drive that carried her interview with Seraph. The words, sometimes mumbled, sometimes clear, washed past AJ's ears. She expected to get a phone call from Charles over this interview.

Finally, she entered her own comments about their conversation and the name Seraph had given her. Elena. *"The streets. Kill,"* Seraph had said. AJ pondered that. It sounded as if Elena was *in charge* of the streets or Michael's gun for hire.

The red words on the computer flashed "Recording Finished" and she pushed up off the floor to get a bottle of water. Considering Seraph's physical condition, she was happy to get what she got. From the beginning, they'd known Seraph lived with Michael and the child. Everything they'd seen had indicated they were simply living together. The thought that she might handle Michael's business was a brand new option. If that was true, Seraph would be the key.

Again, she thought of Katie Blackburn and opened a new file under her name with the basic information. She let that sit for a moment while she checked her personal e-mail.

The first e-mail was a request for dinner next week at a new club from a woman so lovely that most people took a breath when she smiled. The woman was her confidential informant, code name "Star", and she was more than merely beautiful. She was warm and smart, but an addict. For the last few weeks, AJ had exploited Star's weakness for women every chance she got. More than a meal had already been offered, but AJ had held it to a simmering flirtation. Hopefully, she'd get her introduction into the real money of Milwaukee, maybe even Michael, the next time they met. AJ stared at the screen. But now that they had Seraph, that might change.

The next e-mail was from her friend Tom Perry. It was a forwarded cartoon about the military, and she laughed out loud. After graduation from West Point, they had served their first assignment together in Ecuador, something she had loved almost to the point of obsession but learned to hate. She loved the military to this day and was proud of her service.

The third e-mail was a puzzle. The address was familiar, but she couldn't pinpoint who belonged to "T5525." Something about it rang a bell, but for the life of her nothing came forth.

Suddenly, she remembered that she'd forgotten to add the information about the Blackburn woman's car, and she clicked back to the new file for Katie Blackburn. Because of the storm tonight, they'd left Katie's car at the station. Every flat bed and tow truck had been in use helping stranded or crashed vehicles. The CSUs had notified her that they'd get it to the impound lab tomorrow to go over the entire car. One of Bonnie's photos was of the floor of the back of Katie's car, and she attached it to the file. Seraph was tall, and a big man, alone, could have gotten her into the car. Michael was big. If it had been a woman, it would have taken more than one, but Seraph had mentioned Elena and the snow. At the office, she'd thought it was the work of a woman. Seraph had confirmed her gut feeling.

AJ stared at the screen and thought about the interview with Katie Blackburn. She was a cop's kid for sure. She'd watched Katie's eyes cruise Bill's office. AJ leaned forward and shuffled her notes beside the laptop. When Bonnie had called, she had said that she and Katie were old friends, but she'd mentioned something else. A woman named Lu Wright. That was familiar.

She looked over her shoulder. Her jeans were still on the couch where'd she'd left them, and AJ dug the bar napkin out of the pocket. Lu Wright was the woman she'd given CPR to at the Copper Penny earlier today. They'd taken her—where? Probably the detox hospital in Franklin. She searched the data from the metro files and found the paramedics' trip sheet. They had taken her to St. Luke's for her heart. "Oh-oh," AJ muttered to herself. Katie Blackburn was the hospital's contact for Lu Wright.

AJ checked to see if Lu had a police record. Yes, three drunk and disorderly and public intoxication. So Katie knew Lu Wright?

When she'd rushed down the stairs to collect Katie Blackburn tonight, she'd seen Katie's frustration and anger, followed by a heartbreaker smile that had made her mouth go dry. All through the interview those startling gray eyes had flashed with intelligence. She had a nice body too. A deceptive body, actually. Katie appeared small and delicate, but when AJ had watched her run across the street to the Copper Penny, she'd hurdled a snowbank in a quick, athletic leap that had made her grin. If Katie hadn't been able to find a way home tonight, AJ would have driven her wherever she was going in one of the agency vehicles. An attractive woman like her would have plans on a Friday night.

With a sigh, she tucked Katie away and went back to work. Another of her informants, Claudia—or Frog, as she was known on the streets—had left her a message to get in touch. She hauled herself up from the floor and stretched with a groan. The name Frog always made her smile. She had been downtown with Bill Whiteaker before Christmas when they'd hauled the young girl in on suspicion of drugs for the fourth time in less than three weeks. She was wearing an orange jacket with a big green frog on the back, and the local cops had begun to call her Frog. After reading her personal information, AJ had talked to her and negotiated an arrangement. She'd also seen to it that she got a new coat.

AJ sorted through a bag of old clothes she kept in the closet. She needed to blend in on the streets when she met Frog tomorrow. She tossed the clothing she wanted on the couch. Worn out, she bent

to turn her laptop off but saw the remaining e-mail, the "T5525."
She paused, scanned the address once again, and opened the e-mail.

Six words hung in front of her. *"It's been years. Can we talk?
T."*

She stared at the screen. *"T"* was Dana Taylor, her ex-lover.
Her ex-lover who lived with her ex-best childhood friend, Rachael.
No, she sure as hell wasn't going to answer. She hit Save and shut
the computer down.

In bed, she listened to the wind blow snow against the window.
"Women," she said. *I'd face a gun any day before facing Dana
Taylor and Rachel.* Because of them, she'd spent time in a hospital
when she'd returned from Ecuador. Because of them, she knew
exactly how cruel and indifferent people could be, even best friends
and lovers. She hated betrayal with all her soul.

She had been so broken after Ecuador that it had taken all her
courage to fall into bed with another woman. The second woman
had been almost as hard, but the third one had been exactly what
she'd intended. A physically satisfying but emotionally empty one-
night stand. And that's what she'd had ever since.

As sleep overtook her, she gripped the little gun under her
pillow, hard.

CHAPTER SIX

Bright sunshine shot off snowbanks as Katie drove the new car into the Franklin Hospital parking lot the next morning. She tossed her sunglasses on the dash and checked out the blue sky above her. Last night's storm was already across Lake Michigan, which meant Milwaukee would now have a couple days of sunshine but very cold temperatures. The readout on the dash of the new car said it was eight frigid degrees above zero outside, and she pulled on her warm gloves.

She'd spent the night at her mother's in her old room, then gone home for a shower and clean clothes. The message she'd expected from Lu's doctor was on her phone. She'd made this trip so often that she was on autopilot.

Her uncle had delivered the new car right to her mother's driveway this morning, and she thanked whatever for the best family in the world. They'd talked over coffee as she'd explained what had happened. Katie had offered her uncle money, but he'd said no and settled for a hug before he left. They'd finish up the paperwork next week at his dealership. The new car, a Chevy Traverse, was classy and drove like a dream. Still, she missed her dad's car.

The hospital lobby was quiet as she approached the main desk. She gave the receptionist her medical power of attorney and stuffed her gloves in her coat pocket while she waited.

"Room at the end, on the left," the woman said with a smile as she handed her a pass.

The light in the hallway had a yellow cast to it, and the air felt thick. She pulled in a deep breath. The closer she got to the room, the slower she walked. Finally, she stopped, studying her boots. *Why am I doing this?* She had tried so desperately for such a long time *not* to love this woman. Just as Lu was an addict, she was too. She had been addicted to Lu. *And I'm here because it's the decent, right thing to do.*

The room was dim, and the only noise a strange, gurgled breath. Lu was curled on her side in an odd position, the covers up to her ears.

"My God," Katie whispered. Someone had cut off most of Lu's hair. It barely covered her ears. And there were restraints on Lu's wrists. This had been a bad one. She bent and gave her a tiny kiss on the cheek just as a nurse walked in. She was a big woman. After a hard look at Katie, the nurse flung open the curtains.

"Ow," Lu said and tried to rub her eyes. Katie stepped back, out of the way.

"Come on," the nurse said, pulling the covers back. All Lu was wearing was a pajama top, and although Katie had seen her naked many times, she was unprepared for this. Lu had been fully shaved and was covered in a creamy white salve. Katie backed toward the lone chair in the room and sat down, shocked.

"What happened to her?" Katie said to the nurse.

"The usual. STD. The men are worse, believe me." The nurse gave Lu's shoulder a quick shake. "Come on, sunshine. It's time to shower and then breakfast."

"Go to hell," Lu said. "I'm not hungry."

"You need a shower first," the nurse said as she undid the restraints on Lu's wrists, and Katie heard the nurse sigh. "You'll feel better."

"Feel better? Give me a fucking drink of whiskey, then I'll do anything," Lu rasped. Katie looked away. That rough voice used to be clear and beautiful. She had loved it.

The nurse turned to Katie. "You have to leave the room while I give her a shower."

Katie immediately reached for her bag, but Lu said, "Katie," with the please-don't-go look that was as familiar to Katie as breathing.

"I'll wait in the hallway," Katie said and left. Outside, she fell back against the wall as her heart pounded. The room had smelled of urine and unwashed skin. "This is the last time I'm going to do this." Lu's face had shocked her. She had stitches on her jaw, above her eye, and her entire face looked haggard.

She heard the toilet flush inside and the shower begin. For the millionth time, she wondered how this had happened. Lu's parents, nationally-known scientists in Madison, had raised Lu and her brothers with love and affection. In Katie's opinion, all the gifts Lu had been born with had been her undoing. Her brilliant mind and eye-catching appearance had only brought her grief. One of the things that had made Katie turn her head the day they met had been Lu's clear voice. She'd been speaking French to an older woman sitting between them. Katie had leaned forward and looked past the woman next to her, only to be impaled on the bluest eyes she'd ever seen. As the years passed, Katie had learned that was one of Lu's little tricks to get someone's attention. Incredibly, Lu spoke at least four languages fluently.

The woman between them had translated with an amused look. "She asked me if I know you? Do I?"

"No," a surprised Katie had answered, still caught by those flirting eyes. Finally, she turned to the woman next to her. "Katie Blackburn, owner of Blue Ridge, Inc."

"Celia King," the woman had answered. "This is my husband's luncheon for new businesses in the area." Celia leaned close. "And we're looking for a new advertising agency," she said with an impish little smile. They had talked throughout the rest of the meal as Katie purposely ignored Lu. Celia had rewarded Katie with an introduction to her husband, and a year later, they were Katie's biggest client. They still were, she thought, staring at the floor. That day, when Katie had left the luncheon, Lu had been waiting for her in the parking lot.

Katie pushed back into the wall. That was twelve years ago.

"Ms. Blackburn. Katie." A man's voice cut into her memories. He was peering out of a doorway to her right.

"Dr. Conor," Katie said with a smile for Lu's doctor.

He didn't return the smile. "Would you come in for a moment? Let's talk about Lu."

"She looks rough. What happened to her hair?"

He took his glasses off and laid them carefully on the desk. Finally, he sighed. "There's no nice way to deliver this information, so here we go. Lu had a heart attack yesterday. I could tell you all the reasons. Do you want them?"

Katie shook her head.

"I know you're the legal contact, but her brother was in town on business. They took her to St. Anthony's cardiac unit, then transported her here. The hospital contacted the family, and they called the brother." He jammed the glasses back on his face. "Her parents arrived early this morning and made some decisions. I'm sorry we didn't reach you, but I did leave a message on your business and home phones."

"I was out for the evening," Katie said, feeling him edging toward worse news.

"They made arrangements at their hospital's cardiac unit in Madison before I even came into the room. Lu will be transported there tomorrow or the next day." He shuffled papers on his desk.

"Is the problem with her heart...fixable?"

"In my opinion, no. Frankly, I'm amazed she survived this heart attack or the DTs. She's still dealing with those."

Katie wiped her sweaty hands on her jeans. "I only want Lu to live. You and I have met here enough to know how I feel."

"Her parents were really upset. I think they were afraid she was going to die before they could get her home. Do you know them?"

"Not very well, but like the parents of most addicts, they've just thrown up their hands. I was at their home for Thanksgiving, probably ten years ago, and that's the only time I've met them."

"You've been good to Lu," the doctor said kindly. "But you'd better—" He abruptly changed the subject. "Her hair. You asked about her hair?" He waited for Katie to say something, but she only nodded. "When she fell, she cut her head on a barstool. St. Anthony's cut the hair."

"I'd better what? What did you start to say?" Katie stood.

"Say good-bye," he answered quietly. "Do you want me to go in with you?"

"No," Katie whispered, "I can do this." She looked at him briefly, then out his window at the sunshine on the snow. *Be careful what you wish for.*

The door was open to Lu's room when Katie went back. Lu was propped up on pillows in the bed. Her hair was still wet, her eyes enormous and dark against her white skin. She merely glanced up as Katie entered but then focused again on the bowl of oatmeal in front of her. The nurse had pulled the chair next to the bed, preparing to feed her.

"May I do that?" Katie asked. The nurse got up immediately.

"Thanks," she said with a grateful look. "If there's a problem, call me."

Katie took the spoon and turned to Lu who was staring into space. "Open up, Lu."

"Katie?" Lu suddenly seemed to realize who was beside her. "Where's that other woman?"

"I'm going to feed you."

"My mind is like a series of doors right now. I never know who'll be behind the door when I open it," Lu said, concentrating on Katie's face. She opened her mouth, slurping the oatmeal. "Sorry." Lu held up her hands in the restraints. "These things won't let me reach my face."

Katie put another spoonful of oatmeal to Lu's mouth. "What happened? I haven't seen you in restraints for a long time."

"I don't know. My brother took me out to eat, then dropped me off at the Copper Penny to meet with some friends. The last thing I remember is singing along with Ella Fitzgerald at the bar. No one in town has that music and…" She trailed off, her eyes fading to blank.

Katie pushed another spoonful to Lu's bottom lip, then into her mouth. They got through the rest of the breakfast in silence. She held toast to Lu's mouth, but Lu refused. Katie did get her to drink some milk. She turned to push the table away when Lu said her name in a very clear voice.

"Yes?"

"Let me go, Katie. Take your coat. Walk out of here, right now."

Katie swiveled and stared at Lu's blank face. "Why?"

"Look at you, all pretty. Bright eyes, that curly black hair. Here, lean down." Her fingers traced Katie's mouth. "You have the most incredible smile." Lu pushed Katie upward as far as the restraints allowed. "I know what I look like and what's wrong with me. I've known for a long time." She looked at Katie as if memorizing her. "Just go. Please."

There was no answer. It was exactly what Katie wanted to do. Not to care for this woman any longer. She looked at the floor and gripped the glass of milk for all she was worth.

"What do you know about your heart condition?"

"That I've finally killed it. The doctor says I'll be lucky to make it another six months. Can we just end this peacefully? I don't want to kill your heart too."

Too late. They stared at each other for a long moment. Katie's heart seized with a mixture of fight or flight, but she put her coat on.

"Good-bye, Lu," she said. She felt a little light-headed as she walked out the door.

CHAPTER SEVEN

Downtown Milwaukee was a mess. AJ wove past monster snowplows and trucks clearing yesterday's storm. The huge snowbanks made street corners dangerous. Thankful for her big agency Suburban, she inched past a large pile of snow and worried about Frog. This much snow often left the homeless buried, and she'd bet anything that Frog had not gone to a shelter.

The street she needed was plowed, but getting to the sidewalk was another matter. The snowbank was as tall as she was. Since she was wearing dirty jeans, two ratty sweatshirts, and an old denim jacket, clothes weren't a worry.

"Oh, hell." She crawled over it and then jammed on sunglasses against the bright sunlight. The parking lot where she usually found Frog hadn't been plowed, and there weren't any tracks in the snow. Hands on hips, she looked for the kid.

Of all her CIs, Frog and Star were special. Frog had pointed out the angels from Michael's street gang and given her names of other small dealers. She was the only person AJ knew who had actually been inside all three houses that Michael owned, including the one where he lived. AJ rewarded her with protection on the streets and occasional money.

Her other special informant, Star, would be her gateway to high-end clients.

The worn-out leather boots didn't do much to keep her feet warm. "Damned snow." She was working with the zipper on the old jacket when something hit her from behind. Suddenly, she was facedown in the snow. She came up swinging, but Frog danced away from her, laughing.

"Where you been, boss?" Frog grinned into AJ's face. Her breath was bitter and awful.

AJ coughed and adjusted her sunglasses. "Aren't you cold?"

Frog pulled AJ to a standing position. Desperately thin, the young girl wore only a ragged hoodie, ripped jeans, and torn tennis shoes. "Cold? No. Feel the sunshine?" She rubbed a handful of snow on her face with a yell.

"Where's your coat? Where did you sleep?" AJ scrutinized Frog. The kid was tweaking so hard that she was almost off the ground. "It's only eight degrees out here."

"I slept in the box in the alley." Frog inched away. Every part of her was in motion.

"Damn, you'll freeze to death. You're supposed to be at the shelter when there's a bad storm." AJ started for the alley, anxious to get out of sight.

"I've got something for you. I heard Michael killed someone yesterday. Someone important." Frog suddenly took off. She ran across the street and was almost hit by a car driving by. AJ slogged through the snow and followed her into the alley.

"What's it worth to you?" Frog scratched her back against the brick wall and AJ saw there were more scabs on her face.

AJ blocked the alley entrance with her body. "I'm always here when you call. Who'd Michael kill?"

"See the money, see the money," Frog began to sing.

Reluctantly, AJ held out some bills but snatched them back when Frog grabbed for them. "Tell me first. Who'd Michael kill?"

"You don't understand," Frog yelled. "I need something now. Got bugs in my mouth." She stuck out her tongue.

"It's just meth-mouth. And you lost another tooth," AJ said, seeing the white coating on the tongue. She held the money in front of her and backed away from Frog's rancid breath. "Tell me first."

"He killed his main woman, Seraph. It's all over the street. The angels are all sad."

"Michael killed Seraph?"

Frog nodded vigorously. "She's dead. Heard the news when I scored, but the stuff was crap. That's why I got bugs in my mouth."

"You don't have bugs. I looked." AJ held the money up again, but when Frog reached, she grabbed a fistful of Frog's hoodie and shoved her into the bricks. "Keep the money, but I'm going to do something before you freeze to death. You're spun." Frog almost knocked them both down, but AJ held her while she called for a police car and Frog yelled. "I'll check on you every day. You're done out here."

"I haven't gone without long enough to be spun. C'mon, help me," Frog wailed, her dirty hair across her face. "You cheated me. You always cheat me. God damn, I hate you."

"Shut up. You're going into treatment." AJ increased her grip. She held Frog firmly with her body. "Listen to me. I'll get you help and maybe, just maybe, you won't die out here. There's a place here in town that'll help you. That's how I'm going to pay you."

Frog sagged against AJ crying as the black and white drove up. The kid looked bewildered as they shoved her into the backseat. Anyone tweaking that hard and long was *spun*, and Frog was *spun*. AJ sat beside her. "Listen, kid, it's what I always say to you. Meth isn't particular. It loves anybody who'll love it. Let's get you fixed before you can't be fixed." She held the cold hand in hers and rubbed it. "Frog, who's Elena?"

Frog wiped her eyes, jerked her hand away, and gave her a sulky look. She turned her head to stare out the window.

"Come on, Frog, who's Elena?"

"Michael's murder woman," Frog said. AJ got out, shut the door, and the squad car pulled away.

Murder woman? AJ leaned against the cold brick of the alley.

God damn, I hate you. AJ squeezed her eyes tight against Frog's words. The last person to say "I hate you" was her best friend, Rachel. Her *ex*-best friend. The day Rachel and Taylor had left Ecuador. Together. And the betrayal always lurked right behind her consciousness.

"Stop it," she muttered and turned to the big cardboard containers in the alley. Too many people slept out here at night; some didn't get up the next day. Something glistened on the snow in the sunlight under two crack pipes. It was an empty eight-ball baggie with a black angel imprint on it. The same black angel that AJ had seen tattooed on Seraph's hand last night. She stuffed the bag in her pocket, dropping to her knees in the snow to check the back of the boxes. She saw Frog's coat and pulled it out. One pocket was empty, but she found another bigger baggie in the other.

"Shit," she said and held up the prescription drugs. Red, yellow, and blue capsules, all unmarked. Meth was bad enough, but this shit was a whole different ball game. Hadn't she drilled it into Frog to stay away from the Oxys, Percocet, Vicodin, or whatever? Stepping out into the sunlight, she turned the baggie slowly. She didn't recognize them. On the other hand, it could be that Frog was selling the pills for food and meth. Maybe it was just street-level commerce. She started back to her car.

Okay, two people, Seraph and Frog, had called Elena a killer. It looked like Michael didn't do any murder himself. Maybe he just directed Elena. Whoever she was. They'd better find out. And fast. She put her sunglasses back on to protect her eyes from the merciless sunlight. She'd shower, change clothes at the station, then try to see Lu Wright at the hospital before the meeting with her group.

❖

Almost an hour later, AJ drove into the Franklin Hospital parking lot. She slowed down. Was that Katie Blackburn leaning against a black SUV, arms clasped about herself? Crying? AJ nudged the big Suburban close to Katie and powered down the window.

"Ms. Blackburn? Katie? Are you okay?"

Katie swung around and swiped at her cheeks. She stared at AJ as if she'd dropped from the sky.

AJ got out of the car, boots crunching in the snow. "Don't cry in the cold. It dries your eyes and tears freeze on your cheeks. Bad for the skin." AJ teased her gently as she opened her car door. "Sit with me. I have coffee."

Katie hesitated, then stepped up into the big vehicle.

AJ poured a cup of coffee from the thermos. Last night, Katie had been angry. Today, she looked as if she might fall apart at any moment.

"Thanks." Katie cleared her throat.

AJ saw her hand shake as she took the thermos cup. "I'm following up on a woman who collapsed at the Copper Penny yesterday. Did something happen in the hospital? Are you all right?"

"It was you who did the CPR on Lu?" Katie said and pushed back her black, curly hair.

"At first I thought she was really drunk, but then I was pretty sure she'd had a heart attack. When Bonnie called, before you came into the station, she mentioned Lu's name. You know her?"

"I know her." Katie stared out of the window. "She's being transferred to Madison, to her family's hospital. Her heart is… damaged." She took a drink of coffee. "Christ," she whispered over a defeated breath. "Do you have any Kleenex?"

"Open the glove compartment."

Katie set the thermos cup on the dash and took several Kleenex. She dabbed at her eyes, blew her nose, and looked at AJ. "Thanks. It's a long story, but it's been over for quite a while." Her eyes still shimmered with tears, but she managed a small smile.

"That's better. There's that beautiful smile," AJ said before she thought. She regretted it as Katie dissolved into tears again. "God, I'm sorry."

"No, it's all right." Katie fluttered a hand at her. "Lu just said the same words this morning…oh, shit." She reached for more Kleenex. "Bonnie mentioned Lu?"

"Bonnie's a good friend to you, Katie."

"Yes, she is. I'm lucky to have her and a wonderful family." Katie wiped her eyes again and looked out her window. "See my new car?"

They both looked at the new black Chevy. "It drives great, but I miss Dad's car. Wait," she said and turned suddenly. "Did you find out why they chose my car?"

AJ took a breath, considering how to approach the question. She wanted to know more about the connection between Katie and Lu Wright. "No reason that we can find—so far. I would let you know if I knew. I stopped on my way home last night and talked with Seraph, the woman who was in your car. She's in no condition to tell us much right now, but she didn't seem to know it was your car. She's so injured that I'm not certain she knew what she was saying."

"What about this new car?" Katie looked at the black Traverse. "Will they come after that? Use it for something else?"

"I honestly don't know." AJ tapped the steering wheel with her fingers. Katie still looked shattered so she changed the subject. "Do you like art?"

"Art?" Katie looked confused.

AJ nodded. "Yes. Art."

"Of course I like art. Why?"

"I hear they have a great new show that opened last weekend. I was thinking of taking a little time away from work tomorrow afternoon to see the new exhibition. Want to go with me?"

Katie's face relaxed and AJ saw that her eyes were clear. "That sounds nice." They stared at each other for a moment, and AJ's gaze slid down to the luscious lips. Katie looked away. "Do you cook?"

Caught looking, AJ's face warmed. "I'm so busy that even if I could, I don't have time." *Her eyes have a touch of blue* ran through her mind. "I can make coffee," she said.

"I'll make you a meal afterward, something simple. Do you like chili?"

"A home cooked meal? I'd almost kill for that. Is two o'clock good?" AJ couldn't stop the grin and it felt good. Katie's face brightened too.

Katie took out a business card from her coat and wrote her address on the back. She handed it to AJ. "I know you already have my address, but this'll save you some time." She handed AJ the empty thermos cup. "Thanks for the coffee. See you tomorrow?"

"Tomorrow," AJ said. Her hand over her racing heart, she waited until Katie got into her car and drove away. "What possessed me to do that?" She laughed at herself. Too damned many tears today, she thought as her phone rang.

"Where the hell are you?" Bill Whiteaker yelled before AJ finished saying her name.

"In the Franklin Hospital parking lot."

"They just wrecked the car we impounded last night."

"The Blackburn car? No. Wait, CSU said they were towing it today."

"They called me this morning and asked if I'd have someone drive it down. Everything else is still being used to dig out of the blizzard. I sent Talley, and I'm not sure he survived."

AJ didn't even say good-bye; she took off, lights flashing, siren on. Talley had been the young rookie with Bill yesterday.

She clenched her jaw as she saw the emergency lights, then the silver SUV and a large semi cab crumpled in the middle of the road. AJ parked behind the police car that blocked the road, careful of the ice that was quickly forming on the pavement as fire trucks poured water on the vehicles. Paramedics loaded a body bag into an ambulance, and AJ's heart sank.

A city cop, the size of a pro linebacker, stepped in front of her, and she almost fell. She held up her badge and he nodded. Bonnie Logan was off to the right with a clipboard in her hands. Bonnie was almost six feet tall, something that always caught AJ off guard. Her blue Milwaukee Police stocking cap was pulled down to her mirrored sunglasses. The squad car was partially up on a snowbank and AJ veered toward her.

"Damn, AJ," Bonnie said as AJ grabbed the car door for balance. "He never stood a chance. I hate this."

"Was anyone with him?"

Bonnie shook her head.

"Where's the driver of the truck?"

"Nowhere to be found." Bonnie pointed north. "Witnesses said a woman was driving, but she ran." Bonnie slid into her vehicle and entered information on her computer.

"The fire truck's made the street into a skating rink." AJ said, looking at the glazed street. "Who's in charge?"

"Bill called me so I'm in charge," Bonnie said but continued to stare at the screen. "Shit, the truck's stolen. Last fall. That figures."

AJ moved cautiously to her left and dialed the office. "Bill? Talley didn't make it, and the car's totaled." She listened for a few minutes. "I'll be back there in a few minutes. I'm sorry about Talley." They talked a bit more before hanging up. She thought of Talley last night in the storm and at the bar as she turned back to the police car.

Bonnie got out of her car and turned her collar up against the occasional bitter breeze. "Would you mind if I notified Katie?"

"No, go ahead. In fact, see Ms.—Katie—in person, if you can. She's having a bad day."

Bonnie stared at her for a minute, then looked away. "How do you know?"

"I just left her at Franklin Hospital. That friend of hers, Lu, is in trouble."

"Lu's always in trouble. I heard about you and Lu, the CPR at the Copper Penny." Bonnie leaned back into her squad car for her gloves. "How'd the interview with Katie go last night?"

"She came in, just as you said she would, but she was really angry. Her father was a cop?"

"Yeah, Katie's got a temper." Bonnie grinned a little and shook her head. "Her father was a good cop until he was injured, then Katie and I worked for him. Got us both through college."

"Katie said Lu's being transferred to Madison. Her parents made the decision."

"Really?" Bonnie's eyebrows shot up. "Must be serious then. Her parents kicked her to the curb years ago."

"I didn't ask Katie for more. She was in pieces at the hospital. I was going into the hospital when Bill called."

"I was on my way to the meeting at the station when they called me about this. Obviously, I'm not going to make it. Will you be there after it's over?"

AJ nodded. "I'll be at the office until four or so. I put one of my contacts into rehab today, and I want to make sure everything's taken care of. Be sure and see the notes from the meeting today since you're not going to be there. I interviewed Seraph last night. I want you to hear that. I want your opinion."

"I'll do that after I've seen Katie," Bonnie said. "Damn, she loved that car. There's going to be some screaming in my future. As for Lu, maybe it's better this way. One way or another, Lu was always a problem."

Two huge tow trucks rumbled up and moved ahead carefully. "Gotta go," Bonnie said.

"Wait," AJ said. "Let's get together. I need more information about Lu Wright."

Bonnie tested the icy street for a few feet before she stopped and turned. "Text me if I don't see you today. Later."

AJ walked back to the Suburban. If Katie was destroyed this morning, this car crash would only add to the demolition. But Katie could recover. Talley would never have that opportunity. She looked over her shoulder at the accident scene one last time.

CHAPTER EIGHT

The stairs at the police station felt steeper to AJ. Or was it that her mind couldn't look away from the body bag at the accident? Voices and the smell of fresh coffee drew her to the crowded conference room. She took a huge bite of a pecan Danish to do something about her empty stomach, grabbed a second piece, and balanced her coffee cup carefully as she made her way back to her chair. Bill dropped into the seat next to her.

"Do you want me to inform the group about Talley?" AJ said.

"No, he was mine, the poor kid." Bill's expression was grim. "Look at this group. They're so young." He stood and waited until everyone quieted. "Something's happened. An hour ago, Talley was driving that vehicle that we impounded last night down to the lab when a semi cab T-boned him. He was killed."

The people in the crowded room froze. AJ felt the silence snap, then echo with hurt. It was their first loss as a team.

"I drove down there." AJ picked up the conversation to give Bill a minute. "I couldn't tell if it was accidental or on purpose, but the driver of the semi fled the scene. Witnesses said it was a female driver."

"Female?" someone said. "Wasn't this the car Seraph was in? Could it have been Michael's group?"

"We don't know, but if it was, it took some planning." With some pride, she looked around the room at her task force. They weren't in uniform, but they defended their country every single day, from the streets to the boardrooms. "Keep your ears open, eyes wide. Somebody may be watching us."

Her phone rang and she started to turn it off but saw the name. "Sorry, I have to take this one. When I come back, we need to talk about the angels." She walked into the hallway and leaned against the wall.

"Allison," Charles said.

"Charles," she said. The conversations with her supervisor always began the same.

"That was an interesting conversation you sent me. Good job."

"Seraph gave us a new slant on Michael. Did you get the impression she ran the operation? Not Michael? Maybe's he's just the money. That's exactly what we want."

"Yes. Another twist."

"Something else. Did you catch her comment about the girls who hid her in the Blackburn car? The name Elena hasn't appeared on our radar. And she said Elena *knew* that she—Seraph—was not dead."

Charles was silent. AJ could almost hear him thinking. "I didn't understand that either. Maybe Seraph was confused, disoriented. I'm frankly amazed you got anything out of her."

"We're going to have to pick up on Elena, fast. Seraph said, 'Elena kills,' and this morning, my informant called Elena 'Michael's murder woman.' Also, the Blackburn woman has a close friend that we have to look at, Lu Wright. It was in last night's report. Oddly enough, that's the woman I did CPR on at the bar."

Charles took a deep breath. "Elena? I agree. She must be real, or two people wouldn't have mentioned her. By the way, I want Seraph in the apartment we always use and someone with her, round the clock. I have to go to Missouri, but I'll stop to see you first, and talk with her. Something else. I spoke with Seraph's doctor, the same one you talked to. He could release her to us tomorrow. Did you see the injury?"

"I did. A lot of stitches. She said it was a baseball bat." AJ paused. "They're releasing her tomorrow? That's faster than I would have thought, but frankly, I don't know how safe she is there, even with a police presence."

"Apparently, it was Michael that injured her?"

"That's what she says." AJ braced her foot against the wall. "My informant says the word on the street is that she's dead. That's good for us. It gives us more space. Wonder what happened between Michael and Seraph to cause all of this? And did you catch Seraph's remark that there's something wrong with Michael? That he's suddenly violent?"

"Yes," Charles said. "Did you get any more out of the Blackburn woman's car?"

"No. We had a disaster this morning. All of the flat bed trucks and tow trucks are still in use because of last night's storm, so Bill had one of his rookies drive it to the lab. A semi cab hit it and he was killed instantly."

"The hell," Charles said with a surprised breath. "Who was driving the semi?"

"Eye witnesses said it was a woman. It could have been one of Michael's angels. Or maybe I'm just paranoid."

"Damned cluster fuck," he said softly. Charles, once a FBI field agent, was now DEA. He was almost bald, but he had the trim body of a barely-forty-year-old man, a dedicated gym rat. She wondered how he kept the information straight on all three operations. Her operation in Milwaukee was the smallest, and she tore her hair out over the details. "And maybe it was just an accident," Charles said.

"It could have been, but it seems unlikely to me."

"Okay, the minute you have something, let me know." He changed the subject. "How's it going with Star?"

"She asked me to dinner at a new place in town."

"Good," Charles said. "Have a good time."

A beautiful woman and good food. Charles always viewed this as a sort of night off plus an opportunity to gather information. She shifted against the wall but said nothing. AJ felt as if Charles knew exactly where she was every single moment of her day.

"Now that we have Seraph, I may speed up my approach with Star. Her husband, the doctor, always looks at me as if he'd like to do some serious damage."

Charles gave a short laugh. "No comment. I'll call you when I hear from Seraph's doctor."

"If Seraph organized Michael's drug business, she'll also have all the information about Michael that we need—" AJ ran her words fast to stop him from ending the call.

He groaned. "Stop."

"But, Charles, think. Seraph is our big break; this is perfect."

"Allison," he said carefully, "I worked for over a year to do this job right. Identify Michael's suppliers, find out how it's shipped, and if it's moved from state to state. When we know that much, we'll also know where they manufacture it."

She clenched her jaw. "Could we go a little faster? I don't like dead cops on the street."

"We'll talk later," Charles said and ended the call.

She tossed her phone on the windowsill and stared up at the clear blue March sky. "Damn it all to hell." Patience, she reminded herself with a deep breath. This morning had ramped everything up. Finally, she turned back for the meeting.

AJ opened her laptop, trying to catch up with the conversation about a bust last night in north Milwaukee. In an abandoned church of all places. Someone had labeled it a real "Come to Jesus" moment on the report, and AJ smiled at the wisecracks. One of the worst problems with meth was that they could manufacture the drug in the most ordinary places, from back rooms in local businesses to cars. Or upscale neighborhoods to trailers or mobile homes, ranch houses in middle class suburbs, and farms, lots of farms. As the current economy forced farms out of business, dealers grabbed them up by the handful or squatted.

"What's up with your people?" AJ asked the group. Each of them had their own informants that they checked with during the week.

"Still afraid of Michael and his gang," one of the men said. Everyone nodded or added the same words.

AJ studied them for a moment. To a person, they all looked tired. "When I talked with my informant this morning, she told me that Michael had killed Seraph and called her his main woman. She said all the angels were sad. It's good for us to have that out on the streets. We want everyone to think Seraph's dead to give us more time. And before anyone asks, I don't know if Michael knows that she's still alive. My gut feeling, after the Blackburn car incident, is that he doesn't. So when you listen to my interview with Seraph, pay attention. Seraph made it sound as if she runs—ran—the operation. If that's the case, Michael's just the money."

AJ's second in command, Grace, spoke up. "Is she clean?"

"No, she's addicted and it's meth. Worse, she has a concussion. Michael really did some damage to her. If we move her to a safe house, we'll have a doctor in charge with a nurse on-site for a few days."

"We'll have to deal with her, personally?"

"Since we're keeping a very low profile, we'll be in charge of her. Be careful. The symptoms will cross, the concussion and the drugs, and you won't know which is which." AJ paused, considering what to tell them. "They have her on a new drug at the clinic, specifically for depression, but it helps the withdrawal." She turned to Grace. "Would you post that doctor's report at the end of our daily notes?"

"What about sudden temper tantrums, physical violence?" Jock said. "Or uncontrollable sexual urges?" He grinned as he said that, and AJ frowned at him.

"Not in Seraph's case," AJ said. "Cranky, yes, but the hitting or uncontrollable sexual urges, that kind of behavior shouldn't be part of her recovery. The new drug counteracts that." She stared at him for a moment. He knew better.

Bill cleared his throat and gave Jock a serious look. "AJ's right. Be more alert to suicide than violence in Seraph's situation, but the fact that she has a child factors in on our side. Check the new folder on your computers under her name. This is all the information we have on Seraph, including AJ's interview with her last night, plus her past history of treatment. Seraph was the closest to Michael, is actually related to him, and lived with him. Her DOB, birthplace, real name, and everything we could find on her is there, but for our purpose, we'll continue to call her Seraph. I'm with AJ. It sounds as if Seraph was in charge. We lost Talley. Let's not lose Seraph."

AJ held up her hand. "Seraph may be a drug addict, but she's still a human being and she's frantic over her missing little girl. If I hear or see any disrespect, you're gone before you can take another breath." AJ saw they all understood. "That doesn't mean you can't be firm or that you should trust her.

"One other thing," she continued. "Don't lose sight of why we're in Milwaukee. We want Michael, the high-impact dealer with the money, not the local street dealers, not the mules, the lookouts, couriers, or even the bodyguards. There's enough local and federal law enforcement after those people. This team was formed for information. We're after where they get their ingredients, who they're selling to, and where they're cooking. We're not undercover, but we want you to maintain a minimal presence. Don't forget that."

Jock immediately stood. "I don't get this. Why let the dealers go by?"

With a sigh, AJ looked over her group before she spoke. "For those of us who have been doing this for a while, like Jock and me, this is a hard pass, but that's exactly what we have to do. Any arrests go to Bill's team. Let his side of the operation take care of that. Remember, we're not some group of loose federal cannons. We're a combined task force with Bill's local police, reporting to Justice. Keep a low profile." Jock frowned at her. "The angels. I counted more than twenty photos on our board. Jock, what's your estimate?" AJ intentionally picked on him to give him a little moment to show what he excelled in.

"I'm guessing that's low," he said.

There it is, she thought. Where he likes to be and what he's good at.

"A lot of them have kids and live-in boyfriends. When I see them, they're usually in groups of two or three, always with small children. It's so normal that no one really looks twice. The paraphernalia I saw was in a diaper bag."

"Are you sure they work for Michael?"

"I've seen them before, and one of my informants confirms it. We were in that coffee shop on Harvey and Center, right around the corner from where I get a haircut. I bought the kids some ice cream, and talked basketball to one of their boyfriends."

"Perfect, Jock. Did you get any photos?"

He nodded and looked pleased, which, of course, was what she wanted. The next question was designed to clear Katie from the investigation.

"Do any of you know a woman named Lu Wright? She's connected to the Blackburn woman, the owner of the car that Seraph was found in." No one answered and so AJ went on. "All right, how about an angel called Elena?" Four people held their hands up. "You four, give me everything you know about Elena, no matter how small. Everyone, ask your informants about both women. My informant says Elena is Michael's murder woman, something you'll hear from Seraph on my interview. Anything you find goes on your daily report and the evidence boards in the war room, but pay special attention to Lu Wright or Elena. Talley's death takes this to a new level so bring in anything that you can, no matter how small. And that's all I've got."

The room began to empty. AJ started on notes about her early morning meeting with Frog. Bill would handle the information on Talley.

Bill stayed in the room and shut the door behind him. "I hear you put Frog into rehab."

AJ nodded. "I did. She was in terrible shape this morning." She looked up at him. "And I told Bonnie to stop in, see you, and pick up the information on this meeting. I want her to hear the interview with Seraph. She's Katie Blackburn's friend and has known Lu Wright for quite a while."

Bill shoved his hands in his pockets. "Was that Charles on the phone?"

"Yes. About the interview with Seraph. Also, he wants Seraph in the safe house after the doctor releases her. I'll have Grace set up a schedule when and if that happens."

"Did he say anything about switching Jock out of the unit?"

"We didn't talk about that. He's going to Missouri but stopping here first. Charles has known Jock for a long time so it might be smart to have Charles talk to him, one-on-one."

Bill nodded and left. She checked the clock above the door. There was still time to call Franklin Hospital about Lu Wright to check out the blood work, then swing downtown to check on Frog. She rubbed her eyes and turned back to her laptop. The team should pick up something about Elena and Lu Wright by Monday. If Elena led the street operation, they'd have her under surveillance soon. She began typing and sent her team a note about something she'd forgotten to mention. The tattoo on Seraph's hand.

CHAPTER NINE

"I t's crowded." AJ leaned close to Katie's ear as they moved carefully through the crowd the next day. The Milwaukee Art Museum was jammed.

"Yes, but—" Katie said just as someone bumped her right into AJ's arms. Laughing, they righted each other. "Feel that laid-back Sunday atmosphere?"

"Almost knocked to the floor is Milwaukee's version of laid-back?"

"We take our art seriously," Katie said with a straight face. "What do you want to see?"

"The Paris Posters, for sure. I love the action and all the colors."

Katie smiled but said nothing. Her company, Blue Ridge, had done the museum's catalog for the winter exhibits. Last month, they had finished the museum's spring catalog but, best of all, they had the contract for next year. It was an account she dearly loved.

"Oh, and what's the 'The Layton'?" AJ moved quickly to avoid another collision.

"The Layton Art Collection?" Katie said, threading her way through several people who had stopped in front of her. "It's gorgeous. One of the oldest exhibits here. Follow me. I love this city, and there's lots of interesting information there plus the art."

Several hours later, they picked up their coats at the cloakroom. A tall, well-dressed man stepped out of the crowd, stopping AJ with a hand on her shoulder. AJ introduced him, but it was so noisy that

Katie only heard the word doctor. He barely glanced at her as he stared at AJ.

Katie took both of their coats and moved away. AJ's duster smelled like green plants. Was it spearmint? Whatever it was, it certainly was subtle and sexy when combined with the leather. The same fragrance had been in AJ's car yesterday at Franklin Hospital. Katie took another breath of the scent and turned to the large windows, letting her mind drift.

Last night, Katie had cleaned out the closet where the last of Lu's things had been stored. She'd found an album in the back corner that held old photos of their first trip together. With a pot of coffee perking, she'd sat at the kitchen table, paging through the pictures. *Had she ever been that young?* She had hesitated, then decided that she was tired—and years beyond caring. She had dropped the album in the garbage. With the lights off, she had sat in the dark and stared at the bright stars in the dark winter sky.

Now she looked at the bright sun on the water, tracking it to the horizon. Finally, she turned back to AJ who stood absolutely quiet, focused on the man. Katie's eyes lingered on AJ's lightly muscled body. The navy blue vest covered a long sleeved, white T-shirt tucked into faded jeans. She smiled at the black leather Wellingtons. AJ was definitely a boot woman. The man said something, low and emphatic. AJ nodded abruptly and turned toward Katie with a blank expression on her face. At that moment, Katie decided AJ could be anything or anyone she wanted the public to see.

The cold bit at them as they walked to the car. AJ's rosy cheeks and earmuffs made her look young, her hair lifting with the slight wind off the lake. AJ talked about art while Katie kicked at the snow and felt as if the world had righted itself.

Later, Katie chopped onions and began the chili in her kitchen. AJ sat at the table behind her, staring out into the almost-dark yard, preoccupied and quiet.

"Who was that man at the art museum?" Katie said conversationally but didn't turn around. She heard AJ pull in a long breath.

"I took his wife to dinner a week ago."

Katie glanced over her shoulder. "He looked angry."

"He was." AJ stood. "Could I look at that book on your coffee table?"

"Sure," Katie said as she added the diced tomatoes to the chili. She leaned back a step to see AJ step down into her living room and return with the book. AJ opened it to a page marked with a long black crow feather.

"Eleanor Roosevelt? I've read this biography. Are you a fan?" AJ said.

"As it happens, I am." Katie glanced at her with a smile and watched her study the feather before she went back to the food. "I know she's out of fashion, but I'm a believer."

"That's odd. She's sort of my hero."

"Are you serious? What are the chances of that?"

"Not very good." AJ finally smiled as she began to look at the pages.

"Would you mind a little music?"

"Not at all. In fact, I'd enjoy it," AJ said but didn't look up, absorbed in the book.

Sarah McLachlan began to sing and Katie smiled down at the sink. It was one of her favorites. The windows had steamed over as the kitchen warmed with the cooking food. She hummed along with the music and put the bread in to warm. After stirring the pot of chili one last time, she turned. "Want a beer?"

"Beer's good," AJ said.

Katie took two bottles from the refrigerator. AJ was looking at her, the book held loosely in one hand.

"What?" Katie said.

"This is nice." AJ's mouth lifted a little at the corner. "The kitchen, the music, the smell of food. I like this a lot. Thanks."

"Where do you live? Don't you have meals with co-workers or friends or—" Katie stopped abruptly at the personal question and scrambled to cover her words. "I mean, we all need moments like this every once in a while."

"I have a place up in the Point, just off the lake. It's a tiny, converted carriage house above a garage. One bedroom, a living room, bitty little kitchen, but it does have a stove I never use and a microwave I abuse. That's it." AJ gestured at Katie's living room. "Nothing like this. This is a *real* house. How many bedrooms?"

"Three. It's a single story with a full attic. Everything's easy to get to." Katie wiped her hands on a towel. "Want to see? Bring your beer along for the tour."

AJ nodded and they went to the back of the house. Katie had converted the smallest bedroom into an office and liked it because of the long, narrow windows that overlooked the thick hedge that often brushed the glass. There were two walls of books and DVDs, a long table, and a desk. A lot of her work was done here. Everything about the house had pleased her from the moment she and Lu had first looked at it. *Lu, damn it.* She swung around and looked at AJ.

"You bought this house with someone, didn't you?" AJ leaned against the door.

"Yes. Lu."

"Lu Wright?" AJ said and turned her back to look at book titles. "How long did you live here together?"

Katie sighed. "Almost three years, but that was a long time ago. We owned it together in the beginning, but I bought her out years ago."

"Hey, look at these," AJ said, standing in front of Katie's business plaques and awards. She held up a softball trophy.

"I used to play shortstop." Katie grinned. "We won that year."

AJ pointed at the books. "You're a big mystery nut?"

"My vice. That and movies and music. And I played in a band for years." She pointed at a wall with shelf after shelf of CDs.

"Really?" AJ looked interested. "What did you play?"

"Keyboard and fiddle, or guitar. Mostly rock and roll or blues, but I can do classics if pushed."

"Look," AJ said with a wide grin and pulled two DVDs off the shelf. "You love scary movies. Is this the whole *Mummy* series? It's been years. Could we watch these some time?"

"Of course." Katie smiled. She was happy to hear there might be other days or nights with AJ. "Let's look at the other rooms."

Katie stopped at a doorway down the hallway and held out her hand. "The master bedroom," Katie said in a goofy, presentational voice.

"Great colors. I like blues and the old, faded golds." AJ stepped into the room. "I recognize the design on your quilt. That's a navigator's compass."

"My grandmother made that by hand after I came out to my family," Katie said with a wry smile. "I think she was afraid I'd lose my way."

"Do you use that small fireplace?"

"All the time. After Lu left, I redid this room, the bathroom, and the kitchen." She turned with a sudden laugh. "I have to show you my engineer brother's masterpiece, the bathroom."

AJ followed Katie inside. "Wow. This is different." A large skylight stretched across the ceiling, capturing what was left of the daylight. Delicate earth tones seemed to push the walls out, creating space. Even the air felt bigger. "Unusual," AJ said, turning in the center. "I like the marble effect."

Katie smiled. "Me too, but here's the funny part." She pulled the shower curtain back. "Looks just like a walk-in tub and shower, doesn't it? Look." She opened the wall panel in the tiles. A stainless steel seat swiveled out. "See the braces on the side here?" She pointed at railings hidden behind the shower curtain and the grab bars on the wall. "This is for my future. My brother's convinced I'm going to grow old alone." She demonstrated, sitting on the seat, holding an adjustable shower hose. "I will be a very *clean* old lady."

"Your brother's a genius. I like fix-up stuff too, although I've never tried anything this big. Three rooms. Wow." After Katie stepped out, AJ moved the seat back and forth, then put it away.

"My brother's not a genius; he's just cheap. He got a deal on this from a local hospital supply." They both laughed at that. "I forget it's there. What I really love is the space he created with the skylight and the colors. We had a ton of fun with this." She moved to the door. "Come on. Let's eat. I'm starving."

"Is that homemade bread?" AJ said as she sat at the table.

"My mother's," Katie said and placed a bowl of chili in front of AJ. "Another beer?"

"Thanks, but no. One's my limit."

"How did you like the exhibitions?"

"Loved both of them and that Layton display is a true treasure."

Katie grinned. "And the Bernard Dunstan's. That nude woman, getting out of the bath...You had a funny expression on your face."

AJ paused, spoon midway to her mouth. "That's always a... moment." She reached across for more bread.

"They had the full exhibit up before Christmas. What you saw was only about a third of it. They're making room for the next show but left that part because people loved it so much."

"His women always look so...perky. And I never saw anyone handle blues and grays the way he does." She grinned as she looked up at Katie.

Katie finished her bread and shoved her bowl away with a sigh. "That's enough for me."

"Is there more? It's really good."

"Of course." Katie took AJ's bowl and refilled it.

"I checked your website and saw that you had done the museum booklet on this show. Is that what your business is about?"

Katie took a sip of beer before she answered. "I started the business with print ads. The things you see in magazines and newspapers. Then I played around with billboards for a while, but didn't like it so went into things like the museum booklets. That kind of work is still something I love to do. I hired someone else to do billboards and he's good at it." She smiled at AJ who was eating steadily but paying close attention. "Everything is so digital these days that I had to go back to school for a semester and catch up on computers. I also hired another young guy last fall who's a genius with websites. Now I sell them to businesses. He does the work. I love my job, and thankfully, business is good."

"But it says public relations on your webpage. What's the difference?"

"Ah. That's a whole other world. Come to the office and I'll show you. That's actually my favorite part of my business. For example, I'm just beginning to gather information on a bank that's not doing very well in Milwaukee. I think I know what's wrong so

I'm putting together a presentation. That kind of information goes best with demographics, stats, that kind of thing. I can show better than I can tell."

AJ nodded. "It's a deal. I'll drop in." She pushed her bowl toward Katie. "Let me help you with the dishes. God, that was good."

Together, they cleaned the table and Katie teased AJ. "I'm sending you home with a container of chili. You can just heat it up. Uh, you do have a pot to heat it in?"

"Yes, a few pots and pans came with the place, but honestly, I'll probably use the microwave. Was that really all the bread?"

"Are you begging? Here, crackers ought to do it." Katie opened a tin and took out a sleeve of saltines. She pulled a paper lunch bag from the cupboard and tossed in prepackaged plastic utensils plus a paper napkin.

AJ fished out the plastic utensils. "Okay, enough. I do have silverware." She rolled the beer bottle in her hands. "Katie, I need to ask you some things about Lu Wright."

Katie's hands stopped moving. "Lu?"

"After I did CPR on her, I checked her out. You're her contact and responsible for her insurance?"

"She couldn't hold a job so I just put her on the company insurance. When I first met her, it was only alcohol. She was finishing her doctorate. We dated for several years while I started my business but then took the relationship up a notch, bought this house, and had those years here. Lu was teaching at the university and I was having fun with my little start-up business." She inhaled deeply. "Then came the damned drugs. I'm familiar with pot, but the rest of it scares me to death." Katie held AJ's gaze. "I was never involved."

"I didn't think you were, but—"

"Sure you did, or at least wondered," Katie interrupted with a disbelieving little laugh. "What is your job anyway? Are you a detective?"

AJ went down the front steps to the hall closet to her coat and brought a leather wallet back to the table.

Katie opened it, then looked up quickly. "Are you serious? ATF? I thought you were some new kind of Milwaukee cop."

"Don't be too impressed," AJ said. "I'm not very important, and I've never worked so hard in my whole life. This is my first day off in months. Maybe years."

"But ATF?" Katie repeated and looked up with another tease. "You're a...spy?"

AJ broke into a good-natured laugh. "A spy? That's CIA. You read too many mysteries. I'm just a government employee on loan to Milwaukee and the DEA at the moment."

"No wonder I'm confused. Law enforcement is usually focused and intense."

"It's my day off." AJ smiled and held up her beer.

"Okay, I understand about today." Katie picked up the identification again and stared at it for a moment. "But the night we first spoke, at the police station, I would have expected at least some of that."

"Why? You had a woman in your car who might have been dead. Then we impounded your car. You were angry and upset." AJ regarded her with a small frown.

"Angry?" Katie shot back. "That's an understatement. I was drooling furious. I knew you were going to impound my car. And we know how well that worked out."

"I'm sorry about your car, Katie."

"Poor Bonnie. I almost killed her. Mom and I were having lunch when she called, then she came to the house. I just exploded. I was so rude that my mother actually told me to quiet down." Katie swallowed hard. "I was with Dad when he bought that car. We both loved the thing." She held up her hands. "Listen to me. What am I thinking? It was a car. That's nothing compared to the young cop who was killed. Now I'm the one who's sorry."

AJ was quiet for a moment. "He was the first person to die on my team. Everyone lost on that accident."

Katie picked up their beers and pointed at the big couch. "Let's go to the living room. A fire would be good."

When the fire was going, they settled onto the couch. Katie tucked her leg under her and pulled a book from the shelf on the end table. The jacket showed a tall, black haired woman in a trench coat, pointing a gun down a dark alley.

"See this?" Katie had a wicked expression on her face. "It's about all I know about federal law enforcement. She's FBI, and taller than Bonnie—at least six feet—with searing blue eyes. She's slender but has muscles like steel and a mind like a bullet. One slam from Bren Black's fist, and it's lights out. There isn't anything Bren can't do." She wiggled the book in front of AJ. "Like Bren, is your job"—she made quote marks in the air—"a really big secret?"

"Big secret? No." AJ grinned as she took the book from Katie. "I don't know about Bren, but I worked my butt off, graduated from West Point, and served my military time overseas." She snickered as she read the blurb on the back of the book. "God, who does the research for this stuff? Over six feet tall? I guess most of the women on my team don't stand a chance." She set the book down and smiled at Katie. "I lead a combined agency, working with the local police. We're after specific criminal activity here in Wisconsin. Actually, I could tell you but—"

Katie held up her hand and finished for her. "I know, I know. You'd have to kill me."

"Truthfully? We're here because there was a rumor about Milwaukee, the bones of…" AJ leaned forward and whispered, "Jimmy Hoffa."

"For God's sake, Jimmy—"

"Hoffa," AJ said.

"I can't believe you said that."

AJ laughed again. "I can't either."

"But I did wonder about your job."

"I know you did. I saw you *wonder* when we were in Bill's office."

Katie laughed a little and pushed into the couch. "Then I looked at your card. Just your name. In script?"

AJ shrugged and set her beer on a coaster. "Want to finish discussing Lu? I'd like to clear her out of this investigation."

Her smile suddenly gone, Katie looked away. "I may never have done drugs, but Lu certainly was addictive." She swept a loose curl away from her face. "All those years and I couldn't get away from her. Or stop. I would just go back, go back, go…" Her voice trailed off and she looked up, helpless to explain what had happened to her with Lu. "Did anything like this…someone…ever get to you like that?"

AJ's face changed and her mouth straightened. "Did the drugs end it?"

"Yes. She wouldn't show up to teach her class and not come home for days. I wouldn't know where she was and would end up searching the bars in the city. Dad and Bonnie helped, but we never got ahead of her. You'd never believe how intelligent that woman is."

"Oh yes, I would. Addicts can be highly intelligent and manipulative. Everyone thinks drugs belong to poor, low-life, street people, but that's not the case. Drugs run rampant in white-collar professionals and, in most ways, they're worse. If nothing else, they have the time and means to elude detection. Do you have any idea where Lu got the drugs?"

Katie shook her head. "No. I swear, if I had, I would have turned her in myself. I always thought it was alcohol until I found her stash. Even then I didn't know what it was until I took it to Bonnie."

"What was it?"

"Bonnie said it was cocaine, but there were some pills as well."

They both were quiet for a moment until AJ's phone rang. "I'm sorry, I have to take this," AJ said. She walked away and stepped up into the kitchen area. Her voice was terse, but Katie heard her say "Charles" before she hung up. She turned and Katie stood. "I'd like to stay, but I've got to go." AJ gave her a quick, polite hug, then stepped back with an odd look on her face. "Thanks. I can't tell you how much I enjoyed today and the meal. Let's do it again."

"Cool. Just give me a call." Katie again caught that fresh scent on AJ. Was it a shampoo? A soap? Whatever, it was a beautiful smell and she loved it.

"I will and I promise." AJ pulled on her coat, then was out the door.

Katie stood in the narrow front window, watched AJ's headlights shine through the big tree in her front yard. When they were gone, she turned on the music again, took a bottle of water to the living room, and settled on the floor in front of the fire.

She'd really enjoyed the day and hadn't laughed like that in a long time. At the art museum, AJ had been relaxed, warm, even a little flirty, often leaning into her. Definitely a little flirty. Then there was Allison Jacob, West Point grad and ATF agent. *I'm not important,* she'd said. Like the devil, Katie thought. Anyway, I'd never know if you were. "Jimmy Hoffa," she said with a little laugh and remembered AJ's expression. It was something like an unexpected happy moment.

AJ had avoided the question about being too attached to someone and covered herself, made her eyes go blank.

Katie sipped her water. She liked AJ's intriguing voice and that hug had felt pretty good, not to mention the free, easy way her body moved. Or that teasing, sexy grin. But she wanted the woman behind all those personalities, where the humor and intelligence lived.

For the first time in years, she felt a solid little thrum of attraction and it felt good. *Every time I looked at her, she was looking at me. Those interested, alert eyes.*

CHAPTER TEN

The big agency Suburban groaned with the cold, but AJ ignored it. Her eyes were still fixed on Katie at the window. That hug. Had she lost her mind? When she'd touched Katie's warm skin, it was hard to let go. A little dazed, she looked around the neighborhood.

The area was lit up by a bright winter moon hung on the lip of a cloud. Even in their winter nakedness, the massive old trees were lovely. The houses on the street looked settled, solid, just like Katie's comfortable kitchen, a place where the world felt manageable. Katie had glided in front of her, hands moving confidently over the stove and countertops; her slender, fit, body graceful in the dark jeans and silver-blue tunic, showing off nice shoulders. And breasts.

AJ stiffened suddenly as an unexpected deep tug of sexual attraction lit her up. Surprised, she let the car idle at the stop sign and hugged herself hard. "Wow," she whispered over a breath as it touched her again, soft as a butterfly wing.

"Crap. No damned time." She tossed her earmuffs on the seat. Charles had flown in, just as she'd anticipated. He needed a ride, and he'd whine if he had to wait too long. There was no time to relish this day or how many times her heart had sped up simply looking at Katie.

With a little groan, she forced herself to sort through data for Charles. The first thing her mind lit upon was Star's husband this afternoon at the art museum. His eyes had alternated between fury and sorrow as he'd warned her to be careful of his wife. The doctor's entire rant had been creepy.

Suddenly, an electric blue flash caught her eyes in the side mirror. The only other vehicle on the road was several car lengths behind her as she stopped for a traffic light. Instincts fully alert, she checked the car in the rearview mirror. That car should have caught up with her at the red light. It was large and white with an odd blue hood ornament.

AJ sped up a little, gauging her speed against the next traffic light. The car behind kept the same distance. She made a sudden right turn, then another around a fast food business, speeding behind the building, and back onto the street. She got a good look at the vehicle that was following her, hit the gas, and was out to the interstate in minutes, certain it had been a white, late model pickup. The airport exit to Mitchell International Airport was just ahead, and she hit it fast, praying for ice-free pavement.

Charles's solid frame shoved out of a shadow with baggage in both hands. He tossed stuff into the backseat and settled in beside her. She put the car in gear, checking the rearview mirror just as the pickup came around the corner.

"We're being followed."

"Really? How close are we to the station?" He raised his eyebrows with a little grin.

"Very near. Want to stop there first, before we head over to the clinic to meet Bill?"

"Go for it," he said. "Did you get the plates?"

"Not yet." But no matter how fast or slow she drove, the white vehicle kept a steady distance behind them, just far enough so they couldn't see the driver or passengers.

"Can't catch the tags," Charles said, keeping an eye on the side mirror, "but it does have a strange hood ornament. Something bright blue that's lit up."

The station was coming up on their right when, suddenly, the pickup did a U-turn and sped away. "Whoa," Charles said. "Well, so much for that."

"They must have known we were going to turn in here. Damn," AJ said as she pulled into the driveway. "To the best of my knowledge, I've never been tailed here." She let the car idle, and both of them looked down the road.

"Let's take a moment anyway. I want to talk about Star before we meet with Bill at the clinic. I'll call him."

AJ made coffee while Charles talked with Bill.

"Okay," Charles said and took the cup of coffee AJ offered. "What's up with Star?"

"I'm right at the front with her." AJ took a sip of coffee and held Charles's gaze. "The first time we met for dinner, I played at what she expected. The boy-are-you-beautiful kind of thing with a touch of awe. She was high when I picked her up and drank a lot and offered recreational drugs. But the second meal—last week— was totally different. She paid attention, nursed a glass of wine for two hours, and stayed just high enough to be comfortable. The information that you planted works well. Both she and her husband believe that I'm an art patron getting a feel for the local community on my way to Chicago from Canada. She stayed right on target with that all through the meal. By the way, thanks for the list of their donations to local art. Did you get that from the IRS?"

"Mostly," Charles said.

AJ stretched her legs out. "She was referred to you by the DEA Special Agent in Charge here? Did I remember right?"

"Right, our local guy. He and I go back a long time. We were together in Washington when I was given permission to run this operation and, so far, he's been very helpful. They know she's getting the meth somewhere and then, predictably, shares with her friends. Or sells. They haven't been able to find her source, and it drives him nuts. If you can find the source, it helps him as much as it helps us." He paused to take a drink of coffee, and AJ saw him begin to relax. "So what's next?"

"She's asked me out to the opening of a new club."

Charles considered her for a moment. "This week?"

"Right, but now that we have Seraph, I'd like to keep Star as a contact and nothing more."

"I'd prefer to use them both. If Seraph's telling the truth, then you can use Star just to keep us in the game with her friends. At least for a while." Charles frowned.

AJ leaned toward him. "Her husband stopped me at the art museum today and really ranted. Whoever's selling to her hasn't had time to connect the dots between us, but her husband has, believe me."

"What did he say?" Charles sat up, more alert.

"That his wife has an unfortunate habit and it's costing him thousands of dollars. And that she's more than just eye candy to him. He never once directly mentioned her love of women, but he wants me to stay away from her." AJ shook her head. "None of the background we did on her shows any hospitalization. If he can afford drugs, he can afford hospitalization, and it worries me that he hasn't done that, hospitalized her."

"Thousands of dollars? No wonder her husband's furious."

"I didn't get the feeling it had one single thing to do with money. He certainly made it clear that he didn't want me with her. Unless I was buying art," AJ said dryly. "Not only was he angry, but he was agonized today. That's something else to be careful of. An agonized husband is a huge wild card."

"All right. Your call." Charles shoved his chair back. "What else do you have for me?"

"We've been tracking the girls, the angels, with photos and information."

"Where? Let me see."

They walked to the war room. AJ showed him the photos they'd tacked to the evidence board and the names on the dry board. Michael's name was at the top with a dash and Seraph's name with a question mark.

"You're gonna love me," he said with a grin and set his briefcase on the long table. He pulled out three photos. "The local DEA took these just after the holidays." He handed her three photos. "I asked them about the two names you sent me, Lu Wright and Elena." Charles pointed at the second photo. "This is Elena. The agent that took this photo had just picked up some street intel on her. And you know this one, Lu Wright. This one is from last fall. She's talking to Elena so, at some point, she was definitely involved."

"Elena looks rough." AJ studied the photo of Elena next to a couple, a man and woman, on the street. Tall, long-legged in worn jeans, she was wearing biker boots and her unzipped black leather coat hung on her broad shoulders, casually dominating. Her long hair, straight and black, looked like a smear of ink. "Look at the man beside her. She's in charge." She touched the next photo. "This one…" AJ held up the photo. "Elena and Lu are behind the old foundry works on the river. Damn. I wanted to clear Lu off the list, but it looks like she was in the group too." *And pulled Katie into the mess.* "When I called Lu's doctor at Franklin Clinic, he was almost adamant that her heart's going to give out." She sank against the table. "Did you send these to Bill?"

"I e-mailed them to him before I left the office today." He glanced at his watch. "Let's go meet him and I'll meet Seraph. By the way, we're going to move her tonight."

Surprised, AJ turned to him. "Is she physically able?"

He nodded as they put the photos on the corkboard with thumbtacks. AJ turned off the main lights behind them as they walked toward the stairs, checking the street below her, their own lot, and the bar's parking lot across the street. There was no sign of the white pickup. The bar across the street was outlined sharply in the moonlight. The last time she'd looked at it from this window had been to watch Katie run across the street in the blizzard. She laid her hand on the cold glass as if to hold that image.

Charles waited for her. "Nothing?" he said.

"They may be on a side street. I'll drive the other way, just in case." The zipper on her long duster gave a whine in the quiet office. "You need a warmer coat, Charles. Grab something from the room across the hallway."

❖

Automatically, AJ checked the clinic's parking lot. The white pickup was still a no-show. Where had the truck found her in the first place? It could have been Katie's place if they'd been down the street with their lights off. Maybe they'd followed them from the art museum. Charles said something as Bill and a doctor walked down the hallway with them. After the deep cold, Seraph's room felt warm and steamy. Unzipping her coat, AJ positioned herself for a perfect view of the door while the doctor and Charles explained what was about to happen. A much more alert Seraph paid close attention, her white-blond hair gleaming in the lights.

"Are you certain it's safe outside?" Seraph sounded suddenly young, and AJ looked at her. Even Seraph's eyes were round. It was the voice she used for older men, she was certain of it. This woman had spent time on the streets.

"We're taking you out through the ambulance entrance," Charles said. "The police will lead the way."

"I'm afraid," she said in a low voice, her gaze sliding to AJ.

"We understand." Charles tried to soothe her.

"No, you don't. Some of our people work here."

Everyone was quiet for a moment. "Have you recognized anyone?" Bill said.

"No, but Elena handles the girls. I don't know everyone." Seraph glanced at AJ once again.

When AJ caught Seraph's look, she stared at the floor and pulled in a slow breath. It was as if some women begged silently for help. Her ex-best friend Rachael always had. She was alert to that fragile flicker. Dana Taylor never did, not once. AJ shifted against the wall. Nor did Katie Blackburn.

"We'll be fine," Charles said abruptly. "Get the wheelchair."

Within minutes, they had Seraph inside the ambulance. AJ checked the street and parking lot again, then rode shotgun. The ambulance careened west, circled around the long way, but finally came in through the back alley, lights off. This was a crucial moment, and all of AJ's senses ramped up. The cold bit her skin as she smelled the de-icing chemical on the sidewalk. She checked her weapon and counted the cops around them. It was so quiet she could hear them breathe as they surrounded Seraph to walk her inside. The ambulance pulled away as quiet as it had come.

The apartment was on the first floor of an older building across the street from the city's largest cemetery. AJ had never liked its accessibility. As they entered, she smelled coffee, heard the television go quiet. Seraph stood in the living room, managing to look simultaneously defiant and lost. AJ couldn't stand it and went back outside. She walked down the alley in the silent, cold darkness, then around the neighboring buildings.

The cemetery across the street, the largest in Milwaukee, stretched as far as she could see on either side of her. Utterly still, she listened, her eyes fixed on a large black stone angel about forty feet in front of her. All she could hear was her own heart beating.

When AJ returned, everyone was at the large kitchen table. She made sure the drapes in the front room were closed and tossed her coat over a chair. She sat as far away from Seraph as she could. A mirror hung on the wall off to the side and she caught their reflection in it. How many times had she sat in rooms like this, in this same situation? Too many.

Charles picked up the conversation with Seraph. She was as painfully thin as Frog, and AJ paid attention to her body language for a baseline for the next few days. She would repeat the questions Charles was asking right now, only in a different manner with different words.

"Thank you for cooperating," Charles said, his voice kind.

"I need help and I don't want to go to jail." Seraph pointed at AJ. "She said that you might help me find Meredith."

"We'll do everything we can," Charles said and glanced at AJ for confirmation. AJ nodded and saw Seraph's body relax. *She'd rather talk to a woman and doesn't trust men.* She hoped everyone at the table saw the same thing.

CHAPTER ELEVEN

Running a bit late, Katie hurried into the professional building in downtown Milwaukee. The wind blew the door shut behind her with a loud bang, and she cringed as it echoed in the quiet lobby. She turned to make sure it had closed. A couple came in next and the door slammed with the same loud racket. The man looked familiar, but Katie drew in a sudden breath when the woman shook back the hood of her coat. Had she seen her on television? The movies?

They got on the elevator together and everyone reached for a button. Katie withdrew her hand immediately as the man pushed the button, giving her a hard look. At that moment, she remembered where she'd seen him. He was the angry man who'd talked with AJ last weekend at the art museum. She saw him remember her as well. His face was briefly sad, then stern, and he tightened his arm around the woman.

The elevator doors were almost closed when a hand gripped it from the outside. A tall woman with long black hair, wearing jeans and a leather jacket, held the doors open for a younger woman behind her. They were laughing and paid no attention to anyone else in the elevator.

Katie checked the woman with the man. The woman's ice-blue gaze locked onto hers, unwavering and intense. Waves of chestnut hair surrounded her lovely face. The man increased his grip and the woman stood straighter but continued to stare at Katie.

Uncomfortable, Katie looked away but glanced at the couple again. Now both of them were looking at her, and her face warmed. Worse, he looked fiercely possessive. She pulled in a breath at the invitation in the woman's gorgeous eyes. If this had been a bar, Katie would have expected an immediate offer.

She turned away from them slightly, caught the tall woman in the leather jacket watching her as if she understood the invitation on the other woman's face. She raised her eyebrows slightly at Katie.

When the door opened, everyone started to move. The man and woman stopped, and he nodded at Katie. She walked out ahead of them but still felt the woman's burning gaze. After several steps, she finally took a deep breath. She opened the door to the law firm, an old client. They had called her for assistance with a new advertising campaign.

"What was that?" Katie mumbled under her breath. She was certain those ice-blue eyes were high. Lu's eyes had looked the same many times.

Later that afternoon, Katie returned phone calls in her office before she remembered the couple in the elevator. She found AJ's card and left a message on the phone number printed on the card. She'd like to talk to her about that man and woman. And maybe AJ would be up for another meal. She studied the card for a moment, the unusual script. AJ's genuine smile, quick mind—all her personalities—had been in her mind the whole week. In fact, she'd called her secretary "AJ" yesterday morning. She'd apologized over the laughter as she fled to her office.

"Katie?" Her newest hire leaned into her office. She motioned for him to come on in.

"What's up, Zack?"

With a proud expression, he laid a folder and a disc on her desk. "Look at the sale I just made," he said. He beamed as she jumped up and shook his hand.

"Let's see it. Set your laptop on the conference table." Zack's artwork was far and above anything Katie could do, something she happily admitted.

Her secretary stood at the doorway. "You have a call."

Katie picked up the phone. "Give me a minute, Zack. How about making us both some coffee? Bring it back in with you." She spoke into the phone. "Katie Blackburn."

"I'll take some too," AJ said.

"Some what?" Katie's heart gave a little jump when she heard AJ's voice.

"Coffee."

"Oh, you heard?"

"Never talk when you pick up a phone unless you want the person at the other end to hear too."

"Is this part of your training?" Katie teased her. She sat behind her desk and picked up AJ's business card.

"Oh, please." Laughter trailed through the phone. "I'm so good they didn't have to train me."

"And modest too."

"One of my nicer traits. Did they have to train your famous FBI agent Bren Black, the hero in the book you're reading, or was she just born with all of that knowledge?"

"Not a clue," Katie said with a little laugh. "Are you at work?"

"Offsite. You called?"

"Something happened today. Could I talk you into another dinner at my house?"

"Oh yeah," AJ said immediately. "Wait. I think it's my turn."

Katie watched water trickle off an icicle outside her window. "You'll cook?" She grinned, recalling their conversation about AJ's cooking abilities.

"Would you settle for cereal?"

Katie groaned. "Let me cook something I've never tried before. Want to participate in a food experiment?"

"Love to."

"When?"

"Let's see," AJ said with a breath. "How about tomorrow night? That would be Saturday. Six o'clock?" A man said something and people laughed in the background. "Shut up," AJ said away from the phone.

"Catching a little flack...Bren?"

"This group has a limited intellectual capacity."

"All right, tomorrow night it is." Katie prepared to hang up.

"Wait. What happened this morning? That thing you said on my voice mail?"

"Remember the man at the art museum, the one that talked to you as we were leaving? I was on an elevator with him this morning. He was with one of the most beautiful women I've ever seen, but she looked...wrong."

A sigh echoed through the phone. "It probably was his wife. Where were you?"

"Downtown, at a law office for a meeting with a client."

AJ was quiet for a minute. "The professional building on Madison?"

"Yes."

"How did he seem?"

"Him? Protective as an army. But she was—look, why don't we talk about this tomorrow night?"

"Good idea, but hold that thought for me. Tomorrow night at six?"

Katie heard people talking behind AJ so she confirmed the time and reluctantly ended the call.

Zack stood in Katie's office door with two cups of coffee. "Let's see the proposal," Katie said. He was still energized and she wanted to give him the opportunity to pat himself on the back a little. He plunked his tall, lanky frame in a chair with a happy sigh and opened his laptop. Initially, Katie had hired him on a temporary basis last fall when Lu had brought him by the office and insisted that Katie give him a try. It was probably the only positive thing Lu had done for her. Zack's boyish smile and sandy brown hair seemed to inspire trust in her clients, and she liked working with him.

The client had wanted a theme, plus some small giveaways for folks to carry home once they were in the door. One of the ideas he'd proposed was wristbands along the theme of WWJD, but with the name and logo of the company. Katie looked at his design with a sudden thought.

"Who's doing the sample wristbands for you?" she said.

"Alex, down the street."

"Think you could get him to make me a sample or two?"

"Sure," Zack said and picked up his phone. "I'll do the introductions. You talk with him and tell him what you want."

Katie hung up a few minutes later with a smile. She could pick them up on her way home.

❖

AJ hung up and stared out Seraph's living room window. She was sure that had been Star and her husband on the elevator with Katie, and considering that Star had not shown up last night, she was relieved that the woman was alive. Maybe her husband was clamping down on her. She'd waited at the club almost two hours before leaving, then gone back to the police station and changed clothes. Bill and Charles had come in, and they'd gone over the information that Seraph had given them late yesterday afternoon. She'd called all her team leaders here to catch them up.

"Allison?" Charles called her back to the table in Seraph's kitchen.

AJ sat at the table with the rest of them and opened her own laptop. "Go to the angels folder. Grace has numbered all the photos we have of these girls and we started at number one." AJ and Grace had chased leads on some of Michael's angels and gotten some good looks at the group.

"Look at number one, the first photo, Miss Average Young Mother. Grace and I followed her as she pushed her baby and stroller through Riverside Mall while she window-shopped—and made three sales before we could catch our breaths."

"It would have taken me longer to have found the right shoes," Grace said with a wry expression on her face.

"That's the truth. I've shopped with you. You love to shop," AJ said to Grace. "Anyway, the first buyer, Mr. Prep School, was quick. He came up beside her, flirted a little, and she reached into the diaper bag and handed him something. Bang, he's gone into an electronics store."

"So next up, like three minutes later, is someone I thought was her mother. Both were blondes and tanned. Who's tan in Milwaukee in March anyway?" Grace said and pushed her dark hair off her forehead. "The older woman leans over, says something to the baby, and hands the money off. In the meantime, the angel, the younger woman, stuffs a little paper sack into the older woman's purse. They stand and talk, just like mother and daughter, both of them laughing at whatever. The older woman leaves."

"And that's how it went. All the way down the mall. Grace and I were walking together and could hardly keep up. It was all so—average. So normal. Then this young woman goes shopping for baby clothes, leaving by a front entrance. The whole thing took less than three hours. We did get her license plate and the car's registered to her. Slickest thing I ever saw."

"And that's how it went in every scenario," Grace said. "These girls are good. They act like they're selling Girl Scout cookies."

"We followed numbers one through five. We sat beside them in fast food restaurants or watched them pick up guys on the streets. A few of them met and went to a movie yesterday afternoon." AJ shook her head. "It's a well-oiled machine, believe me, and I think they've been doing this for quite a while. They all know each other."

"Oh, the house." Grace held up her finger. "Look at photo number thirty-three."

"This is a place where some of them live together," AJ said. "We ran the information on this house on North Avenue. Guess who owns it? Michael."

"Nice house," Charles said. "It's kept up. How many girls do you think live there?"

"Not a clue. It's three-story with four bedrooms on each floor. Bet it used to be an old boarding house, but it's had plenty of upgrades."

"Boy, they're young," Charles said as he scrolled through the photos. "Twenties, most of them. Thirties for a few."

"Do you want to talk about Elena?" AJ looked at him.

"Nothing to say. It's like she's disappeared." Charles closed his laptop. "But she drives a big white pickup with a blue, electric hood ornament and that's how everyone knows her. We still don't have a photo, but we're working on it. We'll find it." He reached for a box on the floor just as Bill opened the back door and came inside. He set two grocery bags on the counter.

"Sandwiches," he said with a big smile. Bill leaned over to look at the box Charles had just set on the table. "I see I timed this just right."

"We were about to look at what Seraph finally gave us yesterday," Charles said. "At first, she told us something we've all known. Michael's an assistant vice-president at Benning's, the bank that's taking over a lot of small Milwaukee banks. AJ told her that she'd have to do better than that, and she did." Charles laid a folder in the middle of the table. "Last November, Michael bought a farmhouse in Little Crane, a town about sixty-some miles southwest of here. He's already got someone down there, cooking, and Seraph said he bought two trucks to deliver across state lines. He and a couple of his college buddies have been doing this for several years but just small trade-offs, when one runs low or that kind of thing. Now they're getting organized, and we couldn't be in a better position. Lucky timing, everyone."

AJ studied the first sheet of paper, a plat map of the farmhouse that Michael had purchased. There were photos of the farmhouse, the surrounding land, and several of the little town.

Charles cleared his throat. "Bill, AJ, and I talked to the local law enforcement down there. We didn't give away anything about what we were after but kept the questions pointed at what he's encountered in the area. It wasn't much so, last night, we got together some identification and sent Bonnie Logan and four others down there disguised as state surveyors. They're down there now."

"As you all know, we haven't fully vetted Seraph," AJ said. "And I'm sure we're not going to get more until we find her little girl."

Grace began to put the sandwiches out. "Could we eat first? I'm starving," she said.

AJ nodded and walked into the living room. The late afternoon sun brightened the brown carpeting to about the same color as Frog's eyes. She'd stopped by the detention center this morning and met with Frog. The girl was still sulking, but looked stronger physically. When AJ brought up Elena's name, she saw something that she hadn't seen in Frog before. True fear. Frog wouldn't even make eye contact.

She'd talked to Seraph for a few minutes when she'd arrived here and mentioned Elena but hit a blank wall, just like with Frog. If they found the child, she was certain that Seraph would talk. A faint noise made her turn. Seraph was standing in the doorway.

"What about Meredith?"

AJ stiffened, turned away, and stared at the stone angel across the street. "I don't know," she said honestly. When she turned back, Seraph was gone.

"Allison." Charles pointed at the paper on the table in front of him. "You leave tomorrow; catch up with Bonnie and the boys."

She didn't blink. "Tomorrow? Saturday? Could we set that back a day? Bonnie and the team would be working with the locals today and tomorrow. If I'm in there Sunday by noon, most of the town will be quiet. It'll give them a chance to show me around." Charles gave her a searching look and she raised her eyebrows at him with a small, unspoken challenge.

"All right," he said with a shrug. "I don't want any action. I only want you to confirm that it's Michael's place and what he's doing." He looked at the group. "We swore Bonnie in for temporary duty to give her the same federal status as the agents she's working with."

AJ selected a sandwich and looked at a few photos Bill had laid on the table. "This little girl is out there." She looked across the table at Bill. "I know we can't tip our hand, but what about that house on the north side, the place Michael's stopped at for days? I'd lay money that's where the little girl is hidden."

Bill picked up a photo of Michael going into a large ranch-style house with a box under his arm.

"This looks like diapers or training pants to me," she said and pointed at the box in the picture.

Bill shook his head slightly. "I didn't even notice that."

"I just saw it too," AJ said.

Bill concentrated on the photos as well. "I assigned a detective to tail him when he left the house in the morning. All right, let me handle this one."

"It's huge, a double-wide city lot," Grace said, looking at a city map on her laptop. "The house is secluded in Brown Deer, on the north side of Milwaukee. I'd bet it used to be a farm."

"Anyone grow up on a farm?" AJ said casually.

Grace grinned. "I spent summers on a farm in Illinois. Did you grow up on a farm?"

AJ nodded. No one had ever asked her where she grew up that she could remember, and she kept her eyes down. She could feel them all looking at her. Of the whole group, she was the mystery, but that was her intent. Charles was the only one who knew she'd been raised in a foster home from birth and adopted by the foster family. She and four other girls in Maine. "A farm on the East Coast," she said but heard their busy, unasked questions. They probably figured a gentleman's farm, surrounded by miles of white fences. Maybe horses. She looked up with a smile. "It was a real farm. We worked hard."

"That explains all those muscles," one of the men joked and they laughed together. True, AJ was agile and athletic and could outrun everyone at the table, but she was still a woman who wore dresses in the summer when she felt like it. She held up her right arm and made a muscle. "This is from milking cows." They laughed again, but she could only imagine the crossed images in their minds. Even Charles smiled.

"I'll challenge any of you to bale hay with me. And I don't want any teasing about broken fingernails." She went for a bottle of water, certain that everyone remembered the incident in Arkansas.

"You, in that little plum-colored summer dress and strap sandals," Grace teased her. "Um…*revealing* plum-colored dress."

"Stop. It wasn't that revealing. You know it."

Grace sniggered.

"We were on our way to meet the local law enforcement. I wanted to make a good impression." AJ grinned. There had been unexpected trouble that day and, after taking down a man twice her size, she had flopped down at the table at the local police station, complaining about a broken fingernail. Deceptive, but effective in a summer dress. It was how she led them and she knew it.

CHAPTER TWELVE

"Y ou suck." Katie held a hose from the vacuum cleaner, examining it. "No. The problem is, you don't suck." She gave it a hard shake just as the doorbell rang.

Still holding the hose, Katie opened the door and her mother stepped inside.

"I don't have much time..." Her mother looked at the disassembled cleaner. "Are you and the vacuum cleaner having a private moment? I can come back later."

"We just had a smack-down. I won, but I have to go vacuum shopping."

Her mother took a large grocery bag to Katie's kitchen table. "I made bread. And added some vegetables that we canned last year. It's the last of them, so enjoy." She raised an eyebrow at Katie. "Your sister said that you actually have a dinner planned tonight. Or is it just a rumor?"

Katie smirked and picked up the teakettle to make her mother's favorite tea. "Not a rumor, Mom, but this one's special." They sat at the kitchen table and talked about last weekend at the art museum and AJ.

"Oh, honey." Her mom propped her head in her hand. "She's in law enforcement?"

"But it worked with Daddy."

"Well, sometimes. Your father and that job. He was hardly ever home and was quiet when he was." Her mother began to put the bread away in Katie's freezer. "After Lu? Another difficult relationship?"

"I've just met her, so I don't know if this is a *relationship,* but I'm interested." And maybe it was just a pipe dream, an attraction, but she'd never know if she didn't try.

"I have to go," her mother said. She kissed Katie on the forehead and gave her a hug. "I loved your daddy, honey. That was the important part. Have fun tonight."

Later, when the doorbell rang again, Katie was just finishing the table. She glanced down at herself and the old clothes she'd tossed on after her shower. She'd forgotten to change. She muttered a curse and finger-combed her still-damp hair on the way to the door.

AJ stood on the front porch with a wrapped bouquet of flowers and a bottle of wine.

"Brr, come inside. It's cold," Katie said and took AJ's coat. "Wine, flowers and—" She swallowed. "Nice suit." The beautifully cut black suit somehow elongated AJ and gave her an air of strength. Her hair hung over her forehead. "My God." Katie blinked. "Did you do this on purpose? You've become super-powered FBI agent, Bren Black."

"Stop it. I had to do laundry and it was either this or...." AJ said with that flirty expression that Katie had seen at the art museum. The one that made her catch a breath. "I was on a call today. In fact, my hair's still damp from the shower. It may be frozen." She touched her hair tentatively.

"Do you always wear leather boots?"

"Especially in the winter," AJ said. "In the summer, just about anything goes."

"Oh jeez, look at me," Katie said, showed off her bare feet and legs, tan shorts, and an old Santana T-shirt, one of her brother's castoffs. "I'm late and this was what I had close at hand. If you don't mind waiting—maybe your hair will thaw—I'll change."

"Yes, *look* at you." AJ grinned. "I like Santana and you have great legs. Don't hide them."

Caught off guard at the unexpected compliment, Katie took the wine and flowers somewhat awkwardly and walked toward the kitchen. "I hope you brought your appetite because I made a lot of food." She shook out the pinkish-silver flowers gently over the sink and reached for a vase. "I love French lilacs. How did you know?"

"I didn't. I picked the ones that made me think of you."

Katie held AJ's steady gaze for a beat before turning back to the flowers. "Thank you."

"Don't women bring you flowers?"

"It's been a while."

"Ah, Lu?"

Katie ducked behind the refrigerator door to ignore the question. "Would you like to eat now?" She held out the salad so AJ could see it.

"Now would be great. I'm starving, as usual. I haven't had anything to eat since breakfast." AJ inspected the rainbow bracelet beside her plate. "What's this? WWED?"

"What Would Eleanor Do," Katie translated and hummed a few bars of "God Bless America." She snapped her own band on her wrist. "I couldn't resist."

"Unreal," AJ said, obviously pleased. "Thanks. I've never seen anything like this."

Katie set a loaf of warm bread on the table and smiled when she saw AJ's face light up at the sight. "Don't people give you things?"

For the first time, AJ looked unsure. "No."

Katie handed AJ the bottle of wine and corkscrew, but AJ didn't move. Her face colored just enough for Katie to notice.

"I'm not good at this."

"I see," Katie said and took the bottle back. "I was only giving you the honors." She uncorked the wine, pouring each of them about half a glass. She took a sip. "Nice wine."

"My supervisor recommended it, for the chicken."

"Supervisor? I thought you were in charge?" Katie held the wine up to the light.

"I am, in Milwaukee, but I have to report to someone, and he's in town." AJ took a sip. "I don't have an educated palate. It either tastes good or it doesn't. I like this." AJ gestured at the two mission lights above them. The soft glow of the delicate multicolored glass softened the kitchen. "I meant to tell you the other night that those are beautiful lights."

"My oldest sister is a glass artist. I'm her guinea pig."

"The wood is beautiful." The amber and rose panes of glass highlighted the mellow ash with gold highlights. "That light makes your eyes…" AJ's eyes widened and Katie saw her swallow. "Um, what is that music?" A thin background violin filled the room.

"An eighteenth century Scottish fiddler, Neil Gow. That is, it's his music."

"Is that the kind of fiddle music you play?"

"Yes, but not as well. I love the music."

AJ appeared to have a sudden case of nerves. Katie smiled.

"I can't tell you how I appreciate this meal. Home cooked food is special."

"I have just begun," Katie said as she got up for the entrée and placed three plump Cornish game hens on a serving tray. "Now, prepare yourself. You'll love this." She poured warmed brandy slowly over the birds and held a lit match to it. It went up like a firecracker.

AJ made a muffled sound. "We're on fire."

"No, just the birds." Katie grinned.

"That's a huge fire for such little…chickens?" AJ pushed back into the seat.

"Cornish game hens with a sherry and brandy sideshow," Katie said, proud of the display. They both watched the brief blue-orange flames die out and Katie placed a hen on AJ's plate. "Dig in."

"Are you sure the fire's out?"

"I had no idea you were so easily entertained," Katie said as she added broccoli and pasta to AJ's plate. "There isn't much to these game hens."

"No, you burned it all up."

Katie studied AJ across the table. "Cool. You really haven't seen this before, and it's the first time I've tried it. We're sharing a brand new experience."

AJ sliced off a piece. "Oh," she groaned. "I am going to die. This is wonderful."

Katie began to eat, her eyes still on a slightly new version of AJ. "Where did you grow up?"

"Are you wondering why I've never seen a chicken on fire?"

"Cornish game hen."

"Cornish…whatever. Actually, I grew up on a farm. I'm the oldest and was needed outside so I'm quicker with the livestock and farm machinery than I am in a kitchen. In fact, no contest, I simply am. But I'm good at washing dishes. I also love plants and gardens. Vegetables are pure magic."

"Your parents are farmers?" Katie asked as she delicately took a leg off the hen.

"Yes, and we all worked on the farm where I grew up."

Katie waited for more, but AJ continued to eat. Finally she said, "They adopted me and raised me on the farm in Maine. We worked hard and the farm still supports them."

"You were adopted? Can I ask more?" AJ had more surprises than a magician.

"Ask away. By the way, if you don't want that other chicken, the Cornish thing, I'll eat another one."

"How did you get from the farm to West Point? That's quite a stretch." Katie handed AJ the plate with the remaining hen.

"Not so much. The adults around me not only loved me but made me pay attention to all my schoolwork, and I mean all. Mom had been a schoolteacher, and every evening over dinner, we went over everything. Dad taught me about the land and farming, but most of all, what it is to be a good man. There were five girls there. All of us but one managed to get a scholarship. Since I was the oldest, I was responsible for much of the care and safety of the other girls. My youngest sister is a medic in Afghanistan." AJ frowned at her food. "I can't keep her safe there, that's for sure."

Katie bit her lip, thinking of her next personal question.

"Why did you call yesterday? The man from the art museum?" AJ reached for more bread.

"Yesterday? Oh, the man. We all arrived at the lobby together; that man and woman took the same elevator. I think they went into that enormous suite on the west side of the building. The one with all the doctors?"

AJ shoved the bones on her plate around with a fork. "Probably. If it was the same man, that's his office. He's a doctor."

"His wife, or whatever, is simply beautiful, but I think she was high." Katie saw AJ shift through several answers. "Maybe they're connected to Jimmy Hoffa?"

AJ tossed a piece of lettuce from the salad at her. "Okay, I deserve that. The truth is that I shouldn't talk about it. Was there anything else?"

"Yes. If we'd been at the Copper Penny, not in an elevator, I would have expected her to back me into the wall with more than questions."

"That's probably true, I'm sorry to say. I don't imagine you minded it?" They both laughed.

"I was surprised, that's all." Katie got up and brought the morning paper back to the table. "Actually, it was all kind of strange. Just as the elevator doors were about to close, a tall woman in a leather jacket and biker boots got on with another woman. They were speaking in Spanish and laughing. In the meantime, this gorgeous woman is looking at me like I'm some kind of entrée." Katie saw that AJ's grin had disappeared. "What?"

"That woman, the tall one in the leather jacket? What did she look like?"

"Tough, with black hair down to the middle of her back. Dark eyes. Why?"

"I'm curious, that's all," AJ said and took the newspaper that Katie handed her.

"See that?" Katie pointed at a photo in the "Round the Town" section that featured shots from Milwaukee's nightlife. "Look at you. Great little black dress." She pointed at one of the other two women in the photo. "That's the woman in the elevator that I called you about."

"Damn," AJ said softly. "Don't like to see this. We were at the opening of a new club, testing the menu. Good food, but I liked your meal better."

"Why don't you want to be in the news? That's a really nice dress you're wearing. A little revealing but—" She stopped teasing when AJ frowned at her. When she'd seen the photos in this morning's paper, she'd almost spilled her coffee. The dress was definitely sexy.

"Katie, remember what I do for a living. Like Seraph, I'm part of an ongoing investigation, and the less seen, the better." She grinned. "And don't even go there. I'm not a spy." AJ stood with her glass. "Can we take the wine to the living room and have a fire like we did the other night?" She went down the three steps into the living room.

They sat on the floor as Katie stretched out, wriggling her toes at the heat. AJ curled up next to her, arm on the couch behind them.

"It's still a great photo of you," Katie said. "It never occurred to me that it was part of your job."

"Actually, I'm glad you pointed it out. Was that today's paper?"

Katie nodded. AJ's expression made her decide to let personal questions wait until some other time.

AJ sat up. "I just remembered something. The other night when I got my ID from my coat in the hall closet, did I see a bow and arrows in there?"

"As I told you, I'm not into guns, but I love compound bows."

"Compound bows?"

"My dad used to take me hunting. I can use the others too, the longbows. It doesn't make any difference to me. I've even shot crossbows. Have you ever shot one?"

"No, but it looks interesting. Would you take me sometime?"

"I've got time this week."

"Can't. I have to leave town tonight and I'll be gone for a while," AJ said. "Could we go when I get back?"

"Of course," Katie said. "What's 'for a while'?"

"Probably a few days, maybe until next weekend."

Disappointed, Katie said, "All right, call me when you get back."

"I will." AJ gave her the slowest smile Katie had ever seen. "If it's all right, I'll call you while I'm out of town."

"I'd like that." Katie scooted closer to AJ and picked up her hand, touching the rainbow WWED band. "You're still wearing this? Women today would give Eleanor a lot of satisfaction." She lightly rubbed her hand.

"She knew women could do it all." AJ stretched her legs out close to Katie. "Look at what I do, or my sister in Afghanistan.

Women are fighting all over the world, many in uniform. My team here mirrors what my sister does in many ways. I carry a gun." AJ shifted closer and reached out to move a curl off Katie's cheek. "Is your hair always this curly?" She moved her fingers lightly through Katie's hair.

Certain that the next move would be a kiss, Katie leaned forward, but instead, AJ's fingers only gently moved down her cheek leaving a trail of warmth. Katie exhaled.

"I have to go." AJ was suddenly on her knees, starting to stand. Her voice shook a little as she said, "If I don't reach you, I'll leave you a message. Call me back?"

"You're leaving? But it's early and..." Katie scrambled up, confused.

The closet door was open and AJ held her coat.

Katie caught herself. "Do you have a plane to catch?"

"No, I'm driving."

Katie took a resigned breath. "It's been a long time since I've had anyone here or cooked for someone. Now it's been you, twice."

"I'm glad it was me." AJ put on her coat, took Katie's hand, and tugged her to the door. "I'd like to do it again. And the bows. Don't forget the bows when I get back."

"Of course. As I said, it's been a long time and—oh." Katie was suddenly in AJ's arms. It was so quick she hadn't seen the hands move. Warm breath brushed her ear and she felt a little tremor graze through the arms that held her, then a sigh as a hand caressed her back. More than ready for a kiss once again, Katie moved, but AJ suddenly let go.

"Thanks for the delicious food," AJ said, her voice soft. She opened the door, and was gone.

Stunned, Katie simply stood, staring at the door, her heart still pounding. The scent that she loved lingered and her hands were clenched. "You're welcome," she said to the silence.

CHAPTER THIRTEEN

Completely distracted, AJ sat in the car in Katie's driveway for a moment. She shifted into drive, the car jerked forward, and she slammed on the brakes. "Stop it," she said through clenched teeth, then eased the car into reverse and backed up.

She'd almost kissed her, should have kissed her, but she'd ran. And that hug had been an embrace. Her body was still shaking. She gripped the steering wheel. The delicate bones and warm skin under the thin T-shirt had mixed with Katie's fragrance. Honey? No, more like summer berries and warm, summer nights.

"Not going to happen." It would confuse everything, maybe endanger Katie. "It'd certainly endanger me," she mumbled, but one thing was certain. For the first time since Ecuador, someone had her complete attention. And this woman—Katie—could never be a casual moment.

At the stop sign, AJ automatically checked the rearview mirror, then did a little double take. What was that flash of light? She drove around the block and cut the lights before she made the final turn at the top of Katie's street. There. A white pickup sat in front of Katie's house. Was it the one that had followed her to the airport? The one Charles said belonged to Elena? A tall figure got out and went up the driveway. AJ reached for her weapon, but it was packed in her bag. Instead, she slid her hand into her boot for her little Ruger LCP .380, turned off the interior lights, and got out, straining to see though the dark.

Katie's front light was off, and the only sound was the cold cracking in the trees. A large hedge gave her cover as she checked Katie's house. Had the person gone inside? There was movement to the side, back by the garage. She shifted closer. Someone came down the driveway and paused at the window by the fireplace. AJ scanned Katie's house to see if the kitchen lights were on, but they stayed dark. The person turned quickly and walked back toward the white truck. Was that a man or a woman? When the person opened the door, no interior lights came on, and the big vehicle eased away from the curb. AJ stepped out further to read the plates but couldn't get a good look. She did see the little blue hood ornament, lit up like a beacon as the truck made a right turn at the corner. She tucked the gun in her boot and crunched across the snow to her car. *Options, options*, she repeated to herself, rubbing her cold hands. Finally, she dialed Charles.

"Allison," he said.

"I've got a situation here. After dinner with Katie Blackburn, I left, got to the end of the block, and saw that white pickup stop in front of her house. The same pickup that followed us the other night."

"Are you sure it was the same car?"

"It had that little blue light on the hood," she said and stared down the street at Katie's house. "Charles, if they've followed me, they've got the apartment and Seraph. I'm driving the same agency vehicle I was when I picked you up. Or they could be after Katie."

"Where are you right now?"

The adrenaline from the last few minutes began to leak out of her, and AJ let out a long, slow breath. "I'm down the block, from Katie's—Ms. Blackburn's house."

"Why don't you stay with the Blackburn woman tonight?"

"What?" Her voice tightened at that thought. "All right," she said. "I'll call Grace to check the footprints tomorrow and she should stay at Katie's house for the day. Where are you?"

"Waiting for Bill at his house. His wife cooked dinner for us tonight, but he's late."

"Something else," AJ said. "Last week, Katie was on a business call and ended up in an elevator at the professional building on Van Buren with Star and her husband. That's the building where his office is." She stopped and thought about Katie's words. "From Katie's description, a woman that sounded a lot like Elena was on the elevator too, with a younger woman." AJ cleared her throat. The thought of Katie close to Elena tensed her up again.

"It sounds like Elena's tailing the doctor and his wife," Charles said. "I don't think they have a reason to go after Ms. Blackburn." There was a thick silence as both of them thought through the information and the possibilities.

"One last thing. Check Bill's local paper from today. There's a section on Milwaukee events. My photo's in there with Star, from that second dinner."

"Your photo's in there? Did you say today's paper?"

"This morning's paper. It's just random shots in the social section. We haven't connected Michael to Star yet, but it's possible. They certainly run in the same crowd. And we don't know that he knows whether or not Seraph's alive. There's a million different ways this could go. Tonight, I couldn't see if it was a man or woman. The person was tall and wore something with a hood. It was Elena's truck and the description fits, so I assume it was her."

AJ heard voices. Bill must have returned and Charles hurried. "If nothing else happens, call me tomorrow when you're down there. We'll be in touch."

After they hung up, AJ called Grace and arranged for her to be at Katie's in the morning. She turned the car on, jacked the heater up, and pushed back into the seat, thinking about Charles. After her discharge from the Army, she'd had a friend in the ATF and she'd liked what she'd seen. Charles had just made the move from the FBI to the DEA. They'd met through friends and, later, he'd offered her an interagency job, trained her for undercover, drugs, or anything else he could think of. Over the years, they'd developed a close, unusual partnership. She'd liked the undercover work a lot and stayed there until a drug assignment on the West Coast several years ago. She'd been captured by the dealers and they'd poured cocaine down her throat until she was almost dead.

Charles had got her into the hospital and sat beside her bed until she was human again, then sent her home to recover with her family. Charles had not only taken care of her but, at this point in her life, he was the only one who knew *everything* about her.

She turned the bracelet on her wrist. Damn. It was the wrong time for Katie. She'd been intrigued from the moment she met her, and it was more than just need or desire. Thank God she'd never hidden her preference for women from her team because she might need them to help her keep Katie safe.

Finally, she drove back into Katie's driveway. Any story would do, but she decided on the truth as she rang the doorbell. She exhaled. Every time she went into this house, she came out shaking. The porch light came on again and Katie opened the door.

"AJ?" Katie's eyes widened with surprise followed by a very happy, hopeful smile.

"You were right. We should talk." AJ stepped inside, her heart beating faster when she saw the smile. "Would you make coffee?" She didn't even wait for Katie to take her coat; she hung it inside the closet herself, then faced the confused look on Katie's face.

"Coffee? You came back for coffee?" Katie said over her shoulder as she walked toward the kitchen. AJ's eyes locked on Katie's body. Once she'd looked at her, she'd looked again and just kept looking.

❖

"Are you sure you didn't come back to help me with the dishes?" Katie was rewarded with a smile and she smiled back. *It would be nice if you came back to finish the almost-kiss.* AJ had appeared so serious when she'd opened the door. "No? Coffee first?"

AJ's smile broadened into a grin.

"Fine, we'll have coffee, but only after I finish cleaning the table."

"As I said, it's the one thing I do well in the kitchen."

They were silent until everything was put away or in the dishwasher. AJ had lost the smile somewhere and looked distracted again. Definitely not the kiss, Katie thought as she poured them both coffee. She put her chin in her hands as they sat at the table and raised her eyebrows. "You raced out of here, but now you're back? Something's up."

"Last weekend when I left your house, a white pickup followed me. I wasn't sure if it found me here or at the art museum. It followed me to the airport when I picked up my supervisor and back to the police station that night. Tonight, about the time I got to the stop sign, I saw it again, in front of your house. Someone walked around your house, looked in your windows, then left."

Katie's head jerked up. That was the last thing she'd expected. "Someone followed you and was here, at my house?"

"I'd like to go outside, take a look. Would you mind?"

"I'll go with you." Katie stood.

"No, you don't have—"

"I need to. Let me change clothes," Katie said and was gone.

They walked up the driveway with flashlights, following the footprints under Katie's windows and across the deck in the back.

"Damn," Katie said softly. "It was so quiet in the house that I should have heard something. Wait, I turned the music up a bit. Who was it?"

"I'm not sure. I was across the street." AJ pointed, her breath white in the cold air. "Over there, by that tall hedge."

"You're lucky my neighbors didn't call the cops on you," Katie said. A little hysteria bubbled up inside her and she turned her face away so AJ wouldn't see. "Let's go back inside."

"Hold on," AJ said, shining a light on a print, bending close. "Do those look like a man's footprints, or a woman's?"

"I don't know." Katie squatted down with her flash light. "If it's a woman, she's tall or big."

She stood and AJ wrapped her arm around her waist. "Let's go back inside."

Katie poured them fresh coffee. "What now?"

"One of my agents, Grace, will be here tomorrow, to look at the prints in the daylight and to talk to you. Do you have plans?"

"Sleeping in as late as possible."

"Good. Would it be okay if I stayed here tonight? I'll crash on the couch."

"You're welcome to use the spare bedroom." Katie wrapped her arms about herself to hold her lurching stomach. "The new car's locked in the garage. Are they after that?"

"It's not your car. I'll bet they're after Seraph."

"Isn't she in the hospital?"

"No. She's somewhere else."

Katie tapped her cup with a fingernail, thinking about the information. "I wondered." She held up a hand. "I know. You'll only tell me what I need to know." AJ seemed to relax with that so Katie continued. "And you're here…for protection?"

AJ sipped her coffee. "I notified my supervisor and Bill Whiteaker will make sure this street becomes part of the police patrol. They'll keep an eye on us." AJ took a deep breath and scrubbed her face hard.

Katie took a closer look, suddenly aware of dark circles under AJ's eyes, the tired angle of her body. "Why don't you put on some comfortable clothes while I stoke up the fire? Since you were leaving, do you have a bag? Or you can borrow some of my clothes."

On cue, AJ stood. She went outside to her car for her bag while Katie laid out fresh towels in the bathroom. She checked the spare bedroom and turned on a low light.

Barefoot, AJ wore sweat pants and a faded Army T-shirt when she joined Katie in front of the fireplace. Katie scooted in front of her again. "I checked you out on the Internet. You're a decorated soldier?"

"What?" AJ looked up quickly. "Ecuador, my first assignment? That's on the Internet?"

"What did you do down there?"

"When I was at West Point, my big love was history and constitutional law. That's when I found Eleanor." She pointed at the bracelet Katie had given her. "I wrangled an assignment to our

Embassy in Ecuador to liaise with their military as they sorted out a new function in their government. They were struggling." AJ sighed. "It seemed like it would be a good experience because I was going to get my law degree and maybe teach. And a farm. I wanted to buy a farm. Like that's ever going to happen." She stared at the fire. "I barely have time to breathe on this job, let alone farm."

"There was a man, Thomas Perry, who was also decorated?"

"There were four of us down there. The woman I was living with, my lover, was also part of the team. Then, my childhood best friend was part of a civilian assignment. She was pre-med and managed to get a civilian position with a hospital for part of her training."

"Were they decorated too? I mean, were they injured?"

AJ reached for a couch pillow and tucked it behind her. "Only Tom and I were injured. I spent some time in the hospital there, and again when I came home. It wasn't any big act of heroism or anything."

"The article wasn't specific. I just thought it was cool that you'd been decorated." Katie noticed the unhappy expression on AJ's face. "You don't have to talk about this."

AJ laughed a little. "You must feel like I won't talk about anything." She adjusted the pillow. "We worked in the capital, Quito, one of the most beautiful places I've ever seen. It's right below the Equator—an incredible climate. I truly loved it." She smiled at Katie. "Anyway, that day, Tom and I were sitting on a park bench after work, both of us in uniform, waiting for Dana and Rachel."

"Dana and Rachel?"

"Dana Taylor, my lover, and Rachel, my best friend." AJ wrapped her arms around her legs and rested her chin on her knees. "Tom and I saw men running in the park, chasing two women and some children. We tried to help, took down some of the men, but we both were hurt." AJ took a deep breath. "Remember what you said, that you felt as if you couldn't leave Lu Wright? It is hard to explain, isn't it?"

Katie nodded. "I called it obsession. So did the therapist I saw." She made a wry face.

"That's how I felt about Quito, the job, the people I was with. Obsession, you said? Sure, a little addiction. When that crazy thing happened and the injury, everything finally broke. Then I was ready to leave."

"The men in the park, who were they?"

"Drug dealers," AJ said with a small shrug and held out her left hand. "They didn't shoot. They just hit us. They broke this wrist and one of the men hit me in the head with a piece of wood. I ended up in a cast with a concussion. They kept me in the hospital for days, but I hated that place. Finally, I just checked myself out."

"Against their advice?" Katie gave her a surprised look.

"Everyone was really upset. Came home with a broken wrist, a broken head, and a broken attitude." AJ's face shut down, but Katie was silent, waiting for more.

"Do you have a best friend?" AJ finally spoke, a little wistfully.

"A best friend? Probably Bonnie Logan."

"Right, Bonnie. She's on our team. A good cop," AJ said. "Friends are really important."

"On your team? But she's city police."

"It's a combination of people and agencies. Bill Whiteaker is her primary, but she also reports to me." She pushed her hair back from her forehead. "I'm rambling, aren't I? I'm just tired."

Katie got up immediately. "Do you still see them? Your lover or your friend?"

"Ex-lover, ex-best friend," AJ said, looked away. "I keep in touch with Tom, but I haven't seen Dana or Rachel since then. It ended badly."

"Do you love this job like you did Ecuador?"

"For a long time, I couldn't love anything," AJ said in a tired voice as she stood. She took her laptop from her bag and set it on Katie's kitchen table. "I have reports to enter and then bed. Thanks again, for everything." She bent over the computer.

Katie made sure the fire was out. She glanced at AJ as she turned off the living room lights. She looked exhausted, lost to the work.

Her stomach was still upset as she went to her bedroom.

❖

AJ began to enter the information about the truck tonight and Katie's experience on the elevator, but she stopped typing as Katie left for the back of the house. That smile when Katie had opened the door tonight—she would remember that smile.

The coffee was cold, but she drank it anyway as she heard Katie's bedroom door close. No one had ever asked her if she loved her job. She smiled down at her computer. Even Katie's attention was seductive.

CHAPTER FOURTEEN

M uch later that night, AJ sighed as she settled into the bed in Katie's spare room. She put her gun under the pillow, laced her arms under her head, and stared into the dark. The good news was that Katie was not involved with any of the drugs, despite Lu Wright. The bad news was that Katie had possibly been on the elevator with Michael's worst angel. Then there was the person in the truck, not to mention Star. She had checked her group's information tonight, but there was nothing new on Elena.

The second bad news was that she had to leave Katie alone in all of this. She thought about the two of them outside, looking at the footprints in the snow, the frightened look on Katie's face. Instinctively, she'd reached for her.

For the first time, she had talked to someone other than Charles about Dana and Rachel. How she'd come to love her undercover ops because they let her become someone else, not the woman whose lover and best friend had made her feel like the person no one wanted. In a way, that's what Lu had done to Katie.

And that crazy Internet article. She had no idea what was on there, hadn't even known it existed, but it made her think of Taylor's unanswered e-mail. Dana was so beautiful, and she'd been so rapt that she'd never even noticed the equally smitten Rachel until, one night when they'd all been out together. Even then, it'd taken at least a week for her to understand Rachel's expression. That was when she'd checked herself out of the hospital, gone to a bar for a mind-numbing, blinding drunk, forgettable day.

AJ fell asleep, thinking of Ecuador.

"Allison, get up." Dana shook her hard. Rachel stood behind her.

AJ jerked upright on the couch in her office, knocking the blanket to the floor.

"Cover yourself," Dana said roughly as she went to a knee, reaching for the blanket to cover AJ's nakedness. "Listen, I know you're upset," she said in a softer voice, "but you can't sleep here. Go back to the apartment; I'm staying with Rachel. You're still in a cast, and God knows what shape your head's in." She handed her the blanket. "Christ, you reek of whiskey."

"Fuck off, both of you." AJ took the blanket. "It's none of your damned business where I sleep." She pulled the blanket up to her chin. "Where are my clothes?"

"Hell if I know." Dana looked around.

"Sorry. I am so sorry for everything," Rachel said and bent so close that AJ could smell the familiar shampoo.

"Get out, both of you." She yelled. Rachel stepped back with a hurt expression.

"Hey, babe, stop the yelling," Dana said and tossed AJ's clothes onto the couch.

"I'm not YOUR babe," AJ said to Dana and looked at Rachel. "And I'm not YOUR friend. I'm dead to both of you. Get the fuck out of here."

"No, YOU fuck off and—"

AJ jerked awake, drenched in sweat. She curved back into the warmth of the bed for a moment. Stupid nightmare. She fumbled for the little light beside the bed and saw that it was a variation of the lights in the kitchen. Warm and bright, just like Katie. She fished the little Ruger from under the pillow and pulled on jeans, a turtleneck, and a heavy sweater.

Boots in hand, she crept out into the living room and unzipped the side pocket of her bag for a note pad. Everything in the room, except the white walls, was rose and amber with brown accents, just like the lights in the kitchen. Even in the dim, grainy light of dawn, it was welcoming.

Damn it all, she didn't want to leave Katie. She stared at the blank paper. Finally, she wrote: *Thanks for another delicious meal, nice pyrotechnics show too. I slept well and appreciate the bed. I'll call you, but remember, you can call me. Probably be back by next weekend. I want to learn about those bows. Please be safe. Bren Black (AJ)* She grinned and drew a smiley face after the Bren Black. She left the folded paper between the salt and pepper shakers on the table, zipped her bag, and strapped on her regulation weapon. Finally, she tucked her little gun into her boot and opened the door just as Grace drove up.

"She's still asleep," AJ said as she tossed her bag into the car.

"Charles wants me here. He's going to talk to Ms. Blackburn today."

"Have you ever eaten Cornish...something?"

"The little game hens?"

"Katie cooked them for me last night. They're great." AJ smiled at the thought of the fire at the table.

"Katie? Ms. Blackburn?" Grace turned toward the house. "What's she like, this woman?"

"Nice. Really cute. Funny and smart, but the daughter of a cop. Be prepared, because she'll ask a million questions."

"Your face just lit up." Grace angled her head with a little smirk. "You look rested."

"I'm out of here," AJ said with a non-answer. "I left a note on the kitchen table for Katie. Make sure she sees it, will you?"

Grace pointed at AJ's wrist. "What's that? You never wear a bracelet."

"Huh? Oh, a little something Katie gave me." AJ started for the car but said over her shoulder, "You ask more questions than she does."

"Be careful," Grace said as AJ got into the car.

"I think this is Michael's group, trying to find Seraph. Let me know what you think of the footprints, will you? You'll see more in the daylight than I did last night in the dark, and damned if I know if it was a man or a woman. It was Elena's truck. It had to be her. Watch over Seraph, okay? I don't think the boys are tuned in to how little she trusts them. And, Grace, Katie *is* a little special, okay? Keep her safe for me."

❖

Because the drapes were slightly open, the March sun warmed Katie's face. An odd noise woke her. Then she thought she heard her kitchen cupboard doors close. She sat up so fast that she was dizzy for a moment. The clock said ten o'clock as she moved to the edge of the bed, still carrying the unease from last night. She reached for the long robe over the end of the bed and hurried to the living room, expecting to find AJ rummaging around in her kitchen. A tall, dark-haired woman was looking out the kitchen window with a glass of water in her hand.

"Uh…" Katie cleared the sleep out of her voice. "Hello?" There was an open laptop on the kitchen table.

"Ms. Blackburn," the woman said with a smile. "I work with AJ." She held out her hand. "My name is Grace and I'm going to be here for a while. Our supervisor is going to stop by later to speak to you about last night."

Katie rubbed her eyes. "Is AJ here?

"No, she had to go."

Disappointed, Katie said, "Would you like some coffee?"

"That would be great." Grace closed the laptop and moved out of Katie's way.

As she reached for the coffee, Katie remembered that AJ had mentioned that someone would be at the house today, one of her agents.

Grace sat exactly where AJ always sat. "I like this built-in seat around the table. It's comfortable."

"Thanks. My mom made these padded seats for me. She used to sew for a living." Coffee started, Katie placed a knee onto the seat and looked out at her yard. "Do you work in the same office as AJ?"

"I was assigned to her team over a year ago, in Arkansas." Grace pointed at the coffee table in the living room. "Can I set my laptop over there?"

"Of course. Be comfortable. You joined AJ's team in Arkansas. Is that your home state?"

"No, Arizona."

Katie smiled at her. "Do you miss the desert?"

Grace raised her eyebrows. "Are you kidding? It's cold up here."

Katie got a pan and a mixing bowl out of the cupboard. "Want some breakfast?"

"The last food I saw was a bagel earlier this morning so that would be excellent."

Katie chopped bits of cheese, broccoli, and mushrooms into the eggs and finished the meal with toasted English muffins. Grace ate like AJ, long and lots.

"This is a nice house. Do you own it alone?" Grace said as she got up for more coffee.

"I do now."

"Divorced?"

"As good as," Katie said and brushed away thoughts of Lu. She got up to rinse the plates. "How long will you be here?"

"Until our supervisor talks to you. He'll have more information."

"Your supervisor?"

"Charles Ryan is AJ's supervisor," Grace said.

"I forgot. She said her supervisor was in town." Katie turned the water off. "Did you look at the footprints outside this morning?"

"Yes, first thing. I'm not certain how your situation is going to play out." Grace took the plates out of Katie's hands and began to place them in the dishwasher. "Let me help, then do whatever it is you have to do. I have work to do as well. Did you have plans today?"

"Just work. I'm doing a preliminary presentation next week." Katie moved to the right. "There's soda and water in the refrigerator. Actually, help yourself to anything. Make more coffee if you want.

I'm going to take a shower, get dressed. I'll be in my office, at the end of the hall." She started to leave, but Grace stopped her.

"Wait." She handed Katie a folded piece of paper. "AJ left you a note."

Katie smiled as she took the paper. "AJ's unusual. She seems to have a lot of…personalities."

"Where to begin? She loves fast cars, motorcycles, martial arts…" Grace smiled as her voice trailed off.

Katie's mind flipped to the photo in that little black dress. "She likes motorcycles?"

"Have you seen her car?" Grace looked as if she were about to smile.

"Her car? Do you mean the black Suburban?"

"No," Grace said. "That's an agency car. I mean her personal car. Next time you see her, ask her for a ride in her own car. You'll love it."

Katie thought that Grace was talking about some kind of sleek, fast, sports car. "I'll ask her." She hesitated. She wanted to ask more but instead, turned and left. Fast cars and martial arts? What's next? She checked the spare bedroom. AJ may not know how to cook, but the bed was neat and tight.

Branches scratched against the windows in her office as she turned her computer on. It was twenty degrees today, clear and sunny. That would do for wherever AJ was driving. She read the note. "Bren Black? With a smiley face? Big, tough federal agent," she said with a little laugh. She scanned the few words a couple of times, then propped the note against her monitor. AJ might be back by next weekend? That would be good. It would be even nicer if it were sooner. She heard the TV go on. Grace was pleasant, kind of easy, and Katie was glad she was here.

Last night, unable to sleep, she had stared at the shadows of the streetlights in her bedroom. There had been someone outside her house, peeping into her windows. First, her car and now, her house. AJ had mentioned Seraph, but who were the people in the elevator who had caused AJ to tense up? She'd never admit how much this had rattled her, and she suspected it was just the tip of the iceberg.

Part of it was the woman in her car but could it have been drugs? Her only connection to drugs had been Lu. She had stared into the dark last night, tried to take Lu out of the equation, but she couldn't do it. It had to be her.

Tossing and turning, she'd gone over her conversation with AJ. There had been four of them in Ecuador, including a lover and a best friend. AJ had been in the military and something other than a single fight with drug dealers had happened down there, but she certainly hadn't wanted to talk about it. Maybe *ex-lover and ex-best friend* said it all. Or *broken wrist and broken attitude.*

Last night, she had leaned over in the dark, picked up her phone, and left Bonnie a message. She hadn't talked to her since that day at her mother's and she needed to apologize for at least a few things she'd said. Come to think of it, why hadn't Bonnie told her that she worked with AJ? Bonnie loved to talk about her job.

Still restless, Katie had gotten up and gone in the other bedroom to check on AJ. She had been on her stomach, one hand under the pillow and her hair was tousled. She hadn't even moved when Katie had put an extra blanket over her. *What am I doing here, standing in the dark, listening to her breathe? Go back to bed.*

Katie turned back to the computer. For someone that said she had trouble sleeping, AJ would only have slept that deeply if she felt safe.

Chapter Fifteen

L ater that afternoon, just west of Little Crane Lake, AJ surveyed the unmarked snow of the cornfield in front of her. The clean country air smelled sweet. She took a deep breath and bent to examine the chopped corn stalk at her feet. Bonnie said something that she didn't catch and AJ straightened to look at her.

"The property ends right there, by that hedgerow," Bonnie repeated and pointed to the east. Her tall, muscled body moved easily through the deep snow.

Pines huddled against the fence. "Nice farm," AJ said. She lifted the video binoculars to scan the back of the house. The pine trees to the west were thick, and she noticed the house lights were already on. A plume of smoke vaulted straight up in the still, frigid air. "You've told them that the state wants to buy these ten acres for a highway?"

"I talked with the owner yesterday. Gave him the papers we got from the DOT, and laid the map out beside it. That guy." Bonnie shook her head. "It was almost painful to talk to him. He's young, maybe late twenties, but a zombie and in motion during the whole conversation."

"What's his name?"

"Owen Hood. His parents are dead. The farm on the plat map is named Hood's Hollow." Bonnie tugged her knit cap further down over her ears against the cold. "The house reeked, even with all the kitchen windows open. They're cooking. From where I stood, I could see rubber tubing, faucet couplings, and jars. The usual."

"Not too bright of him to let you inside and let you see all of that. Do you think it's just meth? Or H? Maybe coke, like an all-purpose drop-in?"

"All I could smell or see indicated only meth, but who knows? It could be. He mentioned there was a young woman staying there, but we didn't see her."

AJ nodded. "What condition is the house in? The back windows are open right now." They'd been in meth houses that had maggots in sinks, overflowing toilets, mattresses on the floors. And worse.

"The house? Not as bad as you and I have seen. It's clutter, mostly," Bonnie said as she pushed some snow to the side with her boot. "Even if it's not Michael's, this is definitely something that needs to be closed down. The DEA could do that. Or the locals."

"How many farms have you gotten to?"

"Thirteen. Most of these farms are just hanging on. All the people are older except this guy."

"There are cars in the driveway," AJ said. "Two? I can't see clearly. There are too many trees around that side of the house."

"There was only one vehicle when we were there. Maybe the girl had the other one."

"Maybe, just maybe, we've gotten lucky." AJ hit Record and filmed another slow sweep with her video binoculars. It appeared Seraph had told the truth. "I'll send all of this to Charles and begin to set up surveillance. Did any of the neighbors say anything out of the ordinary?"

"One of them, down the road, complained of the truck traffic."

"What kind of trucks?"

Bonnie held up her hands. "They didn't elaborate. They just said box trucks."

AJ knew farmers paid attention to who was on their land and the farms around them. They took care of one another. The local sheriff had reported missing ammonia about four months ago, but it had stopped. Maybe they shipped it in, like the ephedrine that Jock had dealt with on the Milwaukee interstate. If they were using the house for meth or any other drugs, who farmed this land?

Bonnie dialed her phone as they got back into the vehicle. AJ kicked the snow off her boots and glanced around, reminded of her home, the farm in Maine. The way the trees sat against the uneven land. The same jut of stones. A little ground fog lifted up between the pines, filtered the red setting sun to warm amber and rose, the colors of Katie's kitchen and living room. She idly wondered if Katie liked farms.

"The boys want to meet us for dinner at the local steakhouse," Bonnie said and held up her phone. "Want to go?"

"I'm hungry and don't care what I eat or where," AJ said. She turned the car west. "How big is this town, Little Crane Lake? I know we're sixty-some miles southwest of the Milwaukee area, but I didn't look into it. I figured you'd have all the information."

Bonnie tossed her hat and gloves onto the backseat and flipped her long braid over her coat. "The census has it just under ten thousand, but I don't have a clue if it really has cranes." She stretched her long legs out in the car. "Tell me what happened at Katie's."

"She cooked dinner for me last night. Set some chickens on fire," AJ said with a grin, then tossed her earmuffs and gloves on top of Bonnie's things in the back seat. "I stayed over after I saw that person at her house."

"She set some chickens on fire? You mean she finally tried the Cornish game hens? Heck of a cook, isn't she? That whole family can cook, even the boys." Bonnie reached for her water. "You stayed over?" Her voice was casual, but AJ heard the unasked question.

"Neither Charles nor I thought she should be alone. How'd you know I was there?" AJ turned onto the main highway, headed south.

"She left me a message on my phone late last night. I haven't had a chance to call her back."

"Tell me about Lu. How'd Katie get tangled up with that woman?"

"Oh God, Lu."

"She said she was addicted to her, like a drug."

"Yeah." Bonnie shook her head. "That's what it was like."

"You've known Katie for a long time?"

"Over twenty years. She's my best friend." Bonnie uncapped the water for a drink. "Lu turned her life upside down. I'm sure she's told you about the drugs."

"Yes, she did." AJ remembered the grim expression on Katie's face. "Did any of you ever figure out where Lu got the stuff?"

"That's the hell of it. Even as a cop, Lu completely ran me around the block. We never could pin anything on her. Last year, I was certain Lu was involved with some kind of group. Then you came along and we found Michael and his girl gang, the angels. Damn, those girls are good. I know they're the reason Michael's so successful."

"I hate to think of Katie in all of that. Or in Lu's drugs."

"Katie and drugs? Never. But as you said, Lu was Katie's drug. She just fell in love with the wrong person." When AJ didn't answer, Bonnie continued. "I don't want Lu to die, but I'm glad she's out of the picture. And that Katie's finally done with it."

AJ still said nothing, only stared at the road, thinking of holding Katie, her warm body. All these empty years, she'd tried to fill herself with work, but Katie had opened something…a door? The dim space inside felt odd.

"Did she tell you she used to play in a band?"

AJ snapped back to the conversation. "She mentioned the band and played some music."

"She hauled out the fiddle?" Bonnie looked surprised.

"No. She had a CD on, like background music."

"She plays a lot of old Scottish music. Man, that's a story. She was in a fiddle competition in Madison and won with that music. Lu showed up drunk—and high. Made a mess out of things by getting up, dancing and whistling. It was horrible."

"You were there?"

"I drove Katie over from Milwaukee. She was in terrible shape that last summer they lived together. She's not very big and had lost weight during the struggle with Lu. Her whole family was there, and they put up with Lu for a while until Katie's brothers and father took her out of the building." Bonnie loosened her bootlaces. "Katie's the best I've seen her, right now." She looked at AJ. "Are you interested?"

AJ didn't answer for a moment. "It can't happen, Bonnie. It's too dangerous for Katie."

"Why?" Bonnie raised her eyebrows. "Just because you're up to your neck in all this crap doesn't mean you can't have a life."

"I wouldn't know a life if it sat across from me," AJ said with a short laugh. "I'm sure that was Elena at Katie's house last night, looking for Seraph. I don't want Katie caught up in this mess any more than she is right now." AJ unzipped her coat. "What else does she like, besides music, mysteries, and old movies? Does she work out? Or run, swim, what?"

Bonnie burst out laughing. "It can't happen? But look at you with all these personal questions. Her parents' house is on a lake and she runs out there. She swims a lot. She's a great shot with the bow and the best shortstop our team ever had. Lots of energy." She grinned at AJ. "I can see you're not the least bit interested."

AJ shrugged but couldn't stop her smile. "She's so pretty with that kind of off-hand elegance. We won't even talk about her great legs. Not that I noticed."

"Hell, she's *hot*. Are you kidding? They lined up in college. Men and women."

AJ laughed. "Lined up?"

"*Off-hand elegance?* You talk like a book," Bonnie grumbled. "Say it. She's downright sexy."

AJ took her eyes off the road to glance at Bonnie and, for the first time, did say it. "All right. She's sexy. But she's a lot of other things I really like. Her quick mind, her warmth, and a great sense of humor." She felt her face warm.

"Did you check out her website?" Bonnie smirked.

"Yes, before I interviewed her the first time. Why?"

"There's a picture on there that I took of her." Bonnie smiled across the car. "I think you'll like it. Take a look later." She cleared her throat. "Since you're not interested."

But just not now, AJ thought as the town came into view. No time for Katie. "I'm going to change the subject. We need to find that little girl so Seraph will to talk to us. She's improved physically, but she's not going to give us anything but this farm until she has her child. Then we can settle into a more productive surveillance and do what Charles wants. Tie this group to the other states."

"I'm surprised about Seraph. You and Charles are the best interrogators I've ever been around."

"Thanks, but I'm not. I've been around people that blow your mind away. It's over before you even knew it's started. What did you think of my interview with Seraph at the clinic?"

"From what she said, it does sound as if she was running the show, not Michael. No. I don't mean running it. I mean more like the person who kept it organized and moving."

"I agree." AJ adjusted the car's heater. She angled a look at Bonnie. "Did you ever think of changing jobs?"

"You mean the ATF?" Bonnie turned with a hopeful expression on her face.

"I mean any of the federal agencies. Have you looked into it? You should." AJ slowed the SUV and bent forward to see the storefronts. "Where is this restaurant?"

"I'll tell you when I see it," Bonnie said. "Would I need more education for another job?"

"Not necessarily education in the formal sense, but you'd need more training. You're not going to be a cop forever, are you? Although, good cops are critical. We need them too."

"There it is, the sign with the red rose." Bonnie pointed down the road. "No, I'm not going to be a cop forever, but I could use some direction, AJ."

They parked at the steakhouse. "You could shadow Grace for a while. You've done well. And now that you're a temporary DEA agent, pay attention."

Bonnie laughed out loud. "Grace? She's cute. I'd love to shadow her anywhere." Bonnie leaned into the backseat for their gloves and hats. "How do I set this up?"

"I'll just assign you to her, but I'll clear it with Bill and Charles first. Grace is really my assistant, in a million ways. She could teach you a lot."

Bonnie raised an eyebrow with a wiseass grin.

"We'll talk later." AJ grinned at Bonnie's expression. "Even though I'm assigned to Charles, I'm responsible for the structure of our group," AJ said and took her gloves from Bonnie. Charles would love to have Bonnie work with Grace.

Her phone rang as she locked the car and she motioned for Bonnie to go inside.

"Charles?" she said.

"Allison." He cleared his throat and she braced herself. He always prefaced bad news with a clearing of the throat. "The doctor and his wife were murdered last night or early this morning."

Stunned, AJ stood perfectly still. "Damn," she whispered. "How?"

"As they got out of the car in their driveway. They were shot to death." AJ could hear him breathing.

"I'm sorry, Charles." She bit her lip hard. "How did it go down?" she said, squinting at the traffic through the almost-darkness.

"Execution style." He sounded tired. "Both of them had been on their knees."

"Why? I don't get it. Star made a lot of money for Michael. Or *was* it Michael? What did the CSIs find?"

"I don't know much more. Bill called me from the scene. That house is so secluded no one found them until around noon. We'll have to wait for the ME on that one."

They were both quiet for a moment until Charles spoke again. "Something else. Bill's people picked up Seraph's little girl, late yesterday. She was in that house we looked at. You were right."

"They got the child?" AJ took a big breath. "You didn't tell me about the little girl when we talked last night."

"I didn't know. Remember, Bill wasn't home when you and I were talking. He took the child to the hospital first and had her checked out before he took her to Seraph at the apartment."

"You should have called me back last night." Scattered, AJ leaned against the SUV.

"No time, Allison." He took a deep breath. "I think the child being taken alerted Michael. We're going to have to step this whole thing up a notch. I'm assigning Grace to the Blackburn woman, at least for a while. I'll keep after Seraph."

"Why would he have murdered Star because of Seraph's little girl? That doesn't make sense. Seraph was adamant that Michael knew next-to-nothing about the street operations. Not to mention that he and Elena were fighting. The only connection Star had to any of us would have been that photo in the newspaper, and even then, she only thought I was an art dealer. Something's off. Should I come back?"

"No, stay."

"Again, why didn't you call me last night about the little girl?" She heard her voice rise. "I wouldn't have left this morning."

"Knock it off, AJ. I want you down there, not here. I'll handle this end." In all their years, Charles had never used that tone of voice on her. He was upset too. No, he was frustrated because he couldn't figure it out either. "I'm on my way to the murder scene now and I'll stop at the Blackburn woman's house later. What have you found?"

"The farmhouse is a solid lead. I'm not sure it's Michael's group, but I'll get it all to you tonight. When you're done looking it over, call me." She kept her voice steady. "Any news on Elena? If you remember, we all decided Elena did Michael's dirty work."

"We remembered but she's still in the wind and no one is saying anything. They're all scared to death of that woman."

"All right. Make sure they try to match the prints at Star's with the prints at Katie's. The footprints from last night?"

"When we get around to it, Allison. No one was injured at Ms. Blackburn's."

"I got it," she said through clenched teeth. They ended the call and she shoved her phone back into her coat but didn't move. She'd get Grace to follow up on the prints if no one else did. She was certain that it had been Elena at Katie's last night, looking for Seraph. And, ten-to-one, Elena had done the murders of Star and her husband. If she found Seraph, she'd kill her as well.

AJ turned toward the restaurant. Charles wanted her here? Away from the action? For a moment, she felt cornered. There had been something in his voice besides anger. The DEA was hard to follow. Who knew what they were up to?

What if he had someone deep inside? Like the places she used to go. One thing was certain. If she'd been working this undercover, she'd want to be in that gang of girls, the angels, trying to get right next to either Michael or Seraph. Or Elena. She closed her eyes, resisting the yearning for the freedom of undercover, working alone. God, she was tired of keeping records, the constant responsibility.

"Damn it." She straightened and composed herself for her people inside. Her team worked hard and gave it everything they had. Their operation was small, but it was important. Small things added up in the grand scheme of things.

Star, her husband, and the rookie. Three dead. Christ. All they were after was information. She opened the restaurant door but swallowed hard, not sure if she could eat.

CHAPTER SIXTEEN

M y brain's broke." Katie rubbed her tired eyes, stood, and stretched. It was almost dark. She'd found something that might just wow this client for the first presentation and lost the whole afternoon to the research and set-up. Her stomach rumbled and she glanced at the clock. It was time for dinner.

As she closed the computer, she picked up AJ's note. AJ's arms around her last night had been more than a polite hug. AJ had *held* her. Lord. It was like stepping into sunlight. She studied the vertical, bold handwriting for a moment, thinking about the *Please be safe* that AJ had written. The words spiked a little shot of nerves inside her, but the *remember, you can call me* made her feel better. She tucked the note in her jeans.

The television muted and Katie felt another jitter of nerves. There was someone in her living room today because a stranger had been outside her house last night—less than twenty-four hours ago.

Grace was at the window, talking on the phone with the remote in her other hand. "What? Tell me again, Charles."

Katie opened her freezer in her kitchen. The glazed ham her mother had given her was at the very back, but she patiently rearranged everything to take it out.

Grace caught Katie's eyes as she spoke into the phone. "Let me ask." She smiled and said, "Are you up for a visit from our supervisor now?"

"Ask him if he just wants coffee or would he like to stay for dinner."

Grace repeated Katie's question into the phone. "He says just coffee would be fine."

Katie nodded and set the microwave on defrost. Grace was off the phone but still at the window, quiet. Katie spooned coffee into the basket and poured water into the coffeemaker.

When Grace finally turned, Katie said, "What's up?"

"Our supervisor will explain. He'll be here about the time the coffee's done." She expelled a big breath. "You're liable to see a lot of me in the next few days."

Katie unloaded the dishwasher, put three cups on the table, and prepared herself to answer questions.

After the introductions, the three of them sat in the kitchen. Charles was about as tall as Bill Whiteaker but appeared more vigorous. He didn't have nearly the white head of hair that Chief Whiteaker sported.

"In addition to someone being here last night, something happened that may further affect you and I'm sorry," Charles began. "Worse, I don't know how long this will last."

Katie watched his dark eyes. AJ and Charles Ryan were complete opposites. He was terse and wore authority like a coat.

"Allison told me that you had met a man and a woman in an elevator? You were on your way to a business appointment?" He took the coffee she offered. "Also, there were two other women on that elevator?"

"AJ said the man was probably a doctor and his wife. She didn't comment on the two other women, but it made her tense."

"It was a doctor and his wife and they've been murdered."

Katie shivered with surprise and pulled in a breath.

"I wish I had more information for you but, at this time, I don't."

"Did it involve their car, like mine?" Katie was certain she could feel the hair on her head straighten. "Was it that woman from the paper?" She held up the newspaper photo of AJ.

"Yes, this woman, but no, not their car," Charles said, grasping the cup of coffee with his big hands. "However, I think Grace should stay with you, at least until we understand where this is going. There will be a team out here, later, to check out those footprints."

"All right," Katie said, glad to hear her voice sound calm while her insides shook. "So it wasn't their car or mine. What is it?"

"We honestly aren't sure at this point. My best guess is that they were looking for the woman that was in your car."

Grace stood. "I need to go home for clothes, take care of some personal things. Could someone swing by and stay with Katie?"

"Why don't you go now? I'll stay," Charles said. "I need to ask Ms. Blackburn some questions."

"Katie, please," Katie said with her business smile.

"Okay," Charles said and took some papers out of his briefcase. "This is not a formal inquiry."

"Do I look tense?"

He looked up with an unexpected smile. "A little."

"This is all so crazy. AJ asked me to think of anything or any way I might be connected to that man, Michael, or the woman in my car. Seraph?" She felt herself babbling a little and slowed down. "The only thing I can think of is the woman who used to live with me."

Charles laid an iPad on the table. "Lu Wright? I saw that her name had originally been on this house, but now it's in your name only. Ms.—Katie, I want to be honest. I checked you out thoroughly."

"I would expect that," Katie said. "Lu's been gone from this house for years."

"You've kept in touch with her?"

Katie nodded. "I couldn't live with her alcoholism or drug use, but I was her emergency medical contact as well as her POA. I've told AJ everything. Bonnie Logan also knows Lu."

"Do you have any idea how Ms. Wright supported herself?"

"After she moved? No. She had so many jobs that I lost track of them." Katie stopped, trying to remember. "Honestly, I don't know what she did except that she drove a van."

"Do you know where she was living? I know she's very ill now."

"Her apartment is south of the Copper Penny, the bar across the street from the police station. Lu's in Franklin Hospital, unless her parents have already moved her to Madison."

Something was trying to surface in her memory. "Early last fall, she called and asked if she could come to the house. She wanted a couch we'd bought together. A man drove her van and helped her put it in the back." Katie swallowed hard and looked at Charles. "After she moved, years ago, it was always a bad time for Lu."

Charles gave her a sympathetic look. "I have a brother. He's rarely sober."

"I'm sorry."

"I am too." They both paused as if to collect themselves. "That man that was with her? Do you remember anything about him?"

"Not really. They were here when I got home from work. I wanted to see what she'd taken from the house so I didn't pay much attention to him."

"Was he tall?"

Katie smiled with a little shrug. "I'm only five foot five, so everyone seems tall to me." She scanned him. "Probably about your height. Are you over six foot?"

"I'm just six foot. What color hair, eyes?"

"Brown, but he never took off his sunglasses." Katie got up for more coffee, amazed that she remembered.

Charles bent to his briefcase and laid a few photos out on the table. "Do any of these men look familiar?"

Katie went through the five photos slowly. One was from a police lineup. "Yes." she said, holding up the last photo. "This one— but not the man. The woman he's talking to beside the white pickup. That's the woman that got into the elevator with us, the doctor and his wife." She frowned at Charles. "Wait—that pickup. John, my security man at work…the night Seraph was in my car, the night of the blizzard. He asked me about a white pickup that had been next to my car in the parking lot. Also, something about a hood ornament. How could I have forgotten that?"

"Really?" Charles cleared his throat. "A white pickup? And a hood ornament." He took the photo from her, studying it. "Could we talk to John? Here…" He slid a notepad toward her. "Write down his name. Give him a call, a head's-up so he knows we're coming. Memory's a funny thing, Katie. Given time, it'll usually come to you." He put the rest of the photos away but left the one photo on the table. "Actually, that does it. Ms. Wright has to be the contact, the thing that ties you to Michael." He took another photo out of the briefcase. "This is her, right?"

Katie bent to look at the black-and-white photo in front of her. It was Lu, in a dark van, like the one that had been in her driveway. "Yes," she said, annoyed to hear her voice quiver.

"This was taken after she had met with Michael last fall."

"I didn't know that she knew him. Did she know Seraph too?"

"Since she knew Michael, we're assuming she knew Seraph as well. I know that AJ told you that Michael and Seraph lived together."

"I didn't know anyone that Lu was connected with and I hadn't seen her since last fall, until I saw her recently at the hospital. Everything around Lu was always so fast. That's the whole country these days, not to mention texting, e-mail, Twitter or whatever. You name it, we do it. Sometimes I just turn everything off, sit in the dark and breathe."

"How is your business?"

"It's good. It's a small, niche company. Luckily, the economy hasn't hurt me all that much. If anything, I've grown some." Katie got up to take the ham out of the microwave. "I'm making ham tonight. Are you sure you won't stay?"

"Positive, but thanks." He smiled as she took a glass baking pan from the cupboard. "How has today gone with Grace?"

"She's nice, and frankly, I was glad she was here."

"Grace will be easy to work with. Allison trained her. She's one of the best trainers I have."

Katie turned from the sink. "Have you known AJ for a long time?"

"Years," Charles said and put the photos away in his briefcase.

"Is it true that she likes fast cars and motorcycles? Or is that just one of her many personalities?"

Charles chuckled. "She likes speed all right."

The thawed ham was ready and Katie drizzled glaze on top of it. "She's one of the most interesting people I've met in a long time," she said.

"That she is. I was setting up something and a friend of mine recommended her. Allison was training with the ATF so I called her for a meeting. I'm DEA, and she's been on loan to me ever since." Charles smiled to himself. "That was years ago." He leaned back against the padded seat, relaxed, loosened his tie, and undid the top button on his white shirt. "It's warm in here," he said. He took off his suit coat and Katie hung it over a chair.

"Rumor has it that she likes martial arts?"

"She uses it with her team to cool off the hot shots, and damned if it doesn't work." He raised his eyebrows with a little shake of his head.

"And she was adopted?"

The air suddenly sucked out of the room. Charles's eyes were like stones in snow.

"She told you that?" he said softly.

"We've had dinners together so, naturally, we've talked." Katie felt as though she'd said the wrong thing and felt him looking at her.

"Did she mention her sisters?"

"That she has four sisters? Yes. I know she likes art, knows quite a bit about it. We went to the museum together a week ago. I checked her out on the Internet and asked about her military decoration. The assignment in Ecuador?"

He was waiting, as if there were more, but Katie turned away to finish the potatoes.

"Did she tell you where she is now? Today?"

"No," Katie said, twisting to look back at him. "In fact, I've told you everything I know about her." She sat across the table once again with a reinforcing drink of coffee. "But I know there's more to this than you're telling me. AJ won't say a word. My dad was a cop, and I know you don't drag in the ATF and the DEA over a woman in my car."

Charles stared at her, listening very hard. Katie saw that she'd caught him off guard.

"So, Lu. I'm just guessing that it's drugs, isn't it? That's why Grace is here. The woman in my car, Seraph, was a person of interest, someone that's important to all of you for some reason. And you're not going to tell me anything, are you?"

"Perhaps," Charles said. They challenged each other with a smile.

"And you want Grace here how long?"

"Until we understand why they, or whoever, was here last night."

Katie took a deep breath and tried to find the words that would make him understand. "I'm okay with having someone here for several days. It's not personal, but I'd like to go it alone after that. My father taught me that fear's a good thing, keeps you alert. If there's someone here, I won't pay attention. I'll let things slide, get sloppy." She got up and went back to the potatoes.

"Do you think that's prudent?"

"Probably not."

"I have the authority to do this."

"I'm sure you do."

He sighed but was quiet. Finally, he tipped his cup back, finished it. "We're at a stand-off then, aren't we? Could we just take it day by day?"

"I'll consider that," she said and put the potatoes in the oven.

Chapter Seventeen

No," AJ said out loud to the dark. She sat straight up with her weapon in her hand. Had she yelled? The nightmare left her sweating. She could still hear the warning cries of crows echo over the three bodies in Star's driveway with Katie's slender body curled between the doctor and his wife, one small hand above her head. "Sweet mother," she gasped and pushed herself out of the motel bed before she could examine one more piece of her wrecked inner landscape.

Almost falling, she tangled with her boots by the bed. Righting herself, she stumbled into the bathroom and turned on the shower. A few minutes under the water cleared her head. She hated the dreams where you weren't sure if you slept or lived or what was real.

Wrapped in two towels, she opened her laptop and immediately went to Katie's Blue Ridge, Inc. site, searching for the photo Bonnie had mentioned. There it was, under About Us. A smile spread through her. Katie was turning away from the camera, looking over her shoulder, left hand gripping a briefcase, right hand raised in a good-bye. The full-skirted, knee-length summer dress outlined Katie's body, shifting with her motion. Her curly black hair partially covered the right side of her face leaving only that incredible smile emphasized in the sun. AJ fumbled with her phone and downloaded the photo.

What had Bonnie asked her? *Was she interested?* She certainly was *something*. It had been a long time since she'd talked to anyone or flirted like she did with Katie. AJ held up the phone, looked at the photo again, and debated whether or not to call. What would she say? That she was glad Katie was alive and safe? Or that she'd rather be there, not here? She scowled at the floor and then grinned. Bren Black, super agent, could talk to Katie. Hopefully, Katie would still be sound asleep and she could leave a message.

AJ practiced heavy breathing before she dialed. "It's Bren, reporting in. I'm out of ammo, stuck in a hole in the ground but not sure where." Heavy breathing. "I can hear them coming but don't worry. You know I'll survive." AJ panted into the phone. "I'll figure this out in the next forty seconds. Just turn the page and you'll see what my incredible imagination and ingenuity has cooked up." More heavy breathing. "Have to go. They're almost here." AJ let a long pause go by, then slipped into her calm, emotionless announcer's voice. "Please acknowledge receipt of this message." She hung up with a big grin. Dumb but fun. She began to dress, humming to herself. She stopped when she realized the song was "Secret Agent Man."

Ten minutes later, she was out the door for a run to clear her head. If she stayed on the sidewalks, snow or ice would not be a problem. She jogged in place at one of only three streetlights in town. The quiet night was interrupted by the growl of a diesel motor and she looked over her shoulder. A black Volvo box truck cruised by, headed north. She read the tags, following its taillights until it turned off the main highway.

When she got back to the motel, she ran the license on her laptop. They were registered to a clothing distributor in Pennsylvania. The name was familiar and she searched her notes. There it was. *Today's Fashions.*

The company had trucks stolen in Missouri last fall, including several black Volvo box trucks. That was strange. If this was one of the stolen trucks, they usually repainted the vehicle and changed plates. She sent the info to Charles with her own personal notes, including the plates. Two of her team members, John and Kerry, should be about done with last night's surveillance. If the truck was headed for the farm, they should see it. They were parked behind a deserted barn and silo down the road from the farm, and had a perfect view of Hood's Hollow.

The phone rang and AJ glanced at the clock. It could be Katie but it was Bonnie, asking about breakfast. Hungry, she grabbed her coat just as Bonnie knocked on her door.

Later, over bacon and eggs at the local diner, AJ scanned Bonnie's surveyor clothing.

"Love those bibs."

"Hey, it's cold out there."

"Remember that night out by Lake Michigan?"

They laughed, recalling the night across the street from a drug house close to Lake Michigan in minus-four degrees. The cold had forced them back to the car.

"I worked out at the gym later, just to warm up," Bonnie admitted.

"I've already jogged this morning."

Bonnie paused, her fork halfway to her mouth. "In this weather? Have you lost your mind?"

"A long time ago." AJ reached for the ketchup. "I saw a black truck headed toward the farm, got back to the room and ran the plates. Remember the trucks stolen in Missouri?"

Bonnie nodded but kept eating.

"The license plates confirmed it was one of them. It was headed toward the farm so the boys should have seen it." They both automatically checked their watches. It was about eight o'clock. "Shouldn't they be back by now?"

Bonnie called Kerry on her phone, but he didn't answer. "Not good," Bonnie said as they looked at each other across the table. "They could be asleep. It's been known to happen." They waited until the waitress filled their cups before they spoke again.

"Where are Matt and Jim?" A little warning inched up AJ's spine.

"Asleep. They traded after midnight and I told them to sleep in. Want me to get them up?"

"No," AJ said. "I'll get a car from that rental place, the one with the body shop attached. I don't want any of our agency vehicles out there. The men can drive the state DOT van behind us." She dropped money on the table. "No one's at the farm beside that young guy, right?"

Bonnie shook her head. "No. He said a girl was there. The one we didn't see."

"If they're cooking meth, or whatever, they have to ship the goods somehow. We'll send the boys out in the van to see where we can set up different surveillance spots," AJ said as she stood. "The only new face is me so I'll go to the rental place. Let Matt and Jim sleep for fifteen, twenty minutes, but keep trying to call Kerry and try John. One of them should have answered. Also, I want to stop in and talk with the county and state police here. You come with me." She handed Bonnie a thermos. "Get this filled and yours too. I'll meet you back at the motel." AJ handed her car keys to Bonnie. "Move my SUV to the parking lot behind the motel. We'll put one of those clipboards and survey tripods you guys use into the vehicle I rent, okay?"

AJ walked down to the car rental she'd seen yesterday. The town was awake and she took a thorough look. It was a nice little place with well-kept shops. There was even a small gallery and she slowed to look at the photos in the window. They probably did a good tourist business in the summer because of the lake.

A teenager in a tricked out green Chevy squealed into the driveway of the only fast food business in town. He almost grazed AJ's body.

"Sorry," he yelled. "Late."

AJ lifted her hand. Late for school? He'd looked young enough. The next business was the car rental and she walked through the few cars out front before she went inside. She chose an older brown Chrysler sedan with plenty of room, used one of her three fake driver's licenses, and paid in cash. When she drove into the parking lot at the motel, Matt and Jim were up but unshaven, their eyes weary as they hauled the survey equipment out of the borrowed state DOT van. AJ changed from her duster into a black canvas work coat and a black stocking cap before she got behind the wheel.

She turned in the seat to see everyone in the car. "I'm going to make a pass at the site, then the farmhouse. We'll do a square and come back the same way. I'll get out with the equipment." She pointed at Matt. "You are in charge of the recording. Bonnie, put that big clipboard on the dash so it's visible through the windshield." AJ handed Jim the thermos. "Drink some of this. It'll help. We'll get you some breakfast when we get back." She kept her voice normal and calm. Neither Kerry nor John had answered their phones. Something sure as hell was wrong.

They said nothing on the way to the site. AJ slowed as they approached the deserted barn and silo, just enough for Matt to record the entire drive-by with his phone. Only the back of the black Suburban was visible, but there were multiple tire tracks in the snow.

"Shit," Bonnie said quietly as she tried Kerry's phone again, then John's. No answer. AJ gradually sped up and drove past the farmhouse, doing the square she had described earlier.

"Did you notice the truck tracks at the silo and in the driveway to the farmhouse?" she said. When they came back, she parked about a hundred feet away from the abandoned barn and silo. Out of the car, she hoisted the tripod onto her shoulder and left her sunglasses on. If anyone was watching, they'd only see another surveyor. She opened the plat map she held in her hands.

Crows yelled at one another just as they had in her nightmare earlier. Her eyes on the map, she listened intently but heard nothing except crows. The tripod was heavy as she moved ahead and studied the tire tracks in the snow. There were at least three different tracks, some from a car, but one set was definitely a truck. AJ walked another thirty feet and repeated the process. Now she had a good view of their agency vehicle. Nothing stirred, not even a breeze. She began to walk up the long driveway.

"No," she said involuntarily. She covered her mouth as she saw the carnage inside the big Suburban. What glass was left was covered with blood. Her hands shook as she called 911, the same procedure they would have used in Milwaukee. The state police responded and she gave them the information. With a hard swallow, she tried not to gag. She hated the smell of blood. She squatted down, wiped her eyes, and took deep breaths before she called Charles. All she got was his voice mail so she left a message with the information.

Finally, she called Bonnie in the car, explaining what she was about to do.

She ran back down the driveway and did her best to look like a state employee that had just come upon a horrific crime scene. Her team came toward her as she pointed at the black car and threw the book of maps onto the ground. "Stay back," AJ said, her voice terse and they slowed, then stopped. "Stay right where you are until the state police come." They watched her carefully with anxious faces. Finally, a siren sounded in the quiet country air.

With her back to the farmhouse, she handed the burly trooper her wallet. His eyebrows shot up as he read her ID. She asked him to call his captain immediately. Finally, she walked to her team.

"They're both dead," she said in a low but gentle voice. She watched the shock register across their faces. "If anyone's paying attention to us, this is a very critical moment. Go back. Get into the car. Drive it up here."

"But—"

"Matt, go to the car," AJ said sharply. "Bonnie, Jim, take him back." As one, the three of them turned back to the brown sedan.

"What can I do to help?" The trooper walked toward them, phone still in hand.

"Get someone to tow our car after the ME's done. Is there any place in town that we can put it? Where no one will see it? Our forensic people have to go over it." AJ jammed her shaking hands in her coat pocket.

"The captain already said to tow it to our office. It's about a half mile south of town. We'll put it in the fenced area behind the building."

The warmth slowly leaked out of her and AJ stomped her feet to keep them warm. "Would you look into the barn and the silo? I thought I saw footprints." An ambulance was screaming toward them, followed by a gray pickup. The trooper held up his hand to stop them.

"Is that the ME?" AJ said as she folded the tripod together.

He nodded as a woman in jeans and parka got out. She said something to the EMS, nodded at the trooper, and introduced herself to AJ.

AJ pulled off her glove to take the woman's hand. "I walked up there and came back immediately. I didn't touch anything. The rest of my crew's over there, in the brown car."

"Your supervisor called me on the way over here. You must have called him?"

"Right after I notified nine one one," AJ said.

The ME looked up the hill at the car. "I'll go up alone. The EMS unit will help me."

"Thanks. I don't want my team to see that," AJ said and looked away from the car with the red windows. Jarred to her soul, she stared down at the snow.

"I don't imagine you do. I'll do my job."

AJ nodded and walked toward the brown Chrysler. "Is there any coffee left?" she asked as she opened the door. Bonnie shoved a half cup of coffee into her hands and AJ automatically took a drink. She started the car and turned the heater on high. "I'm sorry," she said and looked away at the fields.

"Are they really dead?" Jim said. He had almost whispered.

"The windshield and side windows are shot out." She cleared the tears out of her voice. "My best guess is that they shot them at the same time. How the hell did John and Kerry let someone get that close?"

AJ watched the trooper enter the barn, then tracked the ME at the vehicle. The woman reached for a camera in her bag and began to take pictures. The EMS team leaned against the ambulance, waiting. One already had a body bag in his hands. Charles would want those pictures from the ME and any forensics.

A gray van parked behind them. She got out of the car and introduced herself to the county CSIs. As she watched the three men walk away she began to tick off the things she had to do. Her gaze slid down the road to the farmhouse, memorizing everything, starting at the top with the old-fashioned cupola. The blood beat in her ears, but she remained perfectly still.

Could she keep anyone safe? *That's five. This is war. Fuck you, Michael. Or Elena. I'm coming after you.*

CHAPTER EIGHTEEN

Downtown Milwaukee was busy as Katie unlocked her car. "How about lunch?" Katie said, resisting the urge to cheer. The bank had granted her an appointment with the senior vice-president next week. Maybe she had the contract.

Grace stepped carefully around the slush on the sidewalk and leaned into Katie's backseat, securing the presentation materials on the floor and backseat. "I'm starving. Can we go to Smitty's? One of their cheeseburgers sounds great right now." She looked across the seats at Katie. "Do you have your business clothes custom made?"

Katie grinned over the headrest at Grace. "My mom and sisters are the clothing mavens. I buy my stuff off the rack and they fit it for me. They all love to sew."

"That's a classy suit. The lines and cut are lovely. That blue-gray does nice things to your eyes."

"Thanks. My family would adopt you for those compliments. This suit is all Mom with the old-fashioned buttons and the wider lapels. She used to own a sewing and alteration business."

"I've got a black suit that could use some work." Grace snapped her seat belt in place. "We wear so much black that I'd like to make some of mine...what? Stand out?"

"Mom would love to do it. Pick out a few things and we'll go over, have some coffee, talk fashion with Mom. She'll be in heaven." Katie blew out a breath and laid her head on the steering wheel. "I'm so relieved this presentation's over that I'd eat snow, but Smitty's sounds better. Thanks for the help." She started the car. "Look at the water on the road. It's a March heat wave. The thermometer says fifty degrees."

Grace shook her head. "Only in Milwaukee."

"Isn't this boring for you? The office or the meetings?"

"Are you kidding? Think about what I do for a living. It's a great change of pace, and that was some presentation. How on earth did you come up with that?"

"This is the biggest business I've ever pitched. I shook all the way through that meeting. Let's face it, Benning's is much more than a bank. They've been in international investment for almost a century. The man who contacted me said that all the presentations they'd seen were clones of each other, including the big New York City agencies. He wanted to know if I could come up with something fresh."

"Well, it's only my non-business opinion, but I think you knocked their shorts off." Grace was looking through her bag but stopped with a frown. "That was Benning's? The sign said Capitol Five Bank."

"Benning's bought them out last month." Katie looked at Grace, wondering why that made a difference. Grace's face had lost the relaxed smile. "At any rate, Benning's has always catered to old business and old money. That's why I suggested changing their approach. I'd like to see them consider the blue-collar market or start-ups. Traditional business is hard-hit right now and lending is slow. Milwaukee's like every other small city. They could use a little cash infusion. And hope."

She turned at a green light and drove toward the lake. "The first day you were at my house, I was researching and caught an online story about the 2006 Nobel Peace Prize winner, Mohammad Yunus. It was his philosophy, microlending, that I wove into the presentation today. It was all through the Milwaukee demographics and our economics. Zack did the artwork, the plasma animations."

"Zack's artwork is stunning," Grace said.

"Bottom line—it's the idea that sells. Zack's artwork gives it an extra zing, dresses it up." Katie parked beside the door at Smitty's.

"My business has two sides. The advertising part that people can see or hear. That would be TV, paper, what have you. Then, what you saw this morning. The presentation. The public relations. They cross, of course, melt into each other." She unsnapped her seat belt and grinned. "C'mon. I'm hungry."

They found a booth at the back and Grace sank into the leather, facing the door. "Last year, the first day I was here, Milwaukee had seven inches of beautiful snow, but the cold that followed was horrible." She took another look around the little restaurant. "I didn't even think to bring gloves when I followed the team up from Arkansas."

"Do you have a specialty?" Katie said. "Or is the team designed that way?"

"Theoretically, I'm the nerd, the tech, the one who does our computer stuff."

"If I'd known that, I'd have asked for help when I was researching." Katie grinned. "Are there a lot of people in your—AJ's—group?"

Grace studied Katie for a moment. "No. In this country, today, there are thousands and thousands of cops and federal agents, working on everything from terrorism to drugs, any kind of criminal activity. Law enforcement is enormous, but so are the problems. Our group has a specific assignment. Is that what you mean?"

"I was only curious about the size of your team, uh, task force." Katie picked up her menu. She already knew what she was going to order but needed a moment to think through her next question. She'd responded to AJ's crazy Bren Black voice mail at the first of the week plus left two new messages. It'd been over three days, but she hadn't heard from her.

Just ask, Katie decided. "Have you heard from AJ?"

Grace's gaze flicked at her for a moment, then back at the menu. "I called her while you were in the shower this morning."

"Oh." Katie bit her lip to keep quiet in front of Grace's neutral expression.

"She's okay, Katie. There's been some difficulty there and she hasn't had much sleep."

Katie frowned down at her silverware. "I don't even know where she is. All of you go…" She searched for the right word. "So fast."

"You were the first thing AJ asked about this morning. She worries about you."

"I know she's busy," Katie said, but Grace's words resonated. *She worries about me?*

"Charles is with her," Grace said as the waitress brought them water.

Katie placed her order then glanced at Grace. How odd that she was sitting in this booth with a federal agent. Her entire life had changed with the dizzying speed of a Fourth of July rocket with that woman, Seraph, in her car. Lu probably wasn't going to live. Then Allison Jacob had walked into her life. Not to mention Michael, Charles, Grace, everyone else connected to all of this craziness. The knowledge that Lu had involved her in this continually rubbed against her mind. No one knew better than Katie how irresponsible Lu Wright was but there were moments when she wanted to scream with all the *not knowing.* She thought of Seraph. If she could confirm how or why Lu had involved her, then she'd be able to understand, get past it.

"Katie," Grace was saying and she snapped back to the moment.

"I'm sorry," she said. "Cotton for brains some days. Do you think I could talk with Seraph?"

Grace's eyebrows shot up and Katie heard her pull in a little breath. "Seraph?"

"The woman who was in my car."

"My God, Katie. No, I don't think so. Why would you want to talk to her?"

"Would you call? At least ask for me?"

Grace stared at her. "They won't…are you all right? I mean, are you scared?"

"Scared? Of course I am." She shrugged a little. "But at the same time, I'm damned mad at Lu. If she wasn't in such desperate health, I swear, I'd go get her and drag her back here."

Grace nodded. "I imagine." She played with a napkin and looked at Katie. "I know you told Charles that you didn't want anyone at your house or with you."

"It's not you. I've simply never been involved in anything like this. I mean, my car's totaled and the cop driving it was killed. That man and his wife were murdered. My life is beginning to resemble the mysteries that I read." She leaned on her elbows and gave Grace her best pitch. "It would make me feel better if I could talk with Seraph, that's all. Dad always said to be prepared for anything. It's the *anything* that can't be taught."

"No, it isn't taught. Don't you have some background in this?"

"Just security," Katie said. "I have a good sense of what's out of place when I'm looking at a scene, a few of the basics, and, of course, I'm familiar with guns."

Grace made a wry face. "Don't even talk to me about your shooting. AJ showed us your shooting range results. You outshot some of us."

"Pure luck if I did." Katie laughed. Grace hadn't agreed to let her see Seraph but looked as if she might at least call someone for her. The worst they could do was say no. In addition to being constantly on guard, she was just plain ticked. The food came at that moment, distracting her. That cheeseburger had her name all over it. She took a big bite, closing her eyes with pleasure. "Death by cheeseburger," Katie said, dabbing at her mouth with a napkin.

A noisy group of young women came into the café and shoved some tables together, joking and bumping each other. Grace was eating but watching the table full of twenty-something girls. Katie glanced at the younger women too. At that moment, they laughed uproariously at something in the newspaper one of them held up.

"Do you know them?" Katie said, noticing the change of expression in Grace's eyes. It was a cop's look.

"Maybe." Grace adjusted her body and squared her shoulders toward the noisy group.

Katie took another bite, savoring the food. "I enjoyed talking with Charles. I think he's proud of AJ."

"I heard about some of that conversation from him. He liked the way you came at him," Grace said with a half-smile. "AJ and Charles are an unusual combination."

"They're close?"

"We're all spooked by both of them and swear they read each other's minds. They've worked together for years. For that matter, AJ's as good as anyone I've ever seen at reading people. It's like she has a sixth sense."

Katie swallowed another bite. "I found her on the Internet, her decoration."

Grace looked at her with a slight frown. "I don't know anything about that. We really don't know much about her background."

"Nor do I," Katie said and shook her head. "I asked and she downplayed it. Said it was no big deal."

"Right," Grace said softly. "I've never worked with anyone that I trust like AJ. The whole team would follow her anywhere. You should see her train new agents, particularly someone who is unusually proud of their guns. The cowboys. Do you know what I mean?"

"Dad called them gun junkies or adrenaline addicts. Or, sometimes, bullies."

"We have one person on our team that's sort of like that. He and AJ have worked together quite a while. Usually, AJ weeds them out, sees that they're sent somewhere else. Unfortunately, those kind of people are needed other places."

"She likes the brains better than brawn?"

Grace looked out of the window. "Physical agility? A must. But brains most of all."

"What about you?" Katie said as she swiped a French fry through ketchup.

"Me? I like getting the bad guy, but killing isn't necessary. AJ always says guns are safety and security but wants them holstered until you have to use them." Grace scanned the table of girls again. "I've never seen her run from a fight. AJ's fearless about a lot of things, but she's not careless."

Katie grinned immediately. Not too fearless when it involved flaming brandy...*or kissing me.*

"By the way, what is this?" Grace touched the rainbow band on Katie's wrist.

"It's an advertising gimmick Zack designed for a company, and I—"

"—had one made for you and AJ?" Grace finished the sentence.

Katie nodded. "We're both Eleanor Roosevelt fans so I had a couple of bracelets made with WWED inscribed on them."

"WWED?" Grace raised her eyebrows.

"What Would Eleanor Do?"

"I gave AJ a bit of a hard time about hers. She—" Grace stopped. "Can I just ask about you two?"

Katie gave a small shrug. "Nothing. Well, unless you count the fact that I'm totally fascinated."

"Fascinated?"

"Don't you dare repeat that. Look, you've read the information on me. You know who Lu Wright is, what our relationship was like."

Grace nodded. "A car wreck."

Katie pointed a French fry at Grace. "When you've survived someone like Lu, AJ's a breath of fresh air."

Katie saw Grace hold back a smile. "You think she's a breath of fresh air?"

"When I first met her, the night she interviewed me at the station, the most I could come up with was that there's a new kind of police woman out there. She's a lot different than Bonnie. I thought she might be a detective."

Grace laughed out loud. "Please, please say yes, that you'll let me tease her about that breath of fresh air."

"I've already teased her about several things," Katie said, thinking of the night that AJ had stayed over. That had been her first glimpse of AJ's professional side, serious and intense. "Does she mind being teased?"

"Not usually. She's subtle, loves to play the roles. Sometimes she's a girly-girl in summer dresses, but she can also wear a business suit or whatever the occasion calls for. Well, you saw the photo in the paper, the little black dress. Seriously, she can do anything from an evening gown to a tux, and always seem perfectly at ease."

"AJ in a tux?" Katie said. That was an interesting thought.

The loud group of women suddenly all laughed again. Grace tossed some money beside their empty plates. "My treat."

Katie stood and patted her stomach. "Thanks. I've grown up on those things. Sometimes I crave them."

"When you get in the car, give me a moment. I need to make some phone calls," Grace said with another glance at the noisy table. "I'll ask about Seraph, but don't get your hopes up."

"Honestly? All I want to know is how Lu involved me in this mess."

Grace shook her head slightly as they went out the door. Katie dialed Zack the minute she got in the car. Grace stayed outside and leaned against the hood, talking on her phone. On a whim, Katie dialed her voice mail and listened one more time to AJ doing an insane imitation of a spy, trapped, out of bullets but, of course, confident that she would survive.

Laughing, she turned the phone off and tapped it against her hand. At the very least, they were going to be great friends, but she hoped for more.

Chapter Nineteen

A loud banging on her door woke AJ. She pulled a sweatshirt over her head and searched for jeans. "Jesus. Stop already," she muttered at the door and flung it open. Charles leaned against the frame.

"Sorry." He hurried by her with a boatload of cold air.

"Have you even been to bed?"

"No. I had two phone calls before I could even take my coat off. I think I've solved the problem, but it needs your eyes." He flopped down on the well-used motel couch. "Make some coffee, will you?" He unloaded his iPad and a bunch of papers onto the coffee table.

She'd only been asleep a few hours. Her mind and body weren't working well together. The coffee pot bounced away from her but she caught it before it hit the floor. Somehow, she got it going and then stood in front of Charles. "Have you been drinking—in addition to what we drank earlier?"

"Yeah." He unraveled a map. "But I'll be fine with some coffee in me." His unshaven face and bloodshot eyes were testimony to the last twenty-four hours.

Yesterday, they'd stood together in a light snow beside John and Kerry's caskets at the Madison airport and waited for the plane that would take the men's bodies home. Earlier, for the first time in her life, she'd had to call the families of the deceased. When they returned, they'd immediately gone to the motel bar without asking each other. The alcohol hadn't even fazed her. She couldn't even remember what she'd drank.

She went back to the kitchen and poured coffee for both of them.

"Lawrence Kelly called tonight. Here's our plan." Charles pointed at his laptop. "We take down the farmhouse, with the help of the locals so they get some credit too, and then set it up again. Only we'll be running it." Lawrence Kelly was Charles's supervisor.

"What?" AJ sat up. "Why would we do that? Is that even legal?"

"So we can track the trucks." Charles gave her an odd look. "Of course it's legal."

AJ leaned closer to see the fuzzy photo on Charles's iPad. It was someone leaving a restaurant. "Is that a woman?"

"Yeah, it's a woman who reports to our Milwaukee DEA. And me, when I'm in town. She did so well in Iowa that Lawrence and I brought her over to Milwaukee when we opened the Howell Avenue Police Station. She's been somewhere in Michael's group ever since. Actually, she's been cooking for Michael."

"You had someone in town and didn't tell me? And a cooker?"

"You were still in Arkansas when I cleared her for this. I was just beginning to gather information."

AJ was startled to see that her cup was only half full. She didn't even remember drinking it. "We could have used her in the last few weeks." She wiggled her finger at him.

"She reminds me of you. Loads of finesse, but not as dependable." Charles stretched his legs out, but he was anything but relaxed. "She'll help us with Hoods Hollow. I'll put her there instead of that kid, that young guy that's out there now."

"Where is she? This—whoever? Still in Milwaukee?"

"No. She's nearby. She says Michael's really unhappy with the kid. It'll be a slam-dunk."

AJ stared at him. "This is crazy and you know it."

"How else are we going to find out where Michael's shipping his meth? Look, all you have to do is get young Owen out. We'll get the local SWAT and Hazmat to help us out. Once that's done, we'll let the house sit for a day or two, insert the woman, and monitor the shipments. If we do this right, Michael will see it as a solution to that fuck-up kid."

"Drink your coffee. And take your coat off." AJ took the coat he handed her and tossed it on the chair. "Charles, are you sure of any of this? And you're sure about this woman?"

"Her information's always been on point. Never had a problem there."

"Sounds too easy, but I'm too tired to think straight." She got up. "Could we go over this again in the morning? It still feels off to me." She set her cup on the table. "Crash on the couch, if you want. Remember the last time I thought something felt wrong and too simple?" She started for her bedroom. "I ended up in the hospital."

❖

The next morning, AJ braced her feet on the coffee table. Charles was at the desk, scribbling things on a pad of paper. "We have to wrap this up or I have to do laundry. I'm running out of clean clothes." She jiggled her foot and tried not to look at the motel's teal-colored walls. This operation might be small, but five dead? The war in the Middle East wasn't the only one claiming American lives.

AJ took her cup to the small kitchenette. "I want a shower and breakfast. Then we'll bring Bonnie and the boys over here and explain all of this to them." The small window over the sink was dirty, but she could see the parking lot. It looked the same as yesterday.

"What do you want me to do after this is over?"

"I want *us* to go back to Milwaukee, work with Seraph, and get the rest of her information. Now that she has the child, we can get the money set up."

"Okay." She turned to Charles. "I don't like this, down here, and you know it. Then we have to do something about Elena."

Charles had obviously slept and looked much more rested than last night. Showered and shaved, he was wearing a suit and tie. Right now he nailed her with a cold look. "You and Bill can handle

Elena. Find her, incarcerate her, and the killing will stop. And I think all Seraph has left is the money. Damn, Allison. I need to know who the businessmen are that are working with Michael, and I don't think Seraph has that information. If we pick up Michael, he'll just lawyer up."

"I think you're wrong," AJ said over a sigh. "Maybe we should all be on meth. It makes you feel as if anything's possible." Charles looked angry, but his phone rang so she went to her bedroom. She rummaged in her bag for the last of her clean clothes. For the first time in over two days, she had something close to energy. She'd better have some fight left in her. They were taking down Hood's Hollow tomorrow morning. The first light sweep of adrenaline washed over her.

That meant the rest of today would be spent in meetings and setup. She'd already picked up the search warrant while Charles enlisted two state SWAT and Hazmat teams. They'd argued over that. Damn it, too many people with too many guns. Guns and meth houses didn't mix. She glanced at him as she went across the hall into the bathroom. He was hunched over his phone, tight as a rock.

Something was out of sync between them today and she couldn't seem to fix it. The only thing they'd agreed on was Jock. Charles had him transferred to the local DEA and Charles had been open to transferring Bonnie over to their task force.

AJ glanced at herself in the bathroom mirror and brushed her shaggy hair away from her eyes. She needed more than clean clothes. A haircut would help.

Before she got into the shower, she leaned against the wall and listened to the messages from Katie that she'd saved on her phone. The first, a response to her crazy Bren Black report, had made her laugh on a day when it was hard to even find a smile.

"Bren," Katie had said in an exasperated tone of voice. "The jet. Or the car. Where's your head, girl? Bren always has one of two things nearby. An incredibly fast car—or a jet. Somewhere. Look around you. It's hard to hide either one of those items. And get out of that hole." And that's all she'd said with a laugh before she'd hung up.

The second message was different. Katie had asked for a ride in her car. Her *personal* car. Wait until she got her hands on Grace. God only knew what Grace had told her. She brought up the photo on her phone, the one off of Katie's website and it gave her the first real smile of the day.

"Stupid. Why didn't you kiss her? You wanted to." She gave the shower handle a hard twist. "I'm kissing her the next time I see her, and I don't care if we're in the middle of Wisconsin Avenue in downtown Milwaukee."

❖

Katie pulled into one of the parking spaces behind the apartment building. The big Suburban vehicle parked there was like the one AJ had driven.

"Ready?" Grace said, adjusting her weapon.

"Is this kind of thing really all that unusual?"

"I've never seen it before," Grace said. "You and Charles must be channeling each other. AJ would never have allowed this."

"I thought you said they were together?"

"She was gone when I called, and I'll bet anything he won't tell her because they're so busy. He did tell me to keep it short. Also, he wants me to record what you two talk about. He's the boss." Grace shook her head as she opened her door. "Wait until I come around. We'll walk in together."

The two men at the kitchen table stood and teased Grace about the doughnuts she'd brought them but quieted when they saw Katie. They did the introductions, and Katie thought Seraph looked much the same as she had in the photograph. She was just as tall as Katie had thought.

Seraph put the toddler on the floor and folded down crossed-legged beside the child. Katie sat nearby, picked up a white stuffed elephant toy, and held it out to the little girl.

"She's a doll," Katie said to Seraph. "She resembles you. The same hair and eyes."

"Thanks." Seraph's face flushed a little. "I'm lucky to have Meredith back."

Not certain what Seraph meant, Katie didn't ask. "How are you feeling?"

"A lot better than when you last saw me," Seraph said. "It was your car, wasn't it?"

Katie nodded. "You scared me to death."

"I hardly remember anything about that night." Seraph ran her hand through her hair and looked at Katie. "You're smaller than I remember."

Katie didn't answer but looked up at Grace. "Would you like to sit here with us?"

Grace settled to the floor and laid a small recorder in front of her.

"I have some questions," Katie said. "Part of the deal I made to be able to talk to you was that they be allowed to record us, and I'm supposed to make it short. Do you mind?" Katie clasped her arms around her knees.

With a deep breath, Seraph looked down at her little girl. When she raised her face, Katie saw understanding, but also sadness. "Are you law enforcement? I thought you owned your own business."

"How did you know that I own my business or that I'm small? You've seen me before?"

"Once. Lu pointed you out and talked to me about you."

"Lu," Katie said softly. Again, she held out the toy to the child.

Meredith got up and ran to the window. "No?" she said, pointing out the window.

Seraph laughed and it made her seem younger. "Yes, honey, *snow.*" The happiness lingered when she turned back to Katie.

"How did Lu Wright fit into this?" Grace stepped into the conversation.

Seraph gave Grace a quick look. "Lu and her little guy pal were part of Elena's backup on the streets."

"Guy pal? Michael?" Grace said.

"No, not Michael. A different, younger man. As I told Charles, the setup was simple. I coordinated everything from the house.

Elena ran the streets, and Michael handled the business sales. Half of the department at his bank buy from us on a regular basis." She turned back to Katie. "Lu said it was time for you to get a new car so, if we ever needed one, look for yours. She gave your car key to Elena."

Katie forced a smile. *Damn it all to hell, she had my key?* "I suppose. Did she happen to mention that it was my father's car?"

"I don't think so," Seraph said. "That car was special?"

"My dad's."

"She didn't mention that. Sorry." Seraph's mouth twisted. "I was close to my family."

"Are you from around here?" Katie asked.

"No. Michael and I are cousins. We grew up on farms in Kansas. After high school, I went to California with my boyfriend. Michael went to college. He did well. I didn't. I got into drugs, men, you name it—ended up homeless and on the streets with Meredith. I called him. He had a great job, a home, and needed help with this…business. I'm good at what he needed." She leaned back on her hands. "We were a good team, and I trusted him with my life, but there's something wrong with him now. He scares me."

Katie saw that Seraph had trusted Michael as she had trusted Lu. It occurred to her that everybody here already knew this information, but she was hearing it for the first time.

"Would any of you like some coffee?" one of the men asked. "We have carrot cake, Meredith's favorite." He grinned at Grace. "Or someone brought doughnuts."

"Sure," Seraph said. She held out her arms to Meredith, picked her up, and closed her eyes with happiness. Katie wondered what would happen to her now. Or the little girl.

"Who is Lu's *guy pal* that you mentioned?" Grace said around a bite of cake.

Seraph took milk from the refrigerator and began to break the cake into pieces for Meredith. "I'm not sure who he is. I only know that they worked together from when he was in college and he would crash at her place now and then. His parents live in the city." She was quiet, managing the food for the child. "I can't remember. He has a short name. Things got kind of dicey last summer." She offered Meredith another bite. "Elena and this guy got into a monster fight and Lu got him out of there. Lu told me that Elena pulled a gun on him."

Grace frowned at her. "I thought it was Michael. The man Lu worked with in college."

"No, Michael *met* Lu while he was in college. Michael doesn't do drugs. He was never involved, and he's proud of that. The guy I'm talking about is mid-twenties or maybe older, someone Lu has known for a few years. He worked for her while he was going to college." Seraph frowned, concentrating. "I'm sorry. He belonged to Lu and I only saw him now and then and..." Seraph suddenly stood. "Look." Seraph pointed at the big living room window. She picked Meredith up and held her tightly.

"What is it?" one of the men said.

"At the cemetery. Beside the angel." Seraph sank back into the kitchen chair with Meredith clutched in her arms.

All of them turned to the big window. Grace said, "Katie, go to the doorway, now."

"It's Michael, by the stone angel," Seraph said.

One of the men picked up binoculars and moved quickly to the other side of the window. "It is," he confirmed. "But he's looking to the north, not here."

Grace and Katie grabbed their coats and were out the back door in a hurry, Grace first, then Katie. "I'll drive," Grace said. "Scrunch down in the seat."

Katie lapsed into an angry silence, slouched in the seat with her knees braced on the car's dash. Again, she was in the dark, endless hole that was Lu. "Did you already have that information? And did you see that little tattoo on her hand, the black angel?"

"We knew some of that but weren't certain about Lu, and... shit, we didn't know there was a guy helping her." Grace glanced across the car. "I'm sorry about Lu."

"I'm way past loving her, but I want to stop hating her too. I want the place where I just don't give a damn." Katie sat up, let her feet fall to the floor, and jammed her hands into her coat. Seraph had been exactly what AJ had said. Addicts or criminals were often like the people next door. Or old lovers. "What will happen to Seraph? The child?"

Grace never took her eyes off the road. "This is one time I can honestly say to you that I don't know."

Michael trudged back to his car through the snow, swearing. "Where the hell are you, Seraph?" Three days ago, his contact at the clinic had confirmed she had been alive when they, whoever "they" were, had taken her from the clinic. It'd taken him two more days to find out that she was on this block. Somewhere. That information had cost him a great deal of money. He blew out a breath, frustrated beyond words. All he did was hand out money, but got very little in return for it. Every day, actually every few hours, he checked his offshore accounts. He knew Seraph hadn't given him up. Yet. Maybe she wasn't even conscious. Or maybe she had died, later. Last night, he'd stayed at the bank and began to move the money, but he had to do it slowly so no one noticed.

A random memory of his uncle, Seraph's father, flipped through his mind. "Damn, if the cops don't kill me, when that man finds out, he will," he ranted into the quiet cemetery. When he'd discovered she was still alive, he was both shocked and relieved. All those years, growing up together; of course they trusted each other. The shock of her blood on his floor after he'd hit her with the bat still turned his stomach. Why hadn't he just given her money and sent her away?

Donnie, one of Elena's helpers who did the heavy lifting, was still asleep in the front seat of Michael's sleek sedan. He shoved him hard as he got inside and slammed the door. "Wake up," Michael growled and started the car.

"What's the matter?" Donnie whined as he righted himself. "I haven't been to bed in days."

"If you'd done what I told you to do in the first place and found Seraph, I wouldn't be freezing my butt off out here, at the angel.

That's what I pay you for." Michael took a long pull on his energy drink. "What do you mean? Why haven't you been to bed?"

"I was with Elena, down at the farmhouse, and then in Madison."

"You and Elena were down at the farmhouse? What in the hell were you doing down there?" Michael looked at Donnie. "The regular pick up is tonight." The truck for the out of state load had already come and gone.

"I report to Elena and she reports to you. When she tells me that you say to go to the farmhouse, I go with her to the farmhouse." Donnie spoke slowly and patiently, his eyes dull. "Then we went to the party in Madison at Elena's friend's house."

"I didn't tell Elena to go anywhere," Michael almost shouted. "Did you pick up a load from Owen and Ariel?" He was so angry he spit on Donnie's dirty shirt.

"No, we killed those two men, the ones in the big black Suburban." Donnie's eyes were now wide and frightened.

Michael was so totally caught off guard by this information that he could only stare at Donnie. "You killed two people?" he finally choked out.

"Yeah, the Feds. Elena shot one and I shot the other, just like those other two people. You know, the doctor and his pretty wife."

"Son of a…" Michael said, so confused that he didn't know what to do next. He grabbed his phone and called Ariel at the farmhouse, but no one answered. What the hell? Next he tried Owen, but no answer there either. They had strict orders to have their phones turned on. They shot the Feds? What Feds? And why hadn't either of them called him?

He was as angry as he'd been when he found out about that doctor and his wife. It was Elena again, doing what she damned well pleased. All he'd wanted was information on the blonde with Star in that newspaper photo. He hadn't wanted his friend killed. God. She'd been the source of his best sales. He opened his glove compartment and took out the photo that he'd clipped from the newspaper.

"Do you know these women?" He handed the piece of newspaper to Donnie.

"That's the pretty woman. The one Elena shot." Donnie looked again. "Not the other two women."

Michael put the car in gear and drove toward the house that some of his girls shared. Donnie's impaired mind wasn't to blame, and he did report to Elena. Michael stopped at the curb. "Donnie, go on, go inside. Catch some sleep. Where's Elena?"

Donnie hauled himself out of the car but leaned back inside. "Don't know," he said in a shaky voice. His lip trembled. "She said to be ready tomorrow. Maybe we'll pick up the product, like she always does?"

Michael took another pull on the energy drink. Damn, he was lost without Seraph and Ariel or Lu. There was only one thing he could do. Go to Little Crane Lake and check out Ariel and Owen. No, first, he had to go back to the office and take care of business. He'd get some sleep and leave early in the morning.

Chapter Twenty

The next morning, AJ drove the old Chrysler down the road to the farmhouse through gold and silver ground fog. Locked and loaded, she was fully focused on Owen Hood, running across the floor plan of the house. Charles was less than five miles back with enough people to fight a small battle in Afghanistan. Too many people, she again thought to herself. People get lost in that kind of mob scene, or worse, make critical mistakes. Again, she was trapped in Charles's load of cosmic dust. She tried to adjust the itchy wire taped against her ribs but finally just left it alone.

The car pulled slightly to the right as she slowed in front of the farmhouse and flipped the switch under the dash for the smoke bomb Matt had installed last night. She hit the brakes hard. Smoke belched out from under the hood as the car backfired, sounding just like a gun. "What the hell, Matt," she said and then grinned. She knew the wire she wore had picked up the backfire plus her comment at Matt.

AJ got out of the car and opened the hood. The tailpipe still smoked as she walked along the length of the vehicle. Finally, she took her phone out of the borrowed work coat and faked a call. She looked at the house, then turned away and popped the trunk and stood the DOT tripod against the bumper. They'd kept surveillance all night. So far, the house was quiet. The idea was simply to get Owen Hood outside. Nothing more. "Don't want to blow up the house," she said under her breath as she strode past the SUV in the driveway. She knocked on the door. Nothing. She rapped louder and it opened a crack. A brown eye peeked at her.

"Hi," AJ said and gave it her brightest smile. "My car's broken down and my phone's dead." She held her phone up so he could see as well. The man was wearing dirty jeans and a torn plaid shirt. Dark eyes swept over her and she smiled again. "Do you know anything about cars?"

"No, not cars, but I have a phone," he said, opening the door, but she didn't enter.

"No, that's okay; I don't want to bother you folks this morning." She watched his eyes scan her fake state DOT badge and kept up her smile. "Do you have a cell phone?"

"My cell's dead, but you can use the house phone."

AJ got a complete look at him as he pulled the door open. Sweet Jesus, Bonnie was right, another zombie, even thinner than Frog if that was possible. Then the smell hit her. That distinctive used-diaper odor. Unable to get him outside, she had no choice but to follow him inside.

Newspapers, soda cans, and pizza containers covered every available surface. He turned on a table lamp and pointed at a phone. She swallowed the urge to gag. Yes, they were cooking.

"Thanks," she said with another smile. Owen Hood nervously moved some food containers and papers on the couch and sat down. She dialed the numbers for her own phone in her coat pocket, the one she'd turned off.

"Hey." She began her make-believe call. "That damned car broke down again." She paused. "Right down the road from where we were working. Get out here and pick me up." She stopped talking as if she were listening. "What? I could walk to town before you get here. Do you know it's only twenty degrees outside?" AJ was about to say something else when a young woman in a short bathrobe with wet, blond hair walked into the room.

"Hi," the blonde said, obviously startled. "I didn't know we had company."

There was something vaguely familiar about the girl, but she forged on. "My car won't run and my phone's dead. I really appreciate this." AJ held the phone away from her ear. "Sorry to bother you. I'm part of the state survey team that's working on your acreage out there." AJ pointed at the back of the house. "They always stick me with that useless car; it's the second time it's broken down. I'm talking to them now." She held up the phone and made sure the young woman could see the state ID that hung off her coat. At the same time, she scanned the blonde. She was short and slim with alert brown eyes. Eyes that were scanning her right now. Here's the boss, AJ thought as she put on her sincere face and smiled.

"Do you need a ride to town?" the girl said. "I'll take you."

"Really?" AJ said enthusiastically and turned away, speaking into the phone again. "I think there's someone here who can help me. Hang on just a minute and let me see how long this will take." Out of the corner of her eye, she saw Owen's hand move under a newspaper, followed by a sound she knew as well as her own breath. A shell being chambered in a shotgun. She turned to the big gun in the hands of the little blonde. Owen had a 9mm in his left hand, held sideways in gang style.

She let the phone drop. "Christ, don't shoot—"

The rich aroma of coffee shook Katie out of a gray, cluttered dream. Was that music? She turned over in bed to see the clock. God, it was late. Last night, she'd read until her eyes ached, then stared at the dark, thinking about what Seraph had confirmed. Another Lu-I-don't-care-betrayal. "Well, that's what you wanted to know. Now stop thinking about it," she said to herself. She had no idea when she'd finally fallen asleep last night.

She pulled on jeans and rummaged for heavy socks. Lu had placed her firmly in the middle of this mess where people were getting killed, and it scared the living hell out of her. She opened the drapes and grabbed her favorite Marquette sweatshirt with a quick thought of AJ. Every day, AJ was in this kind of scary living, from the minute she woke up. How did she stand it? Katie pulled on the sweatshirt without bothering with a bra. Everything felt off-kilter and she hadn't been up more than ten minutes.

Grace was at the kitchen counter. She reached up to turn the music off.

"Keep the music on. I like it," Katie said. "Have you been up long?"

"I slept late too. Thought I'd make the house specialty."

Katie poured herself a cup of coffee and watched Grace break eggs into a mixing bowl. "I don't know what's going on with me. I can't sleep, but when I do it's like I've fallen into a cave, black and strange."

"Yesterday was a tad stressful."

"Right," Katie said with a deep breath. "Want to go out tonight? We've been on the go for days. My brain is fried."

Grace took some milk and cheese out of the refrigerator. "I know what you mean. By the way," she said as she laid the cheese on the cutting board. "What did you tell your office staff about me hanging around?"

"That I was thinking of expanding and you were there to look at the operation."

"Good idea." Grace smiled at her. "I checked your entire staff."

"But they wouldn't hurt me or…" And then she thought of Lu.

"Katie." Grace turned with a serious expression. "What would you do if you were me? I'm responsible for your safety."

Katie made a face at her. "All right, but why didn't you tell me?"

"Because I didn't want to go through this conversation we're having right now." Grace held up her hands.

"How did they do? My staff?"

"Fine. Your artist, Zack, is kind of a puzzle, but nothing to be concerned about."

"Okay, but we need time off. Could we go to the Copper Penny tonight with my sister?"

"It's across the street from my office. That's handy." Grace tipped up the cutting board and swept a light shower of chopped onions and shredded cheese into the bowl with a touch of milk. "Your sister's not married?"

"I have two older sisters and two younger brothers. Circle the wagons and I'm tucked safely in the middle. My oldest sister and her girlfriend broke up before Christmas. She's been cranky ever since, but she has a date tonight, so there's hope."

Grace picked up the whisk. "There's always hope."

"My sis is so loyal it hurts. I think she's too good to most of the women she gets involved with and they take advantage of her." She pulled in a long breath. Had she just described herself and Lu? Do families have *loyal* genes?

Grace's phone rang. Katie saw her glance at the readout, then drop the whisk in the eggs. She walked away, down into the living room before she answered. There was a long, intense conversation, but Katie heard the words *Seraph* and *Copper Penny* mentioned over the music. Snow dropped off the pine trees in her yard and she checked the outside thermometer. It was warming up again. Grace hung up but stood at the window, obviously considering the phone call.

"I'll finish the eggs," Katie said.

"Thanks," Grace said but didn't move. She continued to stare out of the window.

Katie picked up the whisk and took her frustration out on the eggs. She poured them into the pan and impatiently tapped her fingers on the counter until they were done.

"Ready," Katie said. She put the food and two glasses of orange juice on the table, but Grace said nothing and they ate in silence for a few minutes. "These are really good," Katie finally said and raised her eyebrows. "News?"

Grace looked up with her fork poised mid-bite. "Yes, there's news. Everyone will be back tonight. Charles said it was all right to go to the bar. He may show up as well since it's across the street from our headquarters."

"Everyone?" Katie said. Did that include AJ? That would be great. She grinned across the table, but Grace was still looking down at her food with that damned distant, professional expression on her face. They finished the breakfast in silence with the music in the background.

"Let me handle the dishes," Grace said. "Do you want to shower? I've already had mine."

"Sure," Katie said and finished her orange juice. "I'll be back in my office after I shower. I need to call my mom. She'll beat my door down if I don't stay in touch."

❖

The floor was harder than AJ anticipated. She hit with a little grunt but ended up on her side, where she'd wanted to be. She'd done the only thing she could think of, pretend to faint.

"Damn," the blonde said but sounded oddly amused. "She fainted."

AJ heard the papers crunch on the couch and prayed they'd both set their guns down.

"Owen, did you call Michael?"

"My phone's dead." He stuttered a little. "It...it's on the charger, but it still isn't working."

"I'll call," the girl said. AJ heard her bare feet on the wooden floor move away. *Michael? Where the hell was Charles?*

The sudden huge noise of the door crashing open was next. AJ rolled behind the big overstuffed chair. She pulled herself up and crouched, watching everyone run through the house. The young woman and Owen had laid their guns down, thank God. AJ was up and had the shotgun and pistol off the couch, headed for the front door. Owen stood in the middle of the room, hands up, unresisting as they cuffed him and pushed him out of the house. He looked just like Frog the morning she'd hauled her in for rehab. That same bewildered expression.

Back inside the house, AJ moved quickly toward the kitchen and listened for the girl's voice in the midst of all the noise. If she'd had one gun, she might have another.

"Clear," a man yelled from the kitchen and AJ moved around him.

"Where's the girl?"

"No girl here," a SWAT team member answered.

"Look for a young blond woman," AJ yelled over the noise. The kitchen was just what Bonnie had said. Rubber tubing, flasks, faucet couplings, cans, beakers, and who knew what else. She heard a group go up the stairs as she looked out the windows. No one. Where the hell was the blonde? She'd come into the living room from the kitchen. The bathroom and pantry doors were open and vacant. The house was surrounded and, if she wasn't outside, she was still here.

Bonnie was suddenly beside her with a SWAT vest on.

"That girl you mentioned was here, and she had a gun," AJ said. "Let's check the basement."

Bonnie nodded as they moved to the remaining door. It was a mudroom with basement steps like the farmhouse where she'd been raised. She paused at the sight of the murky basement. She cautiously took one step at a time into the dark but stopped. It felt off. Something was wrong. Her skin prickled all the way to her feet. There was so much noise from the main floor that she couldn't hear anything. She turned, gripped the bottom of Bonnie's Kevlar vest, and pointed up. Bonnie began to move as AJ felt the air change, a faint whoosh, and something knocked her legs out from under her. Pain ripped through her left leg. AJ pulled Bonnie down with her, tumbling to the bottom. It was the last thing she knew.

Michael pulled his sedan between the deserted barn and silo and watched his farmhouse under siege. "Christ almighty," he said. Two ambulances, diesel engines thrumming in the winter air, Hazmat trucks, state police cars, and people with SWAT vests on. He watched them put Owen in the back of a patrol car, but there was no sign of Ariel.

"Fuck 'em," he said to himself. He'd just rebuild in another empty farmhouse. Or maybe it was time to end it all. He'd thought about that all the way down here from Milwaukee. Owen was dumb as a box of rocks, but Ariel should have gotten out. Michael concentrated on the side of the ramshackle garage. When he'd brought her down here, they'd walked through this drill. He started his car and pulled down the road, then parked behind the last vehicle. At that moment, the side door of the garage opened and a small figure emerged. She was wearing all black with a dark stocking cap, blending in with the crowd in the driveway for a moment. Never hesitating, she moved calmly into the trees. His car door opened and Ariel slid inside.

They drove toward the interstate, Michael's mind trying to line up the information. The locals didn't have a SWAT or Hazmat team, so it was probably state, maybe Feds. Donnie had said they'd killed men with federal IDs.

"What the hell happened?" he said. "Tell me everything."

And Ariel did, including the woman who had said she worked for the state. Her car had broken down, or so she said. The police had come in, and Ariel had hit her with a board in the basement. One woman had fallen on top of the other, both of them out cold. After she changed clothes, she'd locked the basement door deadbolts behind her, ran through the root cellar, and out the side door in the garage. There were so many people in and out of the house that she didn't think any of them saw her move into the thick trees.

Then she told him about the men in the big Suburban down the road, at the barn and silo.

He swerved a little. "Son of a—Donnie just told me that yesterday. I didn't order any hit down here. What the hell is Elena up to?"

Business had been smooth and the level of mayhem under control for over a year, but it had begun to unravel when he'd taken Seraph's little girl. Then the doctor and his wife were shot in cold blood. Now this?

"Did you get anything from the car or the victims?"

"It's all at the house. They had two sets of IDs, one for the state, as surveyors. The other was federal."

He nodded but swallowed hard. "What'd the woman you hit look like?"

"I had just gotten up, showered, and walked into the front room this morning. I was going to ask Owen what he wanted for breakfast, but there she stood." She spoke in a bland, passionless voice, as if she were reading from an instruction manual. It grated on his nerves.

"What do you remember about her?"

"Dark blond hair, dark clothes, and taller than me, with a state ID on her coat." Ariel still spoke in that unemotional voice. "I'm sure I didn't kill either of them."

Michael stared at the cold pavement stretching in front of him. Fuck. All that killing, not to mention Seraph. That settled it. And the woman Ariel clocked in the farmhouse sounded like the same woman that he'd seen in the newspaper with the doctor's wife. He opened the glove box and took out the newspaper photo.

"Is that her?" he said.

"I think so," Ariel said. "The dress changes things, but that's certainly the doctor's wife."

"I'll bet she's federal," Michael said as he put the photo back. All hell was going to break loose. "I can't believe the doctor's wife was talking to them." He tapped the steering wheel. "I have a plan. Call Elena. See if you can get her to meet us at the Copper Penny." Maybe he could bargain with Elena and get out of this mess, once and for all. He'd give her a shit load of money up front, the house, and the lab. There was a nice little condo close to his work that he could buy, and whatever Ariel wanted to do, he'd pay for it.

CHAPTER TWENTY-ONE

The emergency clinic close to Little Crane Lake was modest but efficient. Bonnie poked her head inside AJ's cubicle in the small trauma room. "Anything broken?"

"No." AJ made a face at her. "You?"

"Couple of stitches and bruises." Bonnie stepped inside. She was dressed the same as AJ with a black T-shirt and pants, her flak jacket and coat over her arm. "It's your fault. You pulled me right over the top of you. That cement was hard." Bonnie tried to raise an accusing eyebrow, but AJ saw her grimace. "Feel like going back to Milwaukee?"

"I want out of here." AJ was sweating profusely and hurt like all the hells she'd ever imagined. "Look at you. Sexy cop with that black eye you're going to have. The girls are going to scream for you. I did you a favor. I want to be there when they take the stitches out of your eyebrow. Or what's left of the eyebrow."

"Are you enjoying this?"

"No. I just want my pants back. And if they think I'm going to use crutches, they're crazy."

Bonnie pulled a chair up to the bed. "Did they give you pain meds?"

"Why? Want some? Jealous?" She waved a piece of paper in front of Bonnie.

"Go to hell, Jacob."

"I'm sure I will," AJ said with a sigh. "Here, every four hours unless you're driving."

Bonnie took the paper and tried to read the prescription. "Does anyone in any hospital ever write anything you can read?" She looked up. "Don't worry, you won't be driving either."

"Says who?"

"Charles. He's back there asking if you should have a cast on your leg."

AJ struggled to her elbows. "What? Christ, no cast on this leg. They've already wrapped it with about a million Ace bandages or something. The doctor said the x-ray showed it's the muscles, not the bones." She gave a groan and fell back to the pillow because it hurt, really hurt. She yelled "*Charles*" at the top of her lungs.

"Jesus, AJ." Bonnie quickly stood.

The curtains parted and Charles stared at her, phone in hand.

"Stop it," he said in a low voice. The doctor and nurse behind him looked startled.

AJ said very clearly, "Do not put a cast on this leg. Period."

Charles took a deep breath and looked at the young doctor standing beside him. "See?"

"Ms. Jacob, we were only explaining what—"

"Doctor, I apologize for yelling, but won't this ten-pound wrap hold until we get back to Milwaukee?"

"Yes, it will and no cast. This is exactly what I was telling you earlier. It's compartment syndrome, where the blood collects inside the muscle sheath. I was simply looking at the rest of the leg, making sure that there were no breaks or fractures."

"That's what I thought you said." AJ gave Charles a smug look.

"However," the doctor continued, "there is a surgical procedure you might have to have."

"What?" AJ tried unsuccessfully to struggle back to her elbows. "Surgery?"

Charles looked at her with a smug look of his own as the doctor continued. "It's called a fasciotomy, a fairly simple procedure to relieve the pressure on the muscle sheath. And yes, it can wait until you're back in Milwaukee, but that leg has to be elevated all the way home."

"Allison—" Charles began, but AJ pointed at the phone in his hand.

"Who are you talking to?"

"Grace."

"Fine. Tell Grace to call the department doctor. She has the number, and when we get back, I promise that I'll go to the hospital. Whatever my doctor wants, fine, but only there, in Milwaukee."

Charles had a sly smile on his face. "Deal. But only if I see you take a pain pill so I can put you in the back of the car and drive you home. You too, Bonnie. No driving, either of you."

She and Bonnie looked at each other. Finally, AJ sighed, held out her hand, and took the pill from the nurse. The nurse handed one to Bonnie as well and they both swallowed a pill.

"I'll get this prescription filled," Charles said and left.

"Damn him." AJ sighed and closed her eyes.

The Copper Penny was jammed. It had been another rare warm, mid-fifties March day in Milwaukee and people were treating it like summer. *Did that guy really have shorts on?* Katie could barely hear the music over the voices and pushed her chair against the wall. She had nursed a beer for over an hour while her sister, her sister's date, and Grace tried to talk over the noise. Grace had stared across the room for most of the night and Katie followed her gaze. A man and a small blond woman, their backs to the crowd, were talking to someone in the far corner of the room. Grace had those searching cop eyes just like AJ's. A large group of college kids had pushed tables together so she only got an occasional glimpse of the corner table in the darkest part of the long room. She felt as if she'd seen the man before and frowned at her bottle. What was familiar?

Grace had said AJ was supposed to return tonight, but Katie's phone was silent. She mulled this all over in her mind. How did she manage to become interested in the most unavailable woman on earth? There were plenty of women at the bar. What would any of them do if she just walked up and asked if they'd help her get on with her life? She rolled the bottle in her hands, picking at the label.

Come on, Blackburn. The truth is you're fascinated with AJ and your gut tells you that she's a little fascinated as well. Katie thought she heard Grace's phone ring. Grace went for the door while talking on the phone, her finger stuck in the other ear to hear.

Katie took a drink of warm beer just as Grace returned and sat to her left.

"What's the matter?" Grace said, her eyes drifting back to the table in the corner.

"Didn't you say that AJ was coming back tonight?"

"She is," Grace said as she stood. "I need the bathroom. Come on."

They went toward the back of the room then took a left into the hallway. There was a line so she settled at the end, next to the exit sign.

Grace reached across Katie and opened the exit door a crack.

"What are you doing?" Katie moved to give her room.

"It's hot. We need a little air in here."

Katie settled against the wall and studied her feet, thinking of the leather boots AJ always wore. Suddenly, a gust of cool air hit her, the exit door opened, and she looked up, right into AJ's eyes.

"Oh." Katie gulped as arms held her tight, her face buried in the duster. AJ pulled back only far enough for her to see her face with that wonderful slow smile as she bent. Katie closed her eyes just as a cold mouth touched her lips. She kissed her back, surrounded by fresh air that seemed to blow completely through her. AJ drew away with a dreamy look, but Katie grasped her coat, pulled her back, and kissed her until she felt lightheaded. She hitched a breath as AJ's cool fingers played under her sweater, across her ribs and her belly. Her feet felt nailed to the floor and her body was on fire.

AJ had them hard against the wall. Katie felt AJ's mouth against her ear as she whispered, "God, you taste good. I thought about doing this all week."

"I missed you." Katie swallowed hard. "What are you doing on crutches?"

"A little slip. Come with me right now?"

"Anywhere."

Grace was suddenly beside them with Katie's coat. "Go. Now," she said urgently, but AJ stiff-armed her and kissed Katie one more time. "Come on, girls," Grace insisted while she helped Katie into her pea coat. They were out of the door to the car as fast as AJ could maneuver her crutches.

"Get in the front," AJ said, her voice not entirely steady.

Katie scrambled into the front seat and looked at Bonnie, behind the wheel. "My God, what happened to you?"

"Took a fall with AJ," Bonnie said. "We're on our way to our doctor."

Grace helped AJ into the seat behind them and Katie heard them both swear. The crutches went to the floor with a loud thump. Bonnie had her window down and spoke to a cop in a squad car.

"What's going on?" Katie said.

"They're waiting for Charles. He just went inside the front door."

Katie turned in her seat for another look at AJ. She was propped against the back door, eyes closed. There was a sheen of sweat on her face and her disheveled hair fell down across her forehead. Bonnie had a ferocious scowl of concentration as she began to put the car in gear.

"Wait, stop. You're not in any shape to drive." Katie looked back and forth between them. AJ's eyes popped open although she seemed to have a problem with her focus.

"That's probably a good idea," Bonnie said. She and Katie traded places.

"Okay, where am I going?" Katie said, adjusting the seat.

Both AJ and Bonnie said, "Columbia-St. Mary's."

"The ER," Bonnie added.

When the stoplight turned red, Katie checked them. AJ and Bonnie already had their eyes closed. Katie's heart pounded against her ribs as she touched her mouth and grinned for all she was worth.

❖

The ER was almost as busy as the Copper Penny. Katie stood between AJ and Bonnie, arms around both, while the nurse paged the doctor. A tall, older woman slipped in from the side and looped her arm through AJ's.

"Dr. Light." The woman introduced herself to Katie and Bonnie as she bent to look into AJ's eyes. "I've talked to the people down at Little Crane Lake, Allison. Let's get you into a wheelchair. I can see you've already taken pain medication."

"Oh yeah," AJ drawled with a sideways smile as they negotiated her through a set of doors. A nurse led Katie and Bonnie to a small, well-appointed private waiting room with leather chairs and a big couch. She laid the crutches and AJ's coat on the couch.

"Jesus," Bonnie said. "Could we find some coffee? I'm going to fall over. Did you see those notes from the clinic that AJ's doctor was trying to read? Those scribbles? The medical profession must have some sort of secret code." She lurched into Katie and almost knocked them both over.

"Whoa." Katie held on to her. "Sit down, Ace." She steered Bonnie into a chair. "How many pain pills have *you* had?"

"Charles made us both take a pill. He drove and we slept all the way back."

"I'll get us some coffee." Katie helped Bonnie out of her coat. "Now sit. Don't move." After a conversation with a very nice nurse, Katie came back with coffee from the back room, not the vending machine. She held the cup while Bonnie sipped.

"I feel like I've fallen into the *X-Files*," Katie said. "Tell me what the hell is going on. You know my sister was with us in the bar. Will Grace take care of her? She's going to rip the bar apart."

Bonnie gave a little laugh. "I know your sister, remember? Grace will take care of her. Do you know who was in there?"

Katie helped Bonnie with another drink of coffee. "In where?"

"The Copper Penny. You were sitting across the room from Michael."

"Michael? Seraph's Michael?"

"Seraph?" Bonnie frowned and slurred the word a little.

"I talked to Seraph yesterday," Katie said. "Look, from what everyone has said to me, I know it's drugs. Start from the beginning. Tell me everything."

"You talked to Seraph? How in the hell did you do that?"

"Where is she?" Charles suddenly walked into the room.

"With Dr. Light, through there," Katie said and pointed. He disappeared through the same double doors that AJ and the doctor had gone through.

Bonnie continued as if Charles had not been there at all. "No kidding? Seraph? I've only seen her once after that night when you brought her into the clinic. I thought you always knew it was drugs. Michael's a big dealer here."

Katie stared at her. "So, thanks to Lu, I got into this as collateral damage?"

"Yes, and Christ, that was some pill...hey," she began to laugh. "Remember the night at the beach when Lu took off all her clothes—"

"Shut up." Katie quickly put her hand over Bonnie's mouth.

"Ladies," Charles said, suddenly in front of them again with Grace beside him. "They're going to do one of those fasc-things, or whatever they're called, on AJ. I've got to catch up with the team. Ms.—Katie—can you wait for AJ? The doctor will see that you're informed. It's kind of like an outpatient procedure. Could AJ stay at your house with Grace for maybe a day or so, at least until I get this all sorted out?"

Katie only had time to nod and say "yes" before he was gone again, down the hallway. Grace helped Bonnie to her feet. "Katie, do you mind if I take this one to your house? Let her crash on the couch so when you bring AJ home, we'll all be in one house."

"Go ahead, no problem," Katie said. "Did you explain anything to my sister?"

Grace only grinned as she put her arm around Bonnie and steadied her. "Your sister and her date are having the time of their life right now with a bunch of rookie cops. She's in good hands." She steered Bonnie out of the room. "I'll see you at the house."

Katie took a deep breath and scrubbed her face. "Oh for Pete's sake, it *is* the *X-Files*."

CHAPTER TWENTY-TWO

After they left the Copper Penny, Michael and Ariel drove home. He slowed the car in the alley and stopped at the first of three garages behind his house.

"Ariel, unlock the inside office door, will you? I'm going to check the area."

He leaned against the garage door, listening. The only sound was a dog barking several houses down. The Copper Penny had been crowded tonight. There were more uniforms than usual. He liked drinking where the cops drank and getting close to them just because he could. He'd seen the woman that Lu Wright used to live with. She owned the business where Lu's friend, that young guy, worked. Michael had been looking for Lu since the final day with Seraph, but no luck. Worse, there was no one to ask. If only Seraph was here.

He locked the garage door. Right now, he needed to put his plan in motion. The meeting tonight with Elena had been edgy, confrontational, but when he'd made the offer, she'd looked interested. Once he shut this down, he'd take a vacation.

"Would you get me another bottle of my energy drink? I want to get out of this suit, into comfortable clothes," Michael said.

He unknotted his tie as Ariel disappeared into the kitchen. Elena was a problem. She'd almost been giving *him* orders tonight when they'd talked. Hell, despite everything that had happened, Seraph had never avoided him. Elena wouldn't even return his calls.

If Ariel hadn't set up tonight's meeting, he knew damned well Elena wouldn't have been at that bar with them.

"Thanks. Do you want to get into different clothes too?" he said as she handed him the bottle. "Or just call it a night?" Ariel and Elena shared the house next door. Absently, he opened the top button of his shirt and took a long, thirsty drink of the cold liquid.

Ariel hesitated. "I think I'll just turn in, if you don't mind."

He nodded and started for the stairs. No more mistakes like he'd made with Seraph. And it was time to get away from all of this crap. Ariel said she wanted to finish college. He'd give her the money she needed. She was always there for him, just as Seraph used to be.

Had he broken the law? Yes, but what was the difference? Most of the people he worked around were on the take. Money, drugs, sex, whatever. Everyone had a racket of some kind. Look at the doctor and his beautiful wife. The doctor sold drugs out the back door on a daily basis, and his wife had sold his meth. Hell, the doc was one of his suppliers. He wasn't any different than most. Most of the dealers he knew were just like him, fronting their business with honest jobs.

Seraph. Frowning, he went toward the stairs. He and Seraph had been a good team, but he'd made the mistake. He should have given her the money she'd asked for, sent her home. None of this would have happened if he'd just done that much. He trudged up the stairs and decided to put off work on the computer until tomorrow morning. It would wait. Suddenly his heart began to thud and he was drenched with sweat. What the hell was wrong with him?

❖

AJ woke with a quick, sharp breath. *Hospital.* Was it Ecuador? A faint noise beeped above her. The room was not completely dark but close to it, and God, she was thirsty. She moved tentatively and saw that she was hooked up to some kind of IV drip. No, not Ecuador, with its long wards full of people in beds. Her mind drifted until it finally found Dr. Light in Milwaukee.

They'd done something to her leg. She tried to raise her impossibly heavy head but gave up, sinking back into the pillow. AJ stared at the ceiling and tried to remember what the doctor had explained. Something about opening the calf muscles to drain the blood.

"Shit," she croaked, her dry throat tight. She didn't like hospitals and she hated blood.

Something moved to her right. Katie was asleep in a chair, her head resting on a pillow. She was in jeans and a wine colored sweater, sleeves pulled down over her hands with her feet tucked up under her. AJ tried to focus her eyes, her heart beating a little faster. Did she finally kiss her or was it only the pain meds? Or maybe wishful thinking? She squeezed her eyes shut and remembered the sharp taste of beer mixed with the summer scent of her skin. Katie had grabbed her, kissed her too, pressing her body against her. AJ felt her heart thump hard, her fingers gripping the bed railing.

A nurse was suddenly beside her, hand on her shoulder, studying the monitor above her. She turned the light up a bit.

"You're awake. How are you?" she said.

"Thirsty," AJ rasped.

"I'll get you some ice," she said then moved away.

AJ stared at Katie. *I can't do a thing about how I feel about her. Every part of me leans to her and has ever since that first night in Bill's office.* Katie turned suddenly. AJ looked at Katie's sleepy eyes through the bed rails. There was no space between them again. AJ's fingers twitched.

Dr. Light came into the room with a cup in her hand. "I hear you're thirsty," she said, her voice soft. "Here, put this on your tongue." She spooned an ice chip into her mouth. "The surgery went well and you're going to be just fine. Charles is right behind me." She raised the head of the bed slowly just as Charles came into the room.

"How are you?" Charles leaned over her.

"Ice," AJ rasped. Dr. Light handed her the cup.

"Dr. Light, could you give me a moment? I promise, only one minute and I'll leave," Charles said.

"Okay, but just a minute."

Charles looked at Katie, curled up in the chair, then rested his forearms on the rails of AJ's bed and leaned over her. AJ thought his head looked enormous as he began to whisper to her. "Owen's in custody at the downtown station, tweaking like crazy but singing like a bird," he said. "They're still working on that house down there." He patted her hand and smiled. "We'll park you at Ms. Blackburn's when the doctor releases you."

AJ nodded but fought sleep. The pillow fell off Katie's chair and she watched her pick it up. Katie sat up, stretching with a yawn. AJ kept her eyes on her, wanting to hold her again. Suddenly Katie gave her the sweetest, most intimate smile. She tried to lift her hand to reach for her, but it was too heavy. What had Charles said? She wanted to remind him about Elena.

"Your minute's up, Charles. I need to examine her," Dr. Light said, stepping back into the room. Her voice echoed in AJ's head. "It'll be a while."

Charles gave her a smile and left. Dr. Light checked the monitors. "Let's see how you're doing. It's almost a sin to be as healthy as you are, Allison. Well, except for your leg." She lifted an eyebrow with a little smile and then turned to Katie.

"Will you be caring for her at your house? If that's the case, I need to talk with you. Allison can rest while I give you instructions. Come out to the desk with me. I have a little paperwork for you. The instructions or Q & A kinds of things. The first twenty-four hours will be the most important so we'll keep her here until we're satisfied. Then she can go home with you."

AJ tried to smile at Katie but lost the battle with sleep right at that moment.

CHAPTER TWENTY-THREE

O uch." AJ stiffened as Katie, Grace, and Bonnie maneuvered her onto Katie's king-sized bed the next day. Intense eyes swept up and Katie almost stumbled under the impact of AJ's gaze. The moment she'd put her arm around AJ's compact body at the hospital, she'd trembled.

The doctor had said no heavy covers. Katie pulled her grandmother's quilt off the bed, folding it into the closet. She began to take things to the small, spare bedroom where she'd sleep until AJ was able to get around.

"More alert and ambulatory, that's what the doctor said," Katie said to herself as she tucked various items of clothing into the chest of drawers. Across the hall, Grace was sitting on the end of the bed, talking to AJ and Bonnie.

Thank God she'd cleaned the closet. There was room for her business clothes. As she entered her own bedroom and began to select clothes for next week, she realized the room had gone quiet.

"What?" She turned to them.

"Are you going to be okay with this?" AJ hardly sounded like herself.

"It's just as easy for me to take clothes from there as here. Besides, this is the biggest room. That spare bedroom is too small." She stepped around Bonnie for her dark, pinstriped suit, the clothes for the bank presentation this week.

The dark circles under AJ's eyes stood out against her pale face as she tried to pull herself up. Katie saw her face tighten. "You have a busy week. I don't want to interrupt."

"It's not a problem. Just let me get squared away. How about coffee, anyone?" She caught herself staring. AJ's T-shirt hid absolutely nothing. Quickly, she turned her back and felt her face warm. She took three more outfits out of the closet and left. Bonnie followed her out of the room.

Katie draped the clothes over her arm, hung them in the other bedroom, and went to the kitchen to make coffee.

"Katie, you're not going to wait on us," Bonnie said and turned the coffee pot on. "Let me take it from here. Grab a shower and go to bed. I'll do this."

Hands on hips, Katie studied Bonnie. "You're going to have a heck of a shiner, plus those stitches can't feel good. Can't any of this stuff wait? The doctor said that AJ needs to sleep."

Bonnie picked up the tray with a little laugh. "I've had more rest than anyone. I'll do this, but for the record, I've never known anyone that operates on less sleep than AJ."

"Okay. It's time for her pills." Katie took a deep, tired breath. "Deliver the coffee and meet me in the bathroom. I'll show you the medication."

They met in the bathroom a few minutes later. Katie went through the meds. She shook two pills out for AJ. "This is the antibiotic and here's the pain pill, every four hours. Any of you are welcome to stay here as long as you want."

"Thanks. I'll be working with Grace from this point on so one of us will sleep on the couch in your office. The other will sleep in the living room tonight. Is that okay with you?"

"You're working with Grace? You're Milwaukee police."

"I'm ready for a career change, and they've approved the plan. It's an opportunity, Katie, and I'm interested. Besides, working with a damned cute ATF agent? Never turn that down."

"Damned cute?" Katie smirked at her. "Good for you. If you have a chance to do something you want, go for it. But all of you should rest. The doctor was firm."

"Go to bed, Katie. You're worn out." Bonnie picked up the tray. "We'll sleep soon."

❖

Two days later, Katie felt as if her house had become a kind of command post. People came and went, speaking in low voices. Anytime she would walk past them, everyone would go quiet, something that completely unnerved her. She stubbornly kept to the doctor's schedule with AJ's medication. And made sure that she was up and walking and that she had food. Just as the doctor had said, the incision was healing fast with minimal swelling. She actually liked those moments, changing the dressing, touching the smooth skin and those nice, long muscles. Every time she was in the room, no matter who was there, AJ's eyes tracked her. They kept her going.

In the afternoon, Katie was in her office, putting the final touches on tomorrow's presentation at the bank. She phoned Zack at the office to make sure tomorrow was clear, but as she hung up, she felt something was off and sat absolutely quiet. That was it. The house was silent. She peeked down the hallway. Nothing moved.

AJ was stretched out on her bed, leg elevated properly, watching a light wind blowing fine snow through the trees. Her laptop was open on the bed beside her. She saw Katie and smiled.

"Hey, you."

"Are we actually alone?"

"I'm pretty sure, but you probably should check the living room, the kitchen."

Katie did and came back, sitting on the end of the bed. "We're alone. Bonnie and Grace asked about your car. I told them to park it in my garage."

"Yeah, I know. I gave them the keys. Bonnie's been dying to drive that beast. I told her to be careful." AJ laughed a little. "I'm sorry. This has been a mess for you, and don't tell me it hasn't."

"I won't. We're all doing better than I thought we would. Your doctor called and she'd like to see you tomorrow."

"What time?"

"One o'clock. Will Grace or Bonnie drive you in?"

"Yes, one of the girls. I'd like to get this big wrap off the leg. Grace said you have an important meeting tomorrow? Or did you mention it?"

Katie nodded. "Both of us, probably. The presentation is ready. Zack's going to meet me there. It's at one o'clock, the same time as your doctor appointment."

"How long will your meeting take?"

"Not a clue. I've never done a proposal this big so who knows how long we'll be there." Katie absently played with the sheet.

"Thanks for everything you've done. I'm sorry to be such a pain."

"Don't apologize. According to the doctor, you'll have physical therapy for a while, then you'll be up and running around like nothing happened."

"Can't come soon enough." AJ ran her hands through her hair. "But look what you've done, even the laundry. Then the meals, the meds, the dressing changes—everything, including kicking people out when you thought I needed rest." She began to laugh. "I loved the look on Charles's face when you told him to get out last night. You have a great frown. I almost got up and left too."

"I'm just following the doctor's orders." Katie leaned over and pulled at a lock of AJ's hair. "You look all weirded-up when you do that to your hair. Makes you look like a porcupine."

"Ha, you with the curls. Pity me, please. I need a bath and this hair could stand some shampoo."

Katie held out her hand. "Remember the shower, the engineering marvel my brother installed? Why don't you give it a test run? I've been watching you with those crutches. You're balanced."

AJ grinned. "I can do wheelies with those things. Lots of practice at different times in my life." She took Katie's hand and got out of bed. "Those horrible people are going to be back soon enough. Maybe I can be clean before they all descend on us again." She gestured at the room. "Look how they trashed your bedroom. It makes me mad."

In the bathroom, Katie opened the door in the shower wall and pulled out the seat. "Sit here. Prop your leg there so you stay steady." Katie set some towels and clean clothes on the shelf next to the shower, then hesitated. "You can handle this alone can't you?" The question hung between them until Katie teased AJ with a grin.

"I'd like to say no, but truthfully…" AJ's voice trailed off and she grinned too.

While AJ showered, Katie changed the sheets on the bed and straightened the bedroom. "Pigs," she muttered as she scooped fast food containers, empty paper coffee cups, and more into a trash bag, all the while paying attention to the sounds in the bathroom. When the water went off, she opened the door a crack.

"How did you do?" she said.

"That was heaven. I may be human again. This really works."

"All right, tell me when you're ready for me to come in. I'll help you get dressed," Katie said on her way to the laundry room with an armload of sheets. *Help you get dressed. Am I out of my mind?* She laughed at herself. Just the thought made her shake.

"How are you doing?" she said again at the doorway. The fresh scent of the shower leaked into the hallway.

"Someday, if I ever have my own house, I'm going to have something like this. You can come in if you want."

With a deep breath, Katie went in. AJ wore a white, long-sleeved T-shirt with ATF printed above the pocket and a pair of dark blue shorts. Hair combed, she was brushing her teeth. Katie bit back a tease about superhero Bren Black. A shaft of sunlight from the skylight above held AJ in a misty, golden light. She was every inch a real hero who didn't need extraordinary powers or fictional exploits. Katie uttered an involuntary sigh at the perfect body in front of her.

"How on earth did you do all that by yourself?"

AJ spit into the sink and rinsed her mouth. She capped the toothpaste and turned, balanced on her crutches. "Training."

Katie laughed. "Training? And I—" She never finished because AJ pinned her to the wall, trailed kisses across her jaw, then found her mouth.

Eyes closed, Katie was certain she was going to slide right to the floor and gripped AJ's shoulders for balance. There was that tremor in AJ's arms again.

"I have to touch you. I can't stop."

The words whispered against Katie's ear sent shivers down her spine. Completely lost, Katie kissed her with everything she had. Once again, AJ had moved so quickly that Katie hadn't been prepared. AJ's hard body pushed into Katie and felt so good that it hurt—and the damned house phone began to ring.

"No…not going to answer," Katie said against AJ's mouth, voice trembling.

"They may be on their way here." AJ pushed back on her crutches, her eyes almost black. Katie pulled in a ragged breath, slid away to answer the phone and, of course, it was her mother.

When she was done, she found AJ in the kitchen, leaning over the stove. Katie never hesitated. She stretched across AJ's back, ran her fingers under the edge of the shorts, caressed taut skin over the hipbones. She sighed against her back and wrapped her arms around her. "You smell good."

"I'm going to fall over," AJ said as she collapsed into a seat at the table. "When did you do that?" She pointed at the soup on the stove.

"Earlier. After Charles left." Katie stirred the soup. "You're drinking milk, whether you like it or not. And there are your pills. We'll wrap your leg when we get you back to bed."

AJ's face was happy as she looked up. "Tell me that soup's homemade."

"That's homemade," Katie deadpanned. "But it comes with a price tag."

AJ blew on the spoonful of soup. "Price tag?"

"Every summer we freeze or can food from Mom's garden, even the boys. Beans, beets, corn, sometimes pickles. It's like a rite of passage. These are"—she pushed the bowl closer to AJ—"Mom's tomatoes in the winter. Well, almost spring."

"It's delicious." AJ sprinkled oyster crackers over the bowl. "What's this going to cost me?"

"That was my mother on the phone, reminding me of my sister's birthday party, and you're invited. My family's about crazy with curiosity over you."

AJ's spoon paused. "They know about me?"

"My family's like the old Mafia. They're everywhere, and remember, they know Bonnie. They've been talking to her."

AJ stared at Katie. "A birthday party? Is that the price tag on this soup?"

Katie laughed at the bit of panic on AJ's face. "I'll get you in and out in a hurry. No, the soup's going to cost you the story of what happened to you and Bonnie."

"Bonnie said she talked to you about the drugs." AJ tackled the soup and told the whole story. The farm, Owen and the young blond woman, and what happened in the basement. She clattered her spoon in the empty bowl, rested her elbows on the table, and went quiet.

Katie sensed there was more and waited.

"We lost two more people down there last week. Shot to death."

"Jesus." Katie gripped her spoon and stared at AJ.

AJ scrubbed her hands over her face and leaned back. "Is there coffee?"

Katie got up for a cup and put it front of AJ. "That scares me. It could have been you. Is your job always like this?" She heard her own frightened voice and stopped.

"No, not always."

Katie held up the front page of the paper that Charles had been reading this morning. "See this? They killed another cop in Chicago; that's the most dead in twenty-five years." She gripped the paper so tightly that it crinkled in her hand. "I'm afraid for you."

"It's my job and I believe in it." AJ frowned at the paper when Katie handed it to her. "And it's not just law enforcement that gets hurt or killed. Citizens get hurt, a lot. Our country is dangerous and it always has been. You've read our history." AJ laid the paper on the table. "Charles told me that you didn't want anyone here with you, but please, I don't want you alone. I need you as safe as possible. The fact that Grace was here made my job a lot easier while I was away. I'm afraid for you, too."

"What good does it do me to be safe when you're not?"

AJ looked away. "I don't know how to answer that. It's been so long since I've had anyone to think of besides my team. Or myself."

"And then, when I talked to Seraph—" Katie began.

"What?" AJ's head snapped up. "You talked to Seraph? When?"

"While you were gone."

"Oh, for the love of—" AJ covered her face with her hands.

"Grace talked to Charles." Katie stood. "I needed to know if Lu got me into all of this. Seraph confirmed it."

AJ uttered a little groan. "Did Grace drive you to Seraph's?"

"At the apartment across from the cemetery," Katie said and poured herself coffee. "Michael was at that big black angel and—"

"Michael was there?" AJ's voice went up.

"There was a little black angel tattoo on Seraph's hand. What is that?"

"That's what they're called. Angels. Michael's girl gang." AJ reached across the table for one of Katie's hands. "You saw Michael? I can't believe no one's told me any of this. Crap."

"He never saw me, AJ, and it helped me close the door on Lu. I don't love her and I don't hate her. I am just where I want to be."

They heard the big engine in the driveway and Katie's garage door open. AJ leaned closer. Her voice was soft as her hand slid under Katie's shirt. "I'd love to go to the party this weekend, but think about this. Do you know how much I want my arms around you right now?"

Grace and Bonnie walked in the front door at that moment. Their voices and the fresh air beat them to the kitchen, but Katie was lost in AJ's voice and hands.

Grace laid her laptop on the table. "What is that delicious aroma?"

"Homemade tomato soup. Want some?" Katie blinked and took a deep breath.

"Do you have enough?"

Bonnie laughed and put two grocery bags on the counter. "Katie and her family always have enough. I'm hungry too. Sit down, Katie. I'll put the groceries away and get the soup."

Grace sat next to AJ. "Did you have a bath? You smell like Katie's body wash."

"Yes, and it felt great," AJ said. "Where have you been?"

"We just met with Bill and Charles at Seraph's. Lots of stuff from her." Grace turned to Katie. "Charles wanted me to ask if we could meet here tonight? Just he and Bill and the three of us. Charles worries about all of us being here."

Katie nodded. "I told you. Whatever you need. I've got room."

Grace reached for crackers and picked up her spoon. "This looks and smells so good." She took a taste and closed her eyes. "It's delicious."

Bonnie put the groceries away before she sat down with her own bowl of soup. "Charles said if you had any problems, just let him know. Or tell one of us." She began to eat.

AJ reached for her crutches. "What time tonight?"

"Around seven," Grace said.

"I need to get some sleep before then. The pills make me dopey. Finish your food, girls. I'll see you later." She turned to Katie. "Would you help me?"

As AJ pushed upright, Katie saw her face tighten with the effort. She stood immediately and followed her out of the room.

That night, Charles and Bill arrived on schedule. AJ was on the couch, under a blanket with her laptop braced against her good leg. Bonnie and Grace were sitting on the floor, their backs against AJ's couch. Grace's laptop was open.

"Where's Katie?" Charles said as he placed his briefcase on the floor and sat in the big, easy chair. "I want to thank her and give her a timeline." He took a folder out of the briefcase and looked at AJ. "This won't take long, but I want to catch you up on what we've done."

"Katie's in her office." Bonnie pointed over her head as Bill sank down in the other big chair.

AJ smiled at the group. This wasn't the conference room at the station, but despite her damned leg, it was a lot more comfortable. Plus the pills had her at a comfortable level. Both Bill and Charles were in suits but Bill looked worn out. Charles looked focused.

"Is it cold outside?" she said. She hadn't thought of the weather until this afternoon.

"Hell, yes." Bill smiled at her.

At that moment, AJ realized how much she'd missed Bill, especially his constant humor that hid the sharp mind and all of his experience. She'd worked with a lot of cops, but he was the best she'd ever found.

"Okay, first the farmhouse." Charles looked at her. "It's officially set up as a sting. The state and the local sheriff are going to work with us. Check the file under Little Crane on your laptop, but don't do it now. Look at Grace's screen. I want to get further into what Seraph told us this afternoon, particularly about Michael."

AJ watched Grace's fingers fly over the key board. The screen bloomed with columns of numbers. "What is this?" Grace moved and AJ looked over her shoulder.

"This is the money. Michael's money. He hid it right under the bank's nose as 'prospects' because, after all, that's his job. See how small the accounts are? That would fly under most casual audit's radar. Seraph said they changed the codes on them every three months. Before she and Michael tangled, she'd just changed them so we have time. Grace will flag most of them so no matter how Michael changes them, they'll be tracked."

"I'll show you how I do that when we get back from your doctor appointment tomorrow," Grace said. She looked up at AJ.

"But this next stuff just blew all of us away." Charles nodded at Grace. She changed the screen again to another series of numbers.

AJ scanned the screen. "A series of numbers?"

Grace entered a code over the first column and a name came up. It was Star's husband's name. The doctor.

"I don't understand," AJ said and looked across at Charles.

"The son of a bitch was a supplier. And Star was not only using but distributing and selling." He stared at her with an angry expression. "It's all here. Every supplier and distributor Michael used. I was wrong about Seraph and you were right. She is the key."

"My God," AJ said. She blinked as one local or state location after another scrolled across Grace's screen. She didn't know what to say. "And we all thought it was being shipped into Milwaukee. But we've seen their shipments."

"They use both, but most of these suppliers are in-state," Bill said. "Worse, I know some of these people. There's quite a few local manufacturers and distributors. And professional people like the doctor. This just made me sick. And furious."

"Damn. How do we handle this?" AJ looked at Charles again. "We don't have the manpower, do we?"

"I don't know. I called Lawrence." Charles shook his head. "Michael's money is almost irrelevant when you look at this. Seraph was brilliant with the computer. Lawrence said he wants to work with her."

"Does that mean she won't see the inside of a jail?"

"No, she'll do time, and probably in a different way than the people on this list," Charles said. "It's enormous. And it definitely impacts my other two operations."

"What about the group of girls? Michael's angels. And what about Michael or Elena?" AJ said.

Charles and Bill looked at each other. "We can't find either Michael or Elena. We've picked up a lot of the girls and none of them have seen either of them for at least two, three days. A couple of them saw Michael Monday, but not to talk to."

"And four of the girls had talked to Elena the same day, but no one has seen either of them since," Bill said.

"What about the woman that hit me at the farmhouse?" AJ shifted, looking at both men. She wasn't going to mention the undercover woman now. That was Charles's problem. He didn't meet her eyes, and so she left the question hanging in the air.

"Bonnie. Could I have some water?" Bill said and glanced at Charles before he spoke. "I haven't talked to the kid, Owen. The DEA has him." Charles continued to stare at his iPad and said nothing.

"Okay," AJ said, but it felt off to her. Bill hadn't talked to Owen Hood? "Still, who hit me? Was it the little blonde with Owen?"

"Seraph says her name is Ariel and she's Michael's top cooker," Bill said and thanked Bonnie for the water.

"I'm going to talk with Katie." Charles stood and shut his briefcase. "I want to thank her for everything and give her a timeline for getting us out of here. Grace, you said you have room for AJ at your apartment?"

Grace nodded. "I have a spare room with a bed."

"I do too," Bonnie said. "Charles, follow me. I'll take you down to Katie."

Grace went back to work on her computer. AJ took a drink of water. She knew Charles knew who injured her and damned if she was leaving, no matter what he said.

CHAPTER TWENTY-FOUR

After Bill and Charles had gone, everyone sat quietly for a moment.

"This is huge." AJ finally broke the silence. "I hardly know what to say except that I think I'm due for another pill. Maybe twenty." She sank back into the pillow. "Think of all the hours we've put in out on the streets. Not a whisper of those suppliers, nothing."

"Oh shit." Grace suddenly stood up. "We forgot something that Seraph told us." She grabbed her phone and dialed. "Charles, we forgot a part of the information from Seraph. The personal stuff on Michael."

AJ watched her talk and then stared at the ceiling. What else could there be?

"You want me to tell her? But not Katie. Okay." Grace looked at AJ. She put her phone on the table. "We forgot the personal things that Seraph told us."

"Personal?" AJ said. "How does that impact the investigation? Well, not true. I might want to know why a successful banker at Benning's sells drugs. Other than he wants more money than God."

"That's it," Grace said and Bonnie nodded. "He loves the money. He gets high on the money. At least that's what Seraph says, and that's why he won't do drugs."

"You're kidding. Like a gambling addition?"

"Exactly what she said," Bonnie said.

"It's always been power, sex, or the drug itself. And then again, money is power."

"No, Seraph said it's exactly like gambling. The winning and the adrenaline of beating the odds is his high. And Charles said to tell you that the girls they picked up confirmed that Michael's not himself. They swear he's not a violent man."

"Not a violent man?" Bonnie burst out. "He damned near killed Seraph, not to mention five murders in the last weeks."

"I'm sure it's Elena that does the killing." AJ felt a small surge of energy and sat up again. "We need to find Elena."

"And something else." Grace sat in front of AJ on the floor. "When Katie and I went to Seraph's—"

"Yes, you did. Grace, how could you do that? That was so dangerous with Elena floating around with all her little eyes out there. Not to mention that Michael was across the street."

"I'm sorry. She asked and I called, but you were gone so I had to talk to Charles and he thought it was a good idea. Katie did get something out of that meeting and so did we. Seraph said Lu Wright had a guy pal. Someone that helped her out with the drugs and I've met him. It's Zack, the young man in her office that does all of her animations and artwork."

"For God's sake." AJ just about fell off the couch. "Ouch, oh shit," she said as she moved wrong and a huge pain shot up her leg. "Zack? We can't have Katie out there, alone, with him. She's taking him to the bank with her tomorrow."

"Wait. Slow down." Grace held her hand up. "Charles said to tell you that he'll have someone at the bank with them. They'll cover this. I did a thorough check on Katie's entire office and it looks just fine."

"We've been on these streets for a long time and everything has looked *just fine,* Grace, and look how that's turned out."

Grace shook her head, exasperated. "What I'm trying to say is that Zack was only involved with Lu. And yes, some of the girls in the gang knew him, but Zack and Elena had a big falling out last summer. That's when Lu brought him to Katie's business. He does really well for her and I've never seen him on drugs. And I've seen him quite a bit."

Katie walked into the room. "I'm going to take a shower and get ready for bed. Is there anything any of you need?"

AJ looked at her. So many things went through her mind at that moment that she said nothing.

Katie gave her an odd look. "Are you all right?"

"I'm fine. Is it time for anything? Like pills?"

Katie looked at the clock. "Soon. I'll see you after the shower."

"Okay, I'll talk to you when you're done. Are you ready for tomorrow?"

With a nod and a smile, Katie turned and left for the bathroom.

"We can't let her go alone tomorrow," AJ said. "Grace, are you sure about Zack?"

"Do you think I'd let anything happen to Katie?"

"No." AJ wrapped her arms around herself, suddenly afraid. "Bonnie, you sleep in my bed tonight. I'll sleep out here and catch Katie before she goes. The more she knows, the safer she'll be. She can handle it, no matter what Charles says. If Zack's clean now, there won't be a problem."

❖

Katie jolted awake in the dark room. She could hear breathing.

"Who's there?"

"Me," AJ whispered.

Katie rolled over to her back. AJ was beside the bed, balanced on her crutches.

"Is there room for me?"

"Of course." Katie's heart did a fast-forward as she flipped the bedcovers back.

"Move to your right."

"Are we alone?"

"No. The usual suspects are crashed for the night, and I know you have an important meeting tomorrow, but—"

Katie scrambled to make room. "Are you okay?"

"No." The bed shifted as AJ settled beside her, face so close that Katie felt her breath. "I need to—I'm going crazy, watching you." The sheets stretched tight and suddenly Katie was being kissed urgently.

Katie traced the mouth beside her with her fingertips. "Yes," she whispered.

"Hang on." AJ lifted Katie's T-shirt and had it off before Katie even realized that she'd lifted her arms to help. AJ's T-shirt followed and she lifted Katie on top of her damp skin. "We've got to be quiet," AJ whispered, slipped her hands inside Katie's panties and tugged them down. "Help me." They got the last of the clothing to the floor.

"You start this and don't finish it, I'm going to hurt your other leg," Katie said as hands brushed her throat, traced her collarbone, and settled on her breasts. She pushed into AJ's hands and they both laughed softly. "You're doing it again, like that first night. You stun me."

"Stun you?" AJ smiled and ran her hands through Katie's hair. "I'd like to do more than that."

"Closer," Katie said as she grabbed AJ's shoulders and pulled herself carefully across the hot, slick skin, feeling every tremor beneath her.

"I'd be you if I got any closer."

"Go slow," Katie said. "Be careful of your leg, but we're going to manage this, one way or another." She inhaled fast when she felt AJ's hands slide down the inside of her thighs. "Ahhh. Yes." She tipped her head back with pure pleasure as AJ explored her body. One finger, then two, entered her and a warm mouth found one breast, then the other. She could hear her blood rush. "More," she whispered against AJ's mouth, then kissed her. She came quickly and hard, collapsing onto AJ with ragged breathing. She gripped her shoulders and then rolled onto her back.

AJ turned her head to look at Katie. "Let's do that again."

Katie closed her eyes and grinned with a long, deep breath, then she went up to an elbow, kissed AJ, and peered down into her face. "God, that was good," she whispered. "Yes. Let's do that again. Hold still for me." Her hands and mouth were already wandering over AJ's body.

❖

Milwaukee was as quiet as Michael had ever heard it. He leaned against the cold stone angel in the cemetery. The hard, full moon flooded the area with pale light. Was it the March equinox or solstice? No, it was the equinox, when the daylight and nighttime were almost even. His dad would be getting ready to plant on the farm. He closed his eyes, remembering the smell of gasoline in the tool shed at this time of year.

When Elena had called him today, he had suggested this meeting. He had the cash in his pocket; the plan ought to work. He wanted out and he'd give her everything, the entire business, including the startup cash he had for her tonight. "Done with the whole mess," he muttered to himself. It wasn't fun anymore, and he missed the thrills he'd shared with Seraph, watching the money grow, taking the risks. He wanted out from under this drug crap. Maybe he'd take some time off, go home and see his folks. Or he could hang out at one of the houses he'd bought last year in California and Texas. They were paid for, and besides, he had plenty of money in his legitimate account.

Car doors slammed off to his right, out by the Civil War memorial and he tensed. Better make a good show of it. He unzipped his jacket a bit. "Wish me luck, Ma," he said, his breath puffing out in the cold air. He took a long drink from his energy bottle.

The girls came through the trees and tombstones, none too quiet as he watched them from the shadows. Michael frowned. Elena wasn't with them. Her tall figure would have towered over the five girls that walked toward him.

"Michael?" someone called from the group.

"Hi, girls," he said, walking toward them. "Where's Elena?"

"Not far behind," Ariel said.

"Ariel?" Michael smiled, surprised to see her. He started toward her, but the minute he moved, strong arms wrapped around him from behind and cold metal pressed against his temple.

CHAPTER TWENTY-FIVE

No matter how hard Katie pushed or pulled on the fabric, the lapels on her black pinstriped suit looked wrong. "Dummy. You buttoned it wrong." She grinned at herself and redid the buttons then checked her hair and onyx earrings. The bright white of the silk tee shimmered in the bathroom mirror.

Katie scanned herself one last time. Confident that she looked all-business and ready to meet David Markam, Senior Vice President of Benning's, she checked her watch. She was right on schedule. She'd meet Zack at the coffee shop close to her office and they'd catch a light breakfast.

The house was quiet and she intended on letting them sleep. She'd fallen asleep in AJ's arms and slept like a stone.

She walked carefully by the living room couch so as not to wake Bonnie but stopped with a surprised breath. It was AJ. Heart beating harder, she carefully bent over the back of the couch and watched her sleep. Hair covered part of her face and she could smell soap and sex mingled with the smell of sleep.

A slight ache sifted through her. She'd loved every moment of last night. AJ's body under her and the hot, sweaty skin. Yes, they would do *that* again, many times. Was there anything she didn't like about AJ? Not so far. Wait, yes. There was her job.

Once again, in the middle of that very still, focused place where AJ always seemed to hold her, Katie slowly straightened. With a determined sigh, she left, shutting the door quietly behind her.

The garage was another surprise. AJ's car was not the sleek sports car she had thought it would be. She walked around the somewhat battered vehicle with a curious look. Everyone said AJ loved speed, and that motor had sounded big yesterday.

❖

A hand on AJ's shoulder woke her and she jerked upward. "Hey," she complained and looked at Grace. "What's the matter?"

"Where's Katie?" Grace said.

"I don't know," AJ said and let her head fall back. "What?"

"Katie's gone."

AJ tried to engage her brain. "She's not here?"

"No. Her bed's made and her car's gone."

AJ struggled to sit up. Finally, she got her good leg to cooperate. "What time is it? The appointment's at one o'clock." She put her head in her hands. "Crap, look at the time. The man at the bank is David Markam. Hand me my crutches will you?" Grace helped her up, gathering the pillows and blanket as AJ went for her phone in the bedroom.

AJ realized that Katie had let them sleep. "Grace, call Katie's office. I'll call Charles. Get dressed," AJ said as she dialed the phone. "Damn, I'll—Charles? Katie's gone." She balanced on her crutches. "Remember? She had a one o'clock appointment downtown, at Benning's."

Bonnie slid by her, into the bathroom. AJ sorted through clothes in her bag as she listened to Charles. Suddenly, she stopped. "What?" She let the clean underwear and socks fall onto the dresser. "Yes, I have a one o'clock doctor's appointment. Of course I'm going, but someone should be with Katie."

AJ swung over to the bed on one crutch and sank down. "No, I just woke up. I forgot what Grace said last night. All right, Charles, thanks," she said and hung up. She stared out the window for a few moments, edgy and worried. On paper, Zack looked as if he was behaving himself. If Grace had checked him out, that was good enough. That thought reassured her and she relaxed a little. Charles had said he'd send someone to find Katie and stay with her. That should do it. But where the hell was Elena? Or Michael. She thought about the bank. Was his office anywhere near David Markam's?

Bonnie stood in the doorway with water and pills. "What did Charles say?" she said.

"Exactly what he told Grace last night. That he'd have someone with Katie at the bank." AJ took the antibiotic that Bonnie handed her but broke the pain pill in half. "I don't need the whole thing." She wanted her mind as clear as humanly possible for the doctor. "I need a shower." She hoisted herself upright. "Drive me to the hospital, Grace. Bonnie, stay and let us know if Katie calls or comes home. I'm still not comfortable with this. Katie's office said the meeting's on the fourth floor of the home office, the building close to the lake."

AJ took a deep breath. "I have to go with Charles on this one. Grace, on the way to the hospital I want you to tell me everything Seraph said about Zack." She looked at her legs. "Do either of you have sweat pants that'll fit over my leg? It's too cold outside for shorts and my pants won't fit over this dressing."

"I have sweats you can wear, but you'll have to roll them up." Bonnie grinned at her. "Why don't we grab a bagel before you leave? I'll get things ready while you're in the shower."

Katie stopped at the guard shack at Benning's parking lot, explained her business, and presented her ID. While she waited, she realized that this was the first time she'd been without any of AJ's group in over two weeks. Or was it three? She looked at the incredible blue sky. March would be done soon and here came her favorite season. Spring.

"A guard shack?" Zack asked as Katie parked close to the tall fence next to the street.

"That's the price we pay to do business after nine eleven," Katie said as they walked to the entryway. It was a wonderful bright day and the warming air smelled good. "Have you always lived in Milwaukee?"

"I grew up on the north side with an older brother. My parents spend winters down south. They just got home," he said and held the door for her. "How about you?"

"I'm probably fifth or sixth generation. We've always been here, as far as I know."

They got off at the fourth floor and turned right. The plush carpeting was dark blue and the walls a rich cream that opened into a large open reception area. Katie took a breath to relax and heard Zack do the same.

The receptionist looked up with a smile and asked them to wait. They settled onto the long black leather couch against the wall. Despite Katie's rampaging nerves, the day felt positive. She thought of AJ, asleep on her couch.

"Are you nervous?" Zack said with an unsure smile.

"Sure. Aren't you? Nerves are good for you. They keep you sharp."

"Actually, I think that idea you have is brilliant."

"It's not my idea. I mean, someone else thought of it long before me, but it would be cool to reposition this older, respected institution in this city. Zack, don't believe what you hear on the news. There's money out there, lots of it. I know Benning's has it. I've scouted them for months since the first time I heard they were looking for a new public relations agency."

Zack stacked their bags on the floor. "What do you mean?"

She crossed her legs and wiggled her foot. "If I told you what I really think, you'd believe that I ran around with my head wrapped up in aluminum foil." Katie grinned at him. "I think it's all just politics. For example, why is no one from the Wall Street mess in jail? One thing I'm sure of. I've never seen this country so divided."

He stared at her. "Sometime, when we have a minute, I'd like to talk about that."

"Well, if we get this contract, I'm hiring you an assistant. I'm spending my money." His face was finally relaxed and friendly as Katie studied him. "Zack, how did you meet Lu Wright? She brought you to me because of your art, but I never asked how the two of you met."

"I was in college and she was always hanging around." He looked away, embarrassed, and Katie's antennae went up. Had there been a personal relationship between Zack and Lu? Lu never cared much how she ended the night.

"Did you ever—" Katie stopped, not sure how to proceed. "Did you ever work for her?" That was safer ground, away from the personal issue.

"Uh," he mumbled, his face reddening a bit. "Yeah. Money was tight and I did about anything to make a dollar. "

There was a thin line between his eyebrows and she could see he was uncomfortable. "I'm not exactly bursting with pride over that time in my life."

"What did you do?"

"Ah hell, Katie." He tightened his tie.

What on earth? Suddenly Katie remembered what Seraph had said, about Lu's little "guy pal." Surely not Zack? "I know that Lu sold drugs. Did you help her?"

Zack wouldn't meet her eyes. "Yes, but I never got caught. I got into an argument with one of the angels, their…gang. Elena even pulled a gun on me and—"

"Ms. Blackburn, Mr. Markam will see you now," the receptionist said at that moment.

They were ushered into a beautiful office. The leather chairs were a rich brown with a subtle gray-green carpeting. Katie thought of the phrase *the corner office* as she stepped into the room. Windows ran floor to ceiling, and the view of Lake Michigan was breathtaking.

"Ms. Blackburn," David Markam said and stood, slender in an expensive dark suit. They shook hands and Katie introduced Zack. He indicated two chairs in front of an enormous dark oak desk.

"Thank you for coming," he said. "My board is very enthusiastic about your proposal. Those are fresh ideas for Benning's." He gave them an encouraging smile. "I understand you're the artist?" he said to Zack.

"Yes," Zack said with the warm smile that made him look so trustworthy, "but hardly the brains of the group."

"Still, your talent is remarkable," Mr. Markam said and his smile increased. At that moment, Katie knew he'd researched her and Blue Ridge, Inc., in a million different ways. Well, good, she thought. They'd asked for "new" and that's what she'd proposed. "Ms. Blackburn, you want me to spend a lot of money. Do you understand that?"

She nodded. It would be costly for them to begin. "I do," she said, "but your group asked for something creative that would sharpen your image in Milwaukee."

He tilted his head a little. "And how, in your opinion, would this sharpen our image?"

Katie kept her voice confident. "Your position here, in this city, is that of a conservative banker's group. You've purchased four of our local banks and some of our businesses. I've asked every business I've come in contact with about Benning's. Most felt your interest lies in the more metropolitan areas around us. Chicago, for example." She paused and lifted her eyebrows. She wanted him to verify what she'd just said.

"Perhaps," he finally said with a brief nod.

"The worst I can say is the truth," she continued. "If you truly are interested in repositioning yourself in Milwaukee, microlending is the way. Frankly, it will make you more money than any single thing I can suggest plus bring you further into the community."

He gave a quiet laugh. "Finally, the truth. I take my wife out for a social function and people treat me respectfully, but they're not necessarily happy to see me. I've been doing this a long time, and I know when I'm being politely put in a corner as if I were some kind of corporate raider, there to buy their business."

Katie smiled slightly. He was aware of the growing division between the bank and the community.

"Many of our people here at Benning's encourage that attitude plus an edge of fear. Personally, I don't." Mr. Markam leaned forward. "Frankly, how can I grow this location if people won't talk to me?"

"This is a loyal, hardworking old city. We want to keep the business that we've worked to create and maintain. I know microlending is risky, but in today's economy, what isn't?"

Markam nodded. "My board members have looked at this, but the final decision is mine. I've always felt I understand a good risk when I see it. I'm going to go ahead and give you the green light on this project and I want you to report to a young assistant vice president that works here." He shoved an elegant folder across the desk to her. "Please read this contract carefully. Take several days. Have your legal counsel look at it as well. I think you'll find it to your satisfaction and return it when you've signed it."

He stood and picked up the phone. "Let's talk to the man I'd like you to work with. I'll call him and let him know we're coming. At least, I hope you'll be working with us." Markam dialed his phone, smiling at both Zack and Katie.

"Hi, Shelly, it's David Markam. Where's—" He listened a few moments. "Thank you. No, I'll find him." He hung up with a mildly irritated expression. "I'm sorry. Perhaps I got my wires crossed. I'll have Mr. Cray call your office and set up an appointment. In the meantime, please look the contract over and let me know, personally." He handed Katie two cards and she looked at them. One was Markham's and the other said "John Michael Cray, Assistant Vice President."

They walked back to the elevators. "Oh, baby, we did it." Zack laughed as he punched the button and Katie dialed her office on her cell.

"Is this great or what?" Katie held up the contract. She felt as if she'd just hurdled the moon. "We're going to celebrate tonight. I've got some people at my house that I have to call and then, how about a huge meal with lots of drinks? The whole office and my friends. Maybe some of my family." She couldn't stop smiling. "Pick a place, Zack." Her phone beeped as they got on the elevator.

Zack turned to her. "Katie, about Lu? You're—"

She held up a hand. "I don't think it was a good decision on your part, Zack, but as long as you're no longer involved with any of those people, we're fine."

Zack studied the pancl and frowned. "Did we get into the wrong elevator?" he said.

The phone in her hand beeped again, and Katie leaned into a corner. There were three calls from AJ and two each from Grace and Bonnie. What the heck? "I've got to take some calls." She looked over at Zack. "What did you say—wrong elevator?"

Zack pushed his lanky frame from the wall as the elevator stopped. He turned to Katie. "This is the wrong floor. It says basement." The door opened to the underground parking in the building.

"That's odd. Just hit the first floor button and—" Katie heard running footsteps on cement.

She saw Zack frown as he said, "Elena and—"

CHAPTER TWENTY-SIX

A J pushed herself to a sitting position. "Well?" she said to Dr. Light.

The doctor washed her hands, her back to AJ. "Well, what?"

"How soon can I get back on the street?"

Dr. Light turned with a get-serious look. "It depends on how fast you improve. Remember, the tissues in the back of your leg were opened and have to heal from the inside out. It's called granulating and takes longer than an incision." She made a wry face at AJ's groan. "I know, I know. You're incredibly healthy, and the surgeon did an excellent job, but you're restricted until I tell you otherwise. I'm going to notify Charles and make it official."

"He'll follow that to the letter." AJ whined at the doctor as she tried to get into her oversized sweat pants. "I'm needed out there."

"That may be, but you're not ready." Dr. Light leaned over, gave AJ's borrowed pants a tug, and helped her into her boots. "Where did you get these pants?"

"Borrowed them. What else?"

Dr. Light began to enter information on her computer. "The woman that was here with you the night they brought you in was nice. The cute caretaker? How has she done?"

AJ finally managed to get to vertical. "Katie?"

"If I could get my husband to look at me like she looked at you, I'd take a week's vacation. We'd never leave the house." The doctor grinned.

"She's one of a kind. Completely herself." AJ felt her face warm.

"The way she listened that night was remarkable," Dr. Light said.

"She's remarkable." AJ adjusted herself onto the crutches. "All right, I give up. When can I start therapy?"

"Next week, and you'll probably get rid of the crutches, but in the meantime, nothing but rest." AJ started for the door, but Dr. Light stopped her. "Allison, if you don't take it easy, you'll only prolong the therapy. I'm changing your pain pills to a lower dose, so have this filled. You can take two if needed." She handed her a prescription.

AJ came out of the office and handed Grace the paper. "We have to go to the pharmacy before we leave. Anything from Charles or Katie?"

Grace studied the prescription. "I agree with Bonnie. How does anyone read this stuff?" She started down the hallway to the pharmacy.

"Wait," AJ said, "I asked if there was anything from Charles? From anyone?"

"No. No one," Grace said and took off at a brisk pace with both of their coats over her arm. "I'll be at the pharmacy."

The clock said almost two o'clock. AJ swung along on her crutches until she could see Grace inside the pharmacy, then she found a chair. First, she dialed Charles, but got voice mail. She sent him a text that let him know where she was. When she called Bonnie at Katie's house, it too went immediately to voice mail and she left a message. She tapped her phone lightly on her leg as her nerves dialed up a notch. The person she wanted to talk to was Katie.

She dialed Katie's phone but got voice mail. "Crap. Three times and you're out." She fidgeted in the chair and closed her eyes. She thought of Katie, above her, dark curly hair brushing her with that wonderful little groan. With her head down, she recalled everything she could of last night. Maybe they could try that again tonight.

Grace was still standing at the counter inside, so AJ dialed Katie's office. The secretary told her that Katie had checked in and they were going to stop there first, but they were overdue. AJ verified the address of the bank building, thanked her, and hung up. They were close to the Benning's building. Her instincts went off like warning bells and she moved to the pharmacy as Grace turned.

"We're going to look for Katie. It's only three blocks away."

❖

What blew up? And then Katie's brain registered—gun shot. She shrank back at the sudden, huge noise as Zack blew backward into the wall, staggered forward, then fell to the ground, half inside the elevator, half out.

"Zack," she screamed, her voice echoing in her own ears as she went to the ground beside him. He clutched at his stomach, blood surging through his fingers, his eyes fixed on the cement ceiling above him. "No, no," she babbled and grabbed her phone, dialing 911. Was he breathing? She swallowed hard, trying to clear her jumbled mind. The doors inanely bumped again and again against Zack's legs. She hit LOCK on the control panel. She thought of AJ and hit the speed dial on her phone. AJ answered, and Katie tried to talk but began to cry. Footsteps sounded to her left as three guards ran down the ramp toward her.

"AJ, someone shot Zack. Yes, shot. We're in the underground parking lot at the bank. You're where?" She swiveled to the guards. "Open the gate. The police are here. That's who I'm talking to."

"The doors opened and he went down," she said to the men. They all turned toward the sound of sirens. "I think there was just one shot. I called nine one one, but he hasn't moved and—"

The guard put a steady hand on her shoulder. "We called too when we heard the gunshot."

Katie looked out into the dim sea of parked cars. Someone or something moved between the cars. "Look!" she said to one of the guards just as Grace drove down the ramp, sirens surreal and deafening in the enclosed area. Katie ran toward them as the siren stopped, but the lights still flashed. She grabbed for AJ and began to cry again. "They shot him."

"Katie, are you hurt?" AJ put her hands firmly on Katie's face.
The warmth of AJ's fingers on her skin slowed Katie's mind.
"They shot him," she said and buried herself into AJ's body. More
sirens echoed in the distance.

❖

AJ kept a tight grip around Katie's waist as they watched
the EMTs lift Zack into the ambulance. Katie was past the initial
hysteria, but AJ recognized the focused silence as shock.

"Come on, we'll follow the ambulance." She turned Katie so
she could look into her eyes but Katie only stared with eyes like wet
glass.

"There was someone there, maybe two people," Katie said, her
voice thin and distant. "There." She pointed. "Wait. Our things are at
the elevator." Katie jerked away in that direction and Grace followed.

AJ looked down the row of cars where Katie had pointed. A
voice called to her and she stopped. Charles was running down the
cement, Bill behind him.

"Katie?" he said as he caught up with her.

"It's Zack. Someone shot him. Katie said there was someone
down there." AJ began to move her crutches toward the cars.

They walked along in silence, AJ's crutches making an odd,
echoing noise. Each of them scanned the parked vehicles. "Look."
Charles stooped to pick something off the cement. He held up the
baggy for AJ to see. There were three more beside the next car. Two
cops caught up with them and one held out an evidence bag.

"Maybe Zack and Katie interrupted something?" AJ said as she
went to the next car.

"Maybe," he said. "Someone's back there." He veered off
through the cars and ran with two cops behind him just as a gunshot
scattered everyone.

AJ automatically went for her weapon, then realized she didn't
have either gun because of the doctor's appointment. She saw
Grace grab Katie and push her behind the SUV. Two more gunshots
sounded and Charles called out for AJ.

She found him by a large black pickup. The cops chased someone toward the street. "What the hell?" she said.

Charles was so pale that his face shone in the semi-darkness of the garage. "He shot at me," Charles said as Bill came up beside them. "I think it was a man, wearing a long black coat with a hood."

"We'll handle this," Bill said to AJ. "You get Katie to the hospital with Zack. Check in with either of us when you can."

AJ focused on Katie's shocked face as she made her way back to the car. Grace had just gotten her into the agency SUV. A well-dressed older man headed down the ramp.

"Is that the man you met with? Markam?" AJ opened the door and rubbed Katie's cold, bloody hands.

Katie glanced at the man and nodded.

"Hold on, Grace. I'll say a few words to him." AJ held up her badge to Markam and introduced herself.

"Sir, would you wait beside the policeman and speak to those two men?" She pointed at Bill and Charles.

He took a deep breath. "What happened?"

"Ms. Blackburn said the young man that was with her was shot as they got off the elevator. He's on his way to the hospital."

"The artist?" He looked shocked. "But Ms. Blackburn…"

"She's in our car and we're following the ambulance to the hospital."

He nodded. "Thank you. I'll wait." As they left, AJ saw David Markam step closer to the crime scene at the elevator. AJ thought of Charles in the garage. Where had his protection been for Katie?

❖

It was almost dark by the time they brought Zack out of surgery at the hospital. AJ and Grace had waited with Katie. Charles and Bill had stayed behind at the bank with David Markam.

When Zack's mother and father arrived, Katie left to stand beside them, listening to a nurse. AJ could see that his parents were older and confused. Katie helped the woman with her coat and got them seated.

The minute Katie left, AJ turned to Grace. "Charles said the person he chased had on a long black coat with a hood. That's exactly what I saw that night in front of Katie's house." She picked up Katie's coat and stood. "Let's move closer to Zack's parents, but first I'm going to call Bill for some police presence here."

"I'll give Bonnie another call and update her." Grace took her phone out and began to walk away. "Damn. Just look at Katie's face."

"I know," AJ said. After talking with Bill, AJ watched Katie struggle with her emotions as she tried to reassure Zack's parents. She took a seat close to them and heard Katie say, "I'll be right here, as long as you need me." Her hand rested lightly on the older woman's shoulder.

Katie finally sat beside AJ but stared at the floor.

"How old is Zack?" AJ tried to draw Katie out and get her to talk some of the emotions away.

"He just turned twenty-six."

AJ studied her. "How did the meeting go at the bank?"

Katie blinked and her face gathered a little light. "We got the contract."

"That's excellent. I thought you might."

"I hoped. Zack is so talented." Resignation settled back onto her face. "I was thinking, if he survives—" She suddenly twisted to face AJ. "Did you know that he sold drugs with Lu while he was in college? He told me today."

"We didn't know until Seraph told us yesterday."

The tension around Katie was so tight that AJ could almost hear it hum, see the air vibrate. Grace returned and sat on the other side of Katie.

"He didn't deserve this," Katie said.

Grace said, "No one deserves this."

"I feel as if Lu brought us all here." Katie cleared her throat and AJ saw tears in her eyes again. "What if Zack took Lu's bullet?"

"No, I think Zack took his own bullet." AJ kept her voice soft but firm, trying to lead Katie. "No one made him work with Lu or this group."

Katie looked back at Zack's parents. "Who's Elena?"

"What?' Grace and AJ said.

"When the elevator door opened, Zack said, "Elena and…" just before he was shot. Earlier, when we were talking, he said she'd had a gun on him last summer."

The surgeon walked out at that moment, and Katie shot up from her chair. She and Zack's parents stood together again, listening to the doctor.

"God. Elena," AJ spat out. They both stopped talking as Katie came back to them.

"He'll be in ICU tonight. It's hopeful. The bullet nicked an artery around a kidney, and that explains all the blood, but he may lose a kidney. Look at his parents, all alone. There's no one here with them. I'll wait until their oldest son arrives." They turned toward his parents still talking with the doctor. Katie rummaged in her bag. "Grace, would you or Bonnie get my car from the bank and park it here?" She handed the keys to Grace. "I'll come home after I've talked with Zack's brother."

"We called Bill," Grace said. "He'll post two policemen here. They'll change shifts, so watch for them."

"For Zack?" Katie said and dabbed at her eyes again.

"Yes, for Zack," AJ said.

Katie nodded slowly, then straightened. "You need to be home in bed," she said to AJ. "I'll come home as soon as I can."

AJ stood and put her arms around her but felt Katie stiffen. "We'll be at the house if you need us. All you have to do is call." She'd give anything to take Katie home with them.

"Thank you, both of you," Katie said, distant and formal.

AJ directed her crutches to the door but stopped. She looked back as Katie put an arm around Zack's mother, and her stomach knotted. Katie had used her business voice and the look in her eyes had not been warm.

CHAPTER TWENTY-SEVEN

Charles's SUV was in Katie's driveway when Grace and AJ drove in. Grace slammed the Suburban into park.

"Send Bonnie out. I don't want to go inside," Grace said. "We'll get Katie's car, move it, and pick up some Chinese on the way home. I only want to say this. Where was the person Charles was supposed to have at the bank, with Katie and Zack?"

"Coward." AJ looked up from her phone. Bill had just sent her a text that he'd catch up with her later. "I don't know where that person was, but I'll find out."

"Charles should have let one of us go with them. Did you see her? This was awful."

"I saw her," AJ said softly. *I think I saw her leaving.*

"While you were gone, down in Little Crane Lake, Katie was edgy, but this…"

"I've got crutches. I'll beat Charles for both of us." Resigned to the conversation ahead of her, AJ studied the house. "Something went wrong."

Bonnie and Charles were at the kitchen table, both with a bottle of water in front of them.

AJ sent Bonnie outside to Grace and noticed that the water bottles were still unopened. *He hasn't been here long.* She opened Bonnie's water bottle, studying the pills she'd gotten earlier at the hospital. Her leg was killing her, and she washed down a pill with a long drink.

"Dr. Light called me," Charles said. "You're officially off the street for a couple of weeks."

"Yeah, and I hate this." She stared hard at him, willing him to open up with the things he hadn't told her. "Charles, talk to me. Something's been off since we were down at Little Crane Lake."

Charles frowned at the bottle in his hands and twisted it slowly, but didn't answer. She saw how tired he sat with his shoulders down and dark circles under his eyes.

"What the hell happened to the person that was supposed to be at the bank for Katie?"

"Right after you called from here today, we found Michael, dead."

AJ pulled in a shocked breath. "Where?"

"Shot, sometime last night, across the street from Seraph's in the cemetery." He bumped the table softly with a fist. "Same as Star and her husband. Execution style."

"Why didn't you tell me at the bank?"

"Because you got into the car with Katie and Grace. And left."

"Bill told me to go with Katie. He said you two would handle the bank."

Charles's head came up as if he were hearing her for the first time. "Bill and I haven't had time to talk since we were there. The man Katie met with today, David Markam, is still in shock that one of his finest employees was involved in anything like this. Then I had to give him Seraph's information, that half of his employees at the bank were buying drugs from Michael—John Michael Cray." With a drink of water, Charles shrugged a little. "It wasn't a good day for Benning's. They're working on Michael's computer right now."

"The bank's people or ours?"

"Both. I called Justice. Markam was furious that we hadn't notified the bank." Charles rubbed his temples. "We left Michael's body with the ME and immediately went to his houses for the computers and anything else we could find. We'd been there for less than twenty minutes when you called from the bank." He took a deep breath. "They wrapped up the houses, about an hour ago, and I came over here."

Neither of them said anything. All AJ could hear was their breathing. Finally, she said, "Do you have a clue who shot Michael?"

"We have the girls from his gang that were at the murder scene. Bill's at Central with them."

"While we were waiting at the hospital, Katie told us that Zack confessed to working with Lu Wright and told her that Elena had a gun on him last summer."

"You know how kids like Zack are. They don't believe drugs are a real threat and they need the money, so they do what they do."

"I agree, but the last thing Zack said in the elevator, was 'Elena and...' before he was shot." She stared at the bottle in her hand. "So based on that, I'd have to say Elena shot Zack, but I don't know why."

"I don't either. Yet." Charles loosened his tie and stared out into space. "I feel like I've fallen off the planet. We came out here, looking for suppliers and distributors, keeping a low profile. And it looked so small, compared to Iowa and Missouri. I thought we had time. No one was supposed to get killed. It didn't turn out like anything we thought, did it?" His face had a light sheen of sweat on it.

AJ looked away. "No, it's turned into something else." She took a chance on her suspicions. "Are you ever going to tell me who you have inside? Or Bill?"

"That's going to have to wait until I have further word from her."

She gave a short laugh. "My gut says it's Ariel. Was she the girl from the farmhouse? She felt familiar somehow."

Charles only gave a curt nod. "Your gut's right. Hell, she even looks a lot like you at that age, only shorter. Will you just leave that alone until she's out and safe, the same way you and I always handled undercover? In the beginning, Ariel was just insurance with the local DEA. When this was over, we wanted you to work with her. I don't think that's an option now."

"You're sure Elena killed Michael?"

"I *know* she did. Elena's feeling pretty good about everything right now." Charles shifted to face her and she braced herself for whatever was coming. "How have you felt about leading this task force?"

She hadn't expected that, and AJ gave a short, unhappy laugh. "I've been damned challenged, but I haven't had much time for feelings."

He ran his hands through his hair. "It's your first time. You've done a good job."

"Hell, you can say that with five, no, six, people dead? And the only thing we know for sure is that Elena killed Michael. We don't even know who hit me at the farmhouse, unless it was Ariel." He gave her a dark look. "Afraid I want to go back under?" She was certain that he was setting her up for something.

Charles gave a short laugh. "I *know* you'd rather be out there, away from the daily reports, the team's eyes on you, no matter where you are. All that up-front responsibility." He gave a wry smile. "You're the best undercover I've ever had, damned near transparent, but I need leaders too."

She stared at him for a moment, mistrustful. Charles didn't praise often. "I admit to having my moments about undercover work versus leading a group, but I'm learning. You should have told me about Ariel in the beginning. All you did was make me suspicious. And we disagreed about the farmhouse. I wanted to set it up like you have it now and I told you so."

Charles leaned toward her. "Maybe, but it wouldn't have made any difference. You knew everything you needed to know."

"Except who did the killings. Oh, and did Ariel know we were going to take Hood's Hollow down?"

Charles shifted uncomfortably. "I don't know."

"How the hell could she not have known?" AJ angrily began and then understood. "You lost her, didn't you?" Her voice rose in disbelief. "Charles, just give it to me. This is between us. However you handle your supervisor is up to you."

"Okay, yes, I lost her. I didn't even know she was down at the farm," he admitted. "She finally checked in the night we came back from Madison to Little Crane Lake. By the time I got this sorted out, you were injured and in no shape to do anything."

"I never, ever did that to you. Separated myself," AJ said. "Where is she now?"

"She's with Elena, and I've talked with her every day. And nothing's wrong. She simply couldn't get word to us."

"I don't believe her. I can tell you from experience that there's always a way." She could hardly believe what he'd just said.

Charles reached down to his case and laid a folder on the table. "You may be off the streets because of your injury, but you can work at the station, coordinate the group from there."

"But Elena's still out there."

"Ariel will handle Elena, and I'll back her up. Here's what I want."

AJ interrupted. "Are you sure Ariel's experienced enough to handle someone like Elena? Elena's smart—street smart—and loves to kill. Let's not get this kid killed too."

"Take the time while you're healing, to learn." He hauled things out of his bag but stopped when AJ tried to push herself up with one crutch.

"At least tell me if it was Elena here that night?"

"Yes, she was looking for Seraph. Will you settle down?" Charles closed the folder and stared at her. "Something else. I want everyone out of here tonight."

AJ levered back into the seat. "Tonight?"

Charles held up a finger. "Today at the bank, you only paid attention to Katie. For that matter, your eyes are always where Katie is when she's in the room. Or looking for her when she's not."

"All right," AJ said tentatively. "I admit that's true."

"Stay at Grace's until you can climb the stairs to your own place."

"No." AJ managed to get to a standing position, clenched her teeth so hard that her jaw hurt. "I can lead from here."

"Until we get Elena, it'll be dangerous for Katie if you're here and you know I'm right."

AJ's legs trembled as she reached for the other crutch. "Bullshit, Charles."

"You were right about Seraph, but I'm right about this. Look, twice in your life I've seen you come back from zero. You're going to be one of the best, and we need the best right now. Hell, if I could just bottle that passion you have for this job, we wouldn't be failing in the drug war in this country and we are. The stats are here, in this folder, on this flash drive. Read it, learn." He held up a hand at her. "I'm going to stay firm on this one—" His phone rang and he checked the name then turned away to answer.

AJ got herself away from the table and Charles. At least the pill was blunting the pain. She went to her bedroom. Katie's bedroom.

She threw one crutch on the floor as hard as she could and tried to breathe. "Damn, Charles is right." She looked around the room.

Someone had made the bed; probably Bonnie as she waited here this afternoon. The dressers were clean, her clothes neatly stacked on top of the taller one. Car doors sounded as she opened the closet for her bag, and she heard Grace's voice, then the front door open. She set the bag on the dresser and began to pack clean clothes inside. Charles said something to the girls and the front door closed. Car lights swept across the drapes.

Grace appeared in the bedroom doorway. "The food's on the table. Charles said he'd see you tomorrow." She walked further into the room. "Are you all right?"

"No," AJ said and settled the last bit of clothes into the bag.

Bonnie came up behind Grace and held up something. "I have something I want you to hear," she said. "When I was cleaning today, I found a recording of Katie's music competition in Madison. You have to hear her play that fiddle."

Still angry, AJ looked at both of them. "That would be great and I'm starving," she lied. As they left the room, AJ sat on the bed and wrote Katie a note. "Thanks. Bren Black and the Posse have to go. I'll talk to you soon." She drew a smiley face and the initials, "B.B." She laid the note on the bedside table and turned out the light.

CHAPTER TWENTY-EIGHT

On the dark side of four o'clock in the morning, Katie drove away from the hospital. Milwaukee was deserted with the exception of a few buses and the occasional car. The white noise in her head had finally melted away, but she felt as empty as the city. When Zack's older brother had arrived from Minneapolis, they had talked, but she'd omitted the part about the drugs. Then the brother had asked if Zack was still in his druggie phase. Relieved, she told him what she knew. After exchanging phone numbers, he promised to keep in touch.

Zack's parents leaned against each other in a big recliner, asleep, as Katie gathered up her things, and gave them a last glance. They should be home, tucked in their bed.

She carried that image all through the drive to her own house. Look what Zack had done to them and all because of drugs. Well, she'd caused her own parents a lot of time and worry over her own gigantic failure with Lu.

There were no cars in her driveway, but AJ's car was still in her garage. Exhausted, she stood on the front porch in the dark, trying to get the key in the lock.

"Could have left the porch light on," she said wearily, too tired to work up more than a little irritation.

With as little noise as possible, she tiptoed into the living room. Something felt different. She frowned at the empty couch, placed her bag on the kitchen table, and walked through the house. As she went through the rooms, she turned the lights on. All her clothes were gone from the little bedroom and back in her own bedroom. The drawers were as they used to be. *Before AJ.* She walked back to the kitchen. It was spotless. She turned slowly. Everything was in its place again, but the house felt abandoned.

She walked back through the house turning off the lights. There was a piece of paper taped to her bathroom mirror, but she didn't smile when she read it. Another message from Bren Black. Worry inched its way inside. Was AJ another gigantic mistake, like Lu?

A little light-headed, she went into her bedroom. Her grandmother's quilt was back on the bed. Already half-asleep, she stood, staring at the bed, then down at the blood on her clothes. Mom might know if the suit could be saved. Completely wiped out, she stepped out of her clothes and left them where they fell. Her eyes smarted with tears as she crawled under the sheets and her heart pounded with fatigue. Last night she'd slept in AJ's arms.

AJ dumped her crutches beside the spare bed at Grace's. "Hell of a day." She undressed and left all of her clothes on the floor. Michael was dead, Zack and Katie were at the hospital, and who the hell knew where Ariel or Elena were? And something was way off with that situation. Years of experience set off alarms every time she thought of it. Would Ariel be savvy enough to manage Elena? Or smart enough to save herself?

Over Chinese at Katie's, she'd opened her computer, caught up, and issued her first e-mail in days. It was only a terse message, but it told everyone to contact her. She wanted them to know she was back on the job.

The conversation at the table with Grace and Bonnie had stayed focused on Michael, Elena, and Zack. She hadn't said a word about Ariel. When she'd announced that Charles wanted them out tonight, she'd seen their surprise, but they hadn't questioned her. They'd cleaned their things out of the house and transferred Katie's clothes back to her own bedroom as Katie's music played over them. The music had been energetic, joyful, and tender, just like Katie.

AJ adjusted the pillow under her leg. How many different beds had she slept in recently? Last night, Katie's spare room had been dark and intimate. It had been only them and the quiet, intense sex. What had Katie whispered? *God, that was good.* And then Katie had fallen asleep, so thoroughly that she'd not moved when AJ got up and went to the couch. That had felt good too, just holding her while she slept.

She'd do what Charles had ordered and take this time to learn the whole operation. But she'd also stay in touch with Katie. If Katie would let her. She replayed today and the distance Katie had placed between them at the hospital. There was coolness in her voice and in her eyes.

A doorbell ringing relentlessly woke AJ later. Disoriented, she looked around the dark room, until she heard Grace talking to a woman. Their voices moved closer. AJ pulled the covers up just as the bedroom door opened.

"What is it?" AJ said.

"A woman says she needs to see you," Grace said, her voice low. "She can't reach Charles. It's the woman I saw with Michael at the Copper Penny."

"A woman?" AJ righted herself in the bed and turned on the small bedside light. "Come in here, both of you. Grace, hand me a T-shirt, would you?"

A slender blonde stepped out from behind Grace. "I need help, Allison." AJ pulled the T-shirt over her head. She recognized her instantly from the farmhouse in Little Crane Lake.

"Ariel?" AJ pulled herself up against the headboard, her little Ruger gripped in her left hand under the sheet. "Come here. Sit on the bed." She studied her in the soft light. She was a twenty-something in a light winter jacket, jeans, and hiking boots.

"Charles was supposed to meet me in the alley behind Los Gatos, the Spanish food place on Layton, but he never showed up. He told me that you were here, with Grace."

"Charles said you were with Elena," AJ said and rubbed her gritty eyes. "Grace, you'd better get dressed. We're going out."

"Elena threw a party. Everyone's still there, and Charles isn't answering his phone. I went to his motel, but his car's gone." Ariel was twitchy, shifting on the end of the bed.

"It's okay. We've got you now. How many people are at the restaurant?"

"I don't know, fifteen of the girls, maybe more. I'm sorry to bother you." She stood suddenly as if it were impossible to sit.

"Hand me my bag." AJ sat up, got her feet on the floor, and began to sort through clothes. The girl looked exhausted. "How long have you been without sleep?" AJ pulled a heavy sweater over her T-shirt and searched for thick socks.

"I'm not even sure what day it is." Ariel's light blond hair hung down across her face, and she pushed it back.

AJ's undercover experience kicked in and she remembered the complete exhaustion and ruthless immersion of the job. Ariel should never have left the restaurant, but surely there was some escape plan for her? AJ slipped her little Ruger into her boot and strapped on her weapon. She'd take a look at the place, then call Bill. Or Charles, if she could find him.

It took them less than fifteen minutes to drive to the Layton Avenue address. As they went by the hospital, she asked Grace to see if Katie's car was there. Grace reported that it was gone from where they'd left it. Good, Katie was home and safe. AJ's watch said 4:10 as she continued to pepper Ariel with questions about the people who were with Elena, all the time going over possibilities for Charles.

"First priority, look for Charles's car." They drove around the block, but no car. It was a cool, misty March night and the area was gray to black. Finally, when AJ was dialing Bill, she realized that many of the streetlights were out. He answered in a sleepy voice but came alert when he heard what she said.

"What the hell? Ariel's with you? I thought she worked for Michael?" Bill said as AJ explained Ariel's sudden appearance.

"Where's Charles?" AJ said.

"He was with me, downtown at Central, but left for the airport to pick up his supervisor. Lawrence flew in to handle the new situation with the suppliers."

"We can't find him," AJ said and hoped that Bill understood that she wasn't saying everything.

"I'll get squads there right now. Wait, let's do the SWAT team."

"What now?" Ariel said, her eyes closed as she leaned against the door in the backseat.

"Drive this block one more time, Grace. It's so dark that we need to see what we can again. Ariel, what were your instructions?"

"To let him know when the party was on. You were his backup."

Me? No, Charles would never have done that. Every nerve in AJ's body jumped. She looked away. The kid had just lied.

Grace drove around the block once again, then slowed as they passed the alley behind Los Gatos. They parked at the end of the block and waited. Two large armored vehicles pulled up, the only noise their deep engines thrumming in the dark. Bill pulled up behind their car. Three police cars were across the street. AJ introduced Bill to Ariel, making sure the cops knew who she was.

"Let's get this show on the road." Bill turned to Ariel and offered her a SWAT jacket. She tossed her coat into the car and put the flak jacket over her sweater. "Come with me. You need to show us the layout." He turned back to Grace and AJ. "Stay close."

"We'll be in the alley, by the back entrance." AJ straightened on her crutches.

"Who is Ariel?" Grace walked beside her. "Is she what you thought, the girl from the farmhouse?"

"Yes, and be careful. I don't know her. She belongs to Charles and the local DEA. That's about as much as I know, except that he told me that she's been undercover with Elena. Grace, I'm pretty sure that she just lied to me, so stay alert. And for God's sake, watch out for Elena."

It was damp and cold as she leaned against the bricks of the alley, hand on her weapon. Only one thin light reflected off patches of melting snow on the wet cement. She felt her heart pound hard.

They went in quietly, Bill and Ariel following the SWAT team. All hell broke loose, but she didn't hear any gunshots. A window scraped above them and a figure slithered out off the back of the roof. AJ pointed. Grace moved down the alley as Bill and the SWAT team led handcuffed people out of the restaurant.

"Did you get Elena? Where's Ariel?" AJ recognized several of the women from their photos at the station. "There's over fifteen here."

"Ariel said they've been living in an upstairs apartment." He went back through the crowd and then came back. "She's disappeared."

"Someone went off that roof, down the alley, and Grace took off. Let's go." Bill turned and moved fast with two uniforms beside him. AJ followed them, cursed her leg and the crutches. The final turn threw her into total darkness. She stopped, listening. There was nothing. No light, no noise. She backed against a wooden door then leaned out to look up at the roof, her gun held close. Suddenly, two strong arms wrapped around her, knocking her crutches to the ground, cold metal against her head.

"Finally. I've been looking for you. And Lu's little friend's next," Elena said with a mean little laugh. She jammed her knee into AJ's leg. A huge jolt of pain sucked the air out of her, and AJ grabbed for breath as the arm closed across her throat. As she began to fade, red dots floated across her eyes. Something scraped against brick. Elena shifted with a quick breath just as a gun went off. Elena took AJ to the ground with her, hitting the cement hard.

On her stomach, partially under Elena, AJ drifted and stared at a small patch of melting snow in front of her eyes. No, not snow, flowers. The flowers she had given Katie?

"We're even," Ariel said, sinking beside her with a tired sigh. "I put you on those crutches, so this is the least I can do." She put a hand on AJ's shoulder. "You're bleeding."

"God, I hate the smell of blood. Always makes me vomit. Elena's dead?"

"Yes," Ariel said as she placed her gun on her knee. "Rest a minute. I will too."

AJ's mind circled. Somebody had to have heard that gunshot. She tightened her hand on her weapon buried against her stomach just as a gun was suddenly against her temple again, the metal so acutely cold that it stung. "What are you doing?" she slurred.

"You're next, and then I'm gone."

The silence was thick, dense. AJ couldn't even hear the SWAT team. She moved her gun again under her body to at least try to get off a shot. "Who are you?" she said.

"I'm not sure I even remember. Charles said I was your twin in a thousand ways."

"Charles was wrong. What the hell did you get into?" AJ's heart ran hard with fear.

"Elena. Just money, drugs, nothing personal…" Ariel's tired voice trailed off into a deep sigh. She leaned down, close to AJ but didn't move the gun. Her voice was flat, devoid of emotion. "I've tracked you, Agent Jacob. Right to the doctor and his wife, then the farmhouse."

AJ's mind whirled. "You shot them?"

"It was as easy as taking a breath. Walked right up to them in their driveway. That bitch was going to talk to you, and I knew she'd give us away." Ariel yawned but didn't move her gun. "This worked out much better than I anticipated. Looks like Elena shot you and I shot her. Perfect." She straightened and pushed the gun harder into AJ's temple.

"If I'm going to die here, do me a favor." AJ looked up into the shadowed face above her, the blank eyes. "Move me away from Elena's blood. I hate that smell."

A wisp of a smile crossed Ariel's mouth. She shoved Elena's body backward and pulled AJ onto her back with a little grunt. AJ let her body relax and sag under Ariel's hands. As the gun was back against her head, AJ pulled the trigger on her own weapon and felt the recoil against her stomach. Once, twice. A searing pain ripped the skin on her head and the top of her shoulder.

The gunshots left Ariel hanging in the air for a second before she slumped forward, blood pouring over her face. Footsteps were running as a dark haze took AJ out for a moment.

"Son of a—she's dead." Grace bent over Ariel. "Two. One through the jaw and one through the head. Elena shot her?"

"No, she shot Elena. I shot her before she got me," AJ mumbled, her tongue thick. "Jesus, my leg. Can you get me up? I think she shot me…the shoulder." They lifted her to the crutches. "She was going to kill me. She would have." The world was in slow motion as AJ leaned over, braced her hands on her crutches, and vomited into the blood at her feet until tears ran down her face. Both Bill and Grace put an arm around her until she was finished.

"Damn. Goddamn. The first person I kill is one of our own. Bill, call our contact at Justice." She handed her gun to him. "My weapon. You'll need this when we get downtown."

They sat her on the bumper of the ambulance, cleaned the gash at her temple, and washed the grit imbedded in her face with something that stung. Ariel had grazed her shoulder but cut her head, probably with the gun. AJ found the bottle of pain pills for her leg in her coat and took one. Two men from Justice showed up, and she listened to Bill's calm voice run through the night.

The ME's group walked by her, pulling two gurneys behind them. AJ stopped them and unzipped the body bag for a final check. She brushed the hair off the damaged face and searched for the wire Ariel should have been wearing, but there was nothing. Just a bra and skin.

Ariel may have belonged to Charles, but she was hers too. *We trusted you and you betrayed us.* How had this happened? Had Elena gotten into her head? No, this woman had been smarter than that. Drugs? Maybe. Undercover was a head wrecker. Things happened that never made it to report sheets or into interviews with superiors, but she'd never seen anything remotely like this. "Too young," she whispered into the cool air.

Bill put a hand on her shoulder and guided her back to the ambulance. "AJ, sit down so they can check you out further, make sure there's not a concussion. Be a good girl. Let this young man shine a light in your eyes. Next, you have to talk to your friends from Justice."

Somehow, he managed a cup of coffee for her and they sat there, talking about the last hour. Slowly, she found a little sanity.

CHAPTER TWENTY-NINE

The quiet of the downtown central office was shattered by a loud crack. AJ mumbled "sorry," and relaxed her grip on the plastic water bottle. Her mind was gripped by the image of Ariel's face, that swift second of surprise, the slump of the head... then all that blood. The kid had died sitting straight up.

"Agent Jacob?" The IAD officer searched her face. His pale eyes widened a fraction.

AJ took a tired breath. "Would you repeat that last question?" They were almost done with her statement to the Milwaukee police. Bill sat beside her as her rep. Behind her were the two men from Justice that had taken her statement earlier at the scene.

"The interview is over," he said and closed the file in front of him. It was done.

They made it as far as the long bench down the hallway from the interrogation room before Bill stopped her. "Charles and his supervisor are on their way. Sit. Ease up on that leg. Take a minute." He and the men from Justice walked away.

Too tired to argue, she felt as frail as the battered water bottle she still held. Grace sat beside her with their coats.

"I think it's ruined. Look, it's all bloody." Grace's dark hair fell across her face as she bent over AJ's damaged duster. "Katie's mother could fix this. Did you know she does a lot of Katie's clothes?"

"No, I didn't, but it's just a coat." AJ touched Grace's shoulder. "You were great out there last night. Are you okay?"

"Okay, truth. Did she shoot you or did you shoot yourself?" Grace gently teased and AJ saw her blue eyes assess her.

"Don't know," AJ said with a tired shrug. The adrenaline was finally out of her body and she felt limp. "I'll have to see a shrink over this."

Grace only nodded as her phone beeped with a text. "Bonnie's on her way in. I'll bring her up here," she said as she left.

Doctors, AJ thought. She'd had enough of them after Ecuador and the West Coast snafu. Sometimes it did help to talk to them but, oddly, the only person she wanted to tell was Katie, tell her how young Ariel had looked when she died, the stress and exhaustion disappearing with the breath.

The only other person she'd ever wanted to talk to was Dana, but that was all that Katie and Dana had in common. Well, except for the fact that the first time she'd seen each of them, her mouth had gone dry.

AJ turned the bottle slowly on the bench and watched the reflection of pale sunlight through the water. Suddenly she couldn't find a piece of anger in herself at Dana or Rachel. It no longer made any difference. Maybe it had been the same for Katie after Lu. She finished the water, tossed the bottle into the green recycle bin, and started down the hallway. Her head pounded and her leg hurt. Running on empty, she was ready for another pain pill and some food.

Bonnie and Grace got off the elevator. "Do either of you have water?" AJ held up her bottle of pills. Grace handed her a fresh bottle of water and she tipped the water into her mouth as Charles walked toward them. She turned her head away.

"Bill said you were here," Charles said and opened the door to a room to their right. "Let's use this room. Grace, will you and Bonnie find us coffee and something to eat? I'm starving." Grace made a face at AJ, but they left.

He closed the door behind them. "What the hell happened?"

AJ told the story in an even voice, surprised at the anger she still carried. She explained Ariel at Grace's, the phone call to Bill, and the restaurant. "Elena grabbed me when I came around the corner in the dark, put a gun to my head, kicked my leg. She said she'd been looking for me. And Katie too. I lost it there for a moment. Next I knew, Ariel had shot her and we were down, Elena dead, on top of me." She stared into Charles's eyes. She wanted him to feel that gun and the pain. "Then Ariel sat beside me, said she was sorry about my leg…and put her gun to my head."

Charles's eyes widened. "She put a gun to you?"

AJ tapped the tape at her temple. "One of us even shot my coat and grazed my shoulder." She held up her ruined duster. "It might have been my first shot, the one that hit her in the jaw."

Charles closed his eyes. "Christ. I never saw this coming," he said softly. "Worse, I trusted her. Believed her." He was quiet for a moment and then pulled his phone out and looked through the calls. "Not a single call from her last night." He handed her the phone. AJ checked the calls and he was right. "She was so good on her first assignments. I checked her out constantly but never caught a whiff of anything wrong." He stared over her head at the window. "I can't believe this."

AJ took a tired breath. "I'd like to know what sent her off the rails. We need to know. She was exhausted, but could it have been drugs?"

Charles picked up his phone and spoke to the ME's office. "They're working on her right now. That means we'll know most of it by tonight or tomorrow, at least have the results of the initial tox screen. Tell me again what she said."

"First of all, that she'd killed Star and her husband." Charles looked stunned as she continued. "Apparently, because she was going to rat them out to me, to us. Then, that it was her, Elena, drugs, and money. We'll probably never know about the young rookie cop or John and Kerry—unless Owen Hood and the girls in the gang have some information." She uncapped the water she'd gotten from Grace. "Charles, I'm serious. I want to know about Ariel."

He leaned on his hands. "I'll give you all the information I have. Lawrence Kelly flew in last night. When we heard the news about Ariel this morning, we were just shocked. Nothing in her history pointed to anything like this. She reminded us of you, Allison. Same good, quick instincts and that uncanny ability to blend. Damn, she was just a kid."

"Old enough to kill." She looked away.

"Well, hell, another cluster fuck." He frowned at her.

"We have to do better than this. You should have told me about Ariel. We could have used her. It might have saved her life if I'd have gotten to her in the beginning. If not me, someone who stayed close, like you always did when I was out there."

The knock at the door stopped them both. Grace and Bonnie came in with sandwiches and Bill followed with coffee.

Charles immediately changed the subject. "Bill, we're setting up a plan that includes a position for Grace to run a small college force for a three-county area, stop these kids from smurfing the local pharmacies or anything else you can find. Bonnie will work with Grace as we integrate her into this group."

Bill gave him a wry smile. "Charles, we need good cops too."

"We have an idea for you, Bill," Charles said. "Something else. Lawrence Kelly will keep all of you away from this mess, but he'll need to talk to everyone."

AJ breathed a sigh of relief and took a sandwich as Charles turned to her.

"Allison, even though you're off the streets for a couple of weeks, we've made space for you at the station so you'll find your office is now upstairs by Bill's. I want to work with you and your group as we develop a plan for those suppliers. Get in touch with everyone and have them come in and see you, one-on-one. Then we're sitting everyone down until the plan's in place."

AJ took a cup of coffee. "One last question. Does anyone know what was wrong with Michael? Everyone said he wasn't violent, but look what he did to Seraph."

Charles cleared his throat. "That was Ariel. That energy drink Michael loved? She put just enough meth in it every day to keep him off his game."

"Meth? You have to be kidding me." AJ stared at him. "That's murky, but Ariel gave us Seraph because of that, although she sure as hell didn't mean to."

Charles nodded. "Next up for all of you, Michael's parents will be at the Howell Street Station in three hours. The parents want to send his body back to Kansas for a proper burial and pick up Seraph's child. Allison, meet with them and use Bill's office. Bill, go to Seraph's apartment, bring her down here so we can start the intake process and so Lawrence Kelly can meet with her. Take the child to your office so that Michael's parents can take her." He took another sandwich off the tray.

"I want you to see our latest figures." Charles took some papers out of his briefcase and handed them all a single sheet. "Look at the latest stats. Meth use in the U.S. is up over sixty percent in the last fourteen months, but illegal prescription drugs are ahead of that. Makes no difference what part of law enforcement we're in, we're all going to be very busy."

AJ finished her sandwich, then realized she'd had no idea what she'd just eaten. Roast beef? The ghost of a gun against her temple slithered across her skin, raising goose bumps. She asked to be excused for a moment.

She leaned on the window ledge in the hall. Dead criminals. Dead addicts. Dead rogue agents. Right now, she felt close to dead herself. She was tired of being "on" all the time. Truthfully, after 9/11, there wasn't a person in law enforcement that was truly off duty any more.

She looked down at the blood on her clothes. Michael's parents didn't need to see that. She'd have to change clothes.

She stared out the window at the church next door. The fragile spring sky and sunlight caught a stained glass window. Colors sprayed out across patches of snow. She checked to make sure her phone was on and brought up Katie's photo. She thought again of how they'd left each other yesterday. What if Katie turned away? That made her feel empty inside. Could she take one more inch of—nothing?

Bonnie came out of the room with AJ's coffee and leaned against the wall beside her.

"So I'll be staying here with Grace. What about Katie?"

AJ took a drink of the coffee and held up her phone, and the photo of Katie.

"I took a good picture, didn't I? Bonnie said, studying the photo. "Do something about this. I know it's going to be a mess for a few weeks, but don't lose her."

AJ took a big breath. "Zack may have been too much for her. She may want to lose me."

"Nah, she's tough. Anyone that survives Lu has to be, and don't give me any crap. I know you care. I've watched you two. She was paying attention, all the time. I've never seen her do that, even with Lu."

AJ looked back at the hopeful colors on the patchy snow. "Let's go change clothes. I need to run one more quick errand before we go to Bill's office."

❖

In the dream, Katie was held by a woman she trusted with all her heart. Desperately happy, the bed rocked her gently as her mind tried to climb into consciousness. A soft mouth grazed her cheek, and she smiled but couldn't open her eyes.

"You smell good, feel even better," AJ whispered against her ear.

Katie gave a loopy little sigh, loving the dream.

"I'm on my way somewhere, but I'll be back. If you want me." Fingers and lips brushed across her bare shoulders. "Sleep," she heard as the bed shifted.

Hours later, when she finally did wake, Katie reached for the warm body and hands that had touched her earlier. Or had it been only a dream? Shocked that it was afternoon, she tossed the covers back and headed for the shower.

The warm water on her face woke her. After she stepped out, she glanced at the mirror and saw the paper still taped there. She pulled it off and read it again, then she looked around the room. The bathroom was so clean that the emptiness hit her all over again. It *was* just a dream.

Disgusted, she threw the note in the trash and took her flannel pajamas, the ones with the little rabbits all over them, off the back of the door, dressed, and combed her hair. She stared at the trash can. Finally, she retrieved the paper and headed for the kitchen. Her stomach growled. She'd eat something and go back to bed. The house was too quiet. Worse, it was lonely. All the long years with Lu, and now this.

When she was almost to the table, she stopped and blinked. A large bouquet of French lilacs shone in the afternoon sunlight. She began to smile but felt sudden tears in her eyes as she thought of Zack on the cement at the bank.

She smoothed AJ's crumpled note out on the table. It was just too much. All the fear of the past few weeks rushed inward and she slumped over the table, on top of the note, and began to cry in earnest.

CHAPTER THIRTY

Despite her painful leg, AJ stood when Grace brought Michael's parents into Bill's office. "I'm sorry for your loss," she said as she shook hands with them. Decades of hard work in the sun, rain, and wind marked their open faces and sunburned arms, just as it did her adoptive parents. She swallowed hard, thinking of her parents, and helped Grace and Bonnie with the coffee to keep herself distracted for a moment.

It was a difficult conversation, but she answered every question she could, watching the shock play across their faces as they listened to the tracks of Michael's double life in Milwaukee. AJ avoided as much personal detail as possible, weaving current drug problems into her words, but Michael's mother's eyes never lost their tears.

They were about done when Bill arrived with Seraph's child. Shy, the little blond girl hid against Bill, but Michael's mother gently coaxed her onto her lap.

"Are you leaving for Kansas from here?" AJ turned to Michael's father.

"Yes," he said. "We've already taken care of...the other arrangements." He smiled at Meredith. "And this little girl will be just fine."

When they'd gone, everyone was silent. Bill put his coat on, his face tired, drawn. "See all of you tomorrow," he said and was out the door before any of them could answer.

"I'm tired and damn, still hungry." Grace spoke first. "Come with us to my place. I'll make breakfast for everyone."

A wet, light snow had begun to fall as they left the station. AJ stretched her leg out in the back of Grace's car, leaned against the door, and closed her eyes. Her mind flipped through a slideshow of Michael's parents, how kind they'd been with Seraph's little girl. It was the first time she'd seen the child. That had been worth it, finding her, getting her to the family where she belonged.

Exhausted, she tried to get comfortable.

The girls talked in the front seat. Bonnie's jacket rustled as she turned to look at AJ.

"Is she asleep?" Grace said.

"I think so. See the big pine tree at the corner?"

"The one that still has a Christmas ornament on it? It's March. What's that about?" AJ could hear the smile in her voice.

"Make a right turn there instead of going left toward your place."

"But it's the quickest way home," Grace said.

"Humor me. I've got an idea."

AJ smiled as she listened. A little humor right now would be a good thing. She'd give anything to be back in Katie's big bed, but the chances felt slim to none. When she'd been there earlier, Katie hadn't even woken up. She rested her head on her crossed arms and fell asleep.

❖

Katie dried her eyes and opened her refrigerator. "Come on, Blackburn. You'll feel better when you eat," she said, then glanced out at the living room. Had her words echoed in the empty house? The place felt as if it was caving in on itself.

The refrigerator was a disaster. There were leftovers crammed everywhere. She propped the door open with the garbage can, tossing things into it. As hungry as she was, nothing looked good. It reminded her of the last few days and she was trying very hard not to think of that. She tossed cheese into a pan with a splash of milk then turned the stove on low. A cheese-based soup would be a good beginning. She added some chopped broccoli, some garlic, a different cheese, and more milk. The bread in the freezer sounded good, and she put it in the microwave to thaw.

Music would keep the silence away, but when she hit the button above the sink, her own violin began to play. "What the—where did someone find this?" She examined the disc, then put it back and hit PLAY again. Because of Lu, she'd refused to listen to this after that competition in Madison. "Stupid," she said into the messy refrigerator. That part of her life was done.

Only one onion looked salvageable. "If that part of my life is done, what's ahead of me?" She stared down at the onion in her hands, the skin crinkling in her fingers as she held it. "Mom was right. As long as I'm around AJ, it's going to be more of…this. Worry and fear. Is this a step backward?" She gestured out to the empty house.

Why couldn't she find an average person to fall in love with? Someone who'd be home every night, and there wouldn't be drugs or alcohol. Or someone who didn't carry a gun. She should end this now. She looked down at the pan, suddenly desperately sad, and began to peel the onion.

"I've never remotely come close to an all-purpose soup like this." She began to add onion to the concoction.

Finally, she left the soup to itself and rummaged in her bag for the new contract, then laid it on the table beside the flowers. The contract lifted her heart a little. She hummed along with the music just as the doorbell rang.

"Shit," she said under her breath. "That's probably Mom, or one of the sisters." They'd want to know why she'd been out of touch and then be all horrified over Zack so she'd have to go through all of that again. Worse—they'd make fun of her soup.

She took the bag out of the garbage, tied it, and carried it to the door.

"Hi," Bonnie said. Katie was so surprised that she held out the garbage bag. "Where do you want this?" Bonnie tied the bag one more time and jumped off the porch to the driveway.

Katie pointed. "There, the big blue garbage can beside the garage."

"Anything else?"

Katie shook her head. "Thanks, I'm barefoot. I thought you were Mom or one of my sisters." She looked at the car and Grace waved. "Why is Grace still in the car? Where's AJ? Come in, I'm making soup, or something."

"Could I speak to you inside, alone?" Bonnie's serious expression made Katie uneasy.

Katie reached for Bonnie. "Nothing's happened to AJ?"

"She's asleep in the backseat of the car." Bonnie shut the door behind her. "Would it be okay if we left her here?"

Katie took a deep, relieved breath. "Why?"

"AJ has this weird idea that you would just as soon she'd be somewhere else."

"Where would she get that idea?"

"It had something to do with you, when she and Grace left the hospital yesterday."

"I was so out of it that I don't even remember what I said." She put her hands on her hips. "Where were all of you last night?"

"Charles ordered us out of here. She stayed with Grace, but listen, AJ's not in very good shape. I wasn't with them last night, but she got tossed around some...and other things."

"Tossed around?"

"Her leg's not very good. She may have done more damage to it. Uh, Katie, I try to stay out of your business, but AJ is the most loyal person I've ever known, generous, cute, fun to talk to, and I hear she likes to dance. But she's a loner and all she does is work. You're the first woman I've seen her give more than just a glance and..."

"You sound like you're selling a car." Katie raised her eyebrow. "The answer's no, as long as she has a safe place to stay," she said and turned Bonnie's shoulders to the door.

Bonnie turned back. "You *are* mad. She was right."

"No, I'm not *mad*. I'm just not going to put myself into another situation where the woman I love is always gone and always in danger. And I'm constantly worried and afraid." Katie opened her door and firmly shoved Bonnie forward. Then she saw AJ, out of the car, standing in the light snow. When she raised her head, Katie pulled in a breath. The bandage and scratches on AJ's face said a lot, but the way she stood—Bonnie may have been right about her leg. Was that blood in her hair by the bandage?

"What happened to you?" she called out as Bonnie went down the steps.

"A long night. Do you have coffee?" AJ looked drained.

Katie said nothing for a moment, then said, "Of course. Come on in, all of you."

Bonnie shook her head. "We're on our way somewhere."

"I'll give her a ride home," Katie said and stepped aside for AJ, closing the door behind her.

"You're wearing bunnies?"

"My pajamas? Go ahead, make fun of them, but they're comfortable," Katie said as she stirred the soup, added a little more milk, and took the bread out of the microwave. She turned for another look at the whiskey-colored, button-down shirt, khaki pants, and brown boots. "I like that color on you. How did you manage to get those pants over the wrap?"

AJ took her usual place at the table and yawned. "Grace and Bonnie. Also, the doctor has a smaller wrap on it. It's healing. And thank you for that. The doctor asked about you."

Katie poured coffee for AJ. "I'm experimenting with leftovers for a soup. Want to try some with me?"

"You know me, always hungry. We ate Chinese here, last night, and listened to that music you've got on now. You play beautiful music."

Katie pointed at the bouquet. "Thank you for the flowers. You were here earlier, weren't you?"

"You didn't even wake up."

"When I did wake up, I thought I had dreamed you—until I saw the flowers."

"I wasn't sure you'd want anyone here at your house."

"Yes," Katie said and took a whisk to the soup.

"Yes? You did or—"

"I don't know what I wanted. There was all this white noise in my head. All I could think of was getting away from guns, blood, that racket at the bank."

"How is Zack?"

"When I left this morning, everyone was optimistic. I'll call his brother after we eat." Katie poured soup into each of their bowls. "Milk?" she said as she got two glasses out of the cupboard. "Are you due for pills?"

"Crap...my coat pocket."

Katie stepped down into the living room, headed for the closet. "Have you taken any, today?" She held up AJ's duster. "My God, what happened to your coat?"

"It got shot." AJ said as if it were too ordinary to discuss. "The doctor changed the dose on the pain pills." She rubbed her face. "Dr. Light's not going to be very happy. My leg's a mess."

"It got shot?" Katie stared at her. When AJ added nothing, she sat down instead, held up a spoonful of the soup, plunged ahead, and took a taste. "It's funky but good." She grinned at AJ but her smile faded. The late afternoon sun streamed through the flowers onto AJ's hair, turning it into dull gold. There *was* blood in her hair.

"It's good. Tastes like squash with cheese."

"I'm shocked we're able to eat it." Katie took another spoonful, still checking out AJ's appearance. "Bonnie said you went to Grace's, last night?"

"Charles sent us."

"Why'd he do that?"

"It's complicated." AJ took another spoonful of soup. "Katie, I need to talk."

"I do too," Katie said. "So you stayed at Grace's?"

"No...yes...I went to sleep there but had to get up and leave."

Katie felt there was probably much more. AJ's hand holding the spoon was shaking. She was just hanging on. "You need sleep." She said the words softly.

"I got a few hours. We wrapped everything up last night." AJ ate more and cleared her throat. "Michael's dead and some other people were killed. That part of the operation's over."

"Killed?" Katie heard her own voice rise, but AJ was quiet. "You people talk so matter-of-factly. If you could hear how that sounds. 'Some other people were killed.'"

"We don't take it matter-of-factly, but we talk that way. I know we do. Sometimes we even laugh about inappropriate things."

"Tell me what's going on. You said you need to talk?"

"I'm in an odd place right now." AJ slumped a little further. "Could I tell you the whole thing my way? Promise not to freak out until I get done?"

"I know your job's dangerous."

"But it's also unpredictable, and I think the *unpredictable* is as dangerous as a gun." She took a drink of milk and stared at Katie for another quiet moment. "You're new for me. I want to tell you everything and I don't know why. I've never had to deal with a person like you."

Katie saw AJ's eyes glisten, got up immediately, and put her arm around her shoulders. AJ stiffened, then relaxed. Katie held her against her own body, kissed her thick black lashes, and tasted salty tears. "You need to sleep, but I think I should wash the blood out of your hair first. We'll talk later." Katie took her hand. "Your doctor says I am to take care of you, so let's go."

Katie opened the cupboard in the bathroom and laid out clean wraps.

"Where did you get those?" AJ said.

"The doctor," Katie said and turned on the shower. "It's what I've been using all week."

They stood together under the water as if they'd done it a thousand times. Katie scanned AJ's body. "My God, the bruises. I don't know where to touch you." She carefully washed AJ's hair, but somewhere between the soap and tender care, she stopped, blindsided by fierce desire. She looked up into AJ's eyes that mirrored the same emotions. "What are we—" she started to say just as AJ folded her into her body with a deep sigh.

Eyes closed, Katie smiled into AJ's wet skin. "You need to go to bed." She turned off the shower, wrapped them in huge towels, and helped AJ into the bed. "Be careful of your leg. Wait a minute.

Maybe I should wrap it before…your face, your shoulder…that looks awful." Katie leaned closer to examine the temple then the left shoulder.

"Don't go." AJ reached but Katie quickly moved.

"If I get in bed with you, I'll never get to the wraps or bandages." But by the time Katie got back to the bed, AJ had crashed. She never moved as Katie wrapped the leg carefully, then bandaged the wound on her head and shoulder. Katie examined small scars, nicks, and newly forming bruises. Every part of her wanted to wake her. Instead, she went to the kitchen, cleaned the dishes, and brought pills and water back to the bedroom. She crawled into bed, but when she reached across AJ to turn out the light, she paused. There was no way she could walk away from this woman. Finally, she held AJ's face against her, scared to death. *Keep her alive for me.* She laid a hand on the lean belly, stretched against her, and closed her eyes.

CHAPTER THIRTY-ONE

The cold metal pushed into her head, harder and harder and...all that blood... AJ was freezing but sweating, and her heart pounded with fear just as Ariel took her last breath. "The hell," she said, struggling to breathe, not to gag. She tried to move but couldn't. She opened her eyes and looked into silver eyes above her. Katie's warm hands held her face.

"What's wrong?" Katie whispered. "Are you all right?"

"A nightmare." AJ pulled in a breath as Katie leaned over her to see the clock. Warm breasts brushed her own and AJ clenched. So much was at stake. This felt almost as dangerous as that gun. One touch, sometimes only a look, from Katie resonated through her like sunlight. No one-night stand here. This had *for real* written all over it.

"I'm sorry I woke you." She traced Katie's chin and ran her fingers down the soft skin to her breast. "Go back to sleep."

"Ahhh," Katie murmured. "Won't sleep if you do that." She pushed herself up onto an elbow. "Does your leg hurt?"

"No. Just a bad dream."

"Then tell me. It'll help the nightmares." Katie's arm slipped under and around her, and she tugged her close. "Talk to me."

"When we left here and went to Grace's, you were at the hospital with Zack. The woman from the farm, the one that hurt my leg, came for me. Said she was looking for Charles." AJ kissed the palm of Katie's hand. "This is confusing, so stay with me. When she injured my leg, I didn't know that she was a federal undercover agent."

"She was law enforcement?"

"By the time she came to Grace's, I knew who she was. We drove her to a restaurant where the girls were having a party, the women we've been tracking. I called Bill and he got the police, the SWAT team."

Katie sat up and put a pillow behind herself and one behind AJ.

"None of us knew that she'd turned, gone bad. I found it out just before I shot her, and by shot, I mean as in kill."

"You killed her?" Katie sat up and stared at her.

"I've shot people, wounded them, but I've never killed anyone." She told Katie about Elena in the alley and what Ariel had said, the last second of her life.

Katie started to speak but then was quiet for such a long time that AJ glanced anxiously at her. Finally, she said, "No wonder you had a nightmare."

"Have you ever been around someone that's dying?"

"Yes, I gave my father CPR until the ambulance arrived, not that it did any good, and I held his hand. I know it's not the same thing, but the end result is the same." Katie got out of bed. "I'm going to get us something to drink." She turned on the nightlight as she left.

AJ pushed herself up in the bed. Should she have said anything?

Katie returned with a short, fat crystal glass. "Here," she said, "take a sip."

The drink was sweet, mixed with a bite. "What is it?"

"Jack and juice, my favorite when I have a tough day. And you've had several of those." Katie played with the WWED bracelet AJ still wore, her curly hair a halo in the night-light's faint flame. "Go on. I know there's more."

"When I was on the cement in the alley, I thought I saw the flowers I gave you." AJ looked up at Katie, half expecting her to laugh or at least disbelieve her.

Katie sipped the drink then handed the glass to AJ. "You thought you saw my flowers?"

"I probably shouldn't have told you all of that, should I?"

"I'm scared and angry that someone tried to kill, you but I'm thankful you're here, with me, in my bed. Do you think I'm disgusted?"

"No…yes. I don't know what I think." AJ felt the weight she'd been carrying begin to shift. "It's what I said. I want to tell you everything. I thought you'd turn away because of my job or things like this."

Katie frowned. "You mean the constant danger? Guns, drugs, things that make me crazy? You're right, I don't like it, but it's part of your job. Part of you."

"That and the fact that I have no time to call my own, let alone any for you."

Katie sighed, quiet again for so long that AJ braced herself for the worst. Finally, Katie leaned close to AJ's face. "Did you ever just…know?"

"Know?" AJ's stomach tightened.

"Am I in bed with the wrong woman?" Katie said and ran her hands down the inside of AJ's thighs. "Because I swear, I knew. The minute you introduced yourself at the police station, I knew. That's never happened to me before. And if something had happened to you or you had left, I would have always known. The truth is, I can't stay away from you."

A little magic crept into the room, warm and intimate. AJ touched Katie's face. "That first night? You were adorable and that crazy, curious mind. I think I loved you from that first glance, and I've never believed that is possible."

"Love. What a beautiful word." Katie set the glass on the bedside table. "Let me show you what else I know." She stretched partially across AJ. "I'd better get used to trying to figure out how to do this around bruises and bandages." She lay carefully on top of her. "Does this hurt?"

"You don't weigh anything," AJ said, already aroused. Her breath hitched.

"Enough for you to know I'm here," Katie said, then kissed her. AJ smelled summer and tasted bourbon. Katie's hair fell over her face, a wet, hot mouth trailed across her jaw, traced her collarbone, stopped at the breast. Helpless with need, AJ made a small sound.

"Don't move," Katie whispered against her skin. "I won't hurt you, but I'm going to love you again, somehow. Lord, I want to touch you." Katie's voice trembled as she cupped AJ's breast and grazed her nipple with her teeth. Her fingers caressed her stomach and tracked down across the hips.

Katie was taking her time and AJ urged her on. "Don't stop."

AJ gripped Katie's hips and slid her leg between Katie's. Pleasure moved across her skin, out to the ends of her fingers. It had been a long time since anyone had touched her simply because they wanted to. She whimpered as Katie's warm mouth kissed her hip, and fingers slid into the wet warmth between her legs. AJ rocked them until they drew apart and she simmered on the edge. She somehow held herself together, waiting until she felt Katie begin, then let herself go with a low moan. It was all she could do to breathe and her ears rang. Katie collapsed on top of her, between her breasts, and AJ felt her hands on her hips, hard. She'd just left everything on Katie's body and, hopefully, her heart.

"You need more rest and…more of me," Katie murmured with a happy sigh, curled into AJ, warm and close.

AJ tightened her arms around the fragile bones and soft skin. "Sleep with me," AJ said and closed her eyes.

❖

Deep peace and sunlight on her face warmed AJ when she woke.

Wearing only a smile, Katie perched on the bed beside her with a cup of coffee. AJ reached, but sore muscles stopped her. "Stupid body," she said.

"Not stupid. It's gorgeous." Katie held out the cup to AJ. "I may have added a few of those bruises last night. Not sure." Her amused eyes were sparkling and sexy. "Did you dream?"

"No, thank God."

Katie stretched out beside her. "I'm glad you're here."

"Thank you for saying that." AJ's voice cracked a little. Katie pulled AJ closer and they were quiet, breathing together. AJ slowly rubbed Katie's arm that held her.

"Katie, was what I said too much last night? Is there more you want to say?"

"I thought I was eloquent."

AJ laughed a little and kissed Katie's smiling mouth. "You were."

"Then, what?"

"That Bren Black series, your books? Most of the time she's undercover, and some is based on fact. It's what I always did, until this assignment."

Katie lifted her head with a surprised look. "See, I was right. You really were a spook." She began to laugh.

AJ grinned, reaching for her but forgot her leg. A sudden jolt of pain ran through her and Katie sat up immediately.

"I saw that. You need pills and we need to call your doctor." Out of bed in a quick movement, she held out a hand and got AJ up. Katie held her tightly, wordlessly for a moment before handing her the crutches. "I'll fix breakfast while you clean up. Let's see, you need something to wear. Damn, I only have one other pair of pajamas that'll go over your leg. They don't have bunnies on them but…" She held them up.

"Naked women, painted on…is that black silk?" AJ said. "Do I want to know where these came from?" She examined the clothing. "The women look like you."

"Never mind," Katie said as she helped AJ into the pajamas. "You left your toothbrush here, in the bathroom."

AJ looked down at herself. "Why not just a T-shirt and underwear?"

"It's your call, but if you're here, someone else will be here too. There's always people that need you."

They met at the kitchen table as Katie cooked. Low music played in the background, and AJ's stomach rumbled at the smell of bacon. She rubbed her stomach, examining the pajamas again. A lock inside her clicked open and something comfortable settled as Katie plated the eggs and poured orange juice, then milk. Katie's body matched, even in bunny pajamas. The breasts fit the shoulders and hips, all held together gracefully by those delicate bones. Those capable hands. AJ grinned. Those hands were capable in the bedroom too.

"What?" Katie said with a smile. "You don't like wearing naked ladies?"

"Bonnie called you hot…sexy."

"Now *that's* a good friend, but how would she know anyway?" Katie's face colored and she narrowed her eyes. "You're thinking about last night, aren't you?"

"Bonnie's right." AJ grinned at Katie's flushed face and began to eat as her phone chirped with a text message. AJ read the words from Charles. "Read your e-mail. Get rest. Monday at the office." She showed it to Katie and they grinned across the table.

"He's giving me time off, but damn, my laptop's at Grace's," AJ said just as the doorbell rang. Grace and Bonnie were there with AJ's things.

"Charles called, looking for you," Grace said to AJ. "When I told him that we left you here, he laughed and said you'd need your laptop. We all have a little time off."

AJ opened her e-mails. There were two from Charles and an official department e-mail from Lawrence Kelly. Charles's first e-mail informed her that her office was ready and he'd see her Monday morning. The second was a forward, the ME's results on Ariel. AJ immediately felt the jolt of nerves as she opened the file.

"Here's news on Ariel," AJ said and felt her heart thud, hard. She studied the preliminary tox screen. "It *was* drugs and lots of them. My God, I'm amazed she was able to function." She hit Save and hid behind a drink of coffee, trying to stay steady. "Grace, when you take on your new assignment, we're going to study Ariel and find out what went wrong. Whatever happened to her may give you a lot of information."

She opened the official department e-mail. "Well, I'm stunned," she finally said. "They're sending Charles to Missouri to try to do something with that situation, so he can concentrate on just one state. And me?" Everyone looked at her expectantly. "I just got a promotion. I'll take Charles's position here, reporting directly to Lawrence Kelly, but I'll still work with Bill at the police station. And I have a new office, right next to Bill. The next part of the operation will include more people, and it'll be boots on the ground, girls. When you come in to see me in a one-on-one, I'll lay out what they've proposed." She pointed at Grace and Bonnie. "I'm still your boss."

Grace merely raised her eyebrows and took several pictures in rapid succession with her phone. "Yes, you are, but…" She grinned. "I'll be the only one of your underlings that will have photos of you wearing naked lady pajamas."

❖

AJ called her doctor while Grace and Bonnie were still there and made an appointment to see her, later in the afternoon. After they left, Katie made some phone calls while AJ took a shower. She talked to Zack's brother, and the news was all good. Zack would be out of ICU tomorrow and into a regular room. Best of all, he wasn't going to lose a kidney. A couple more days and they could take him home. Katie grabbed a notepad to write down the calls and checked in with her own secretary who sounded very relieved to hear from her. They talked about Zack and then sorted through the phone calls.

Next, she dialed the number David Markam had left when he called her secretary and wrote his name on the pad. He immediately asked about Zack's condition and then suggested a lunch. Katie agreed, scribbled the time and day on her paper. He'd assured her that the contract was still good despite their "setback." She shook her head slightly. *Setback?* She was certain of one thing. The contract with Benning's would open doors that had always been closed to her, and her Blue Ridge, Inc. was going to take off like a rocket in the next few years. She heard the shower shut off and got up to help AJ.

❖

Later that afternoon, after seeing AJ's doctor, they saw Zack for a few minutes, then stood outside in the hospital parking lot, enjoying the sunny but cool spring day.

"Is there anything you'd like to do?" AJ said with a broad smile. Katie smiled too. She liked the laugh lines around AJ's eyes.

"The doctor wasn't happy, but she was very specific. You need to get off that leg."

"I know, but there's something I want to do. Didn't you say you had wanted to celebrate your contract? I think we should do that. What was the place? A club on the lake?"

"The Blue Pelican." She grinned as she helped AJ into the car.

"I need to go to my apartment for more clothes, and we have to eat. Let me take you out for a nice dinner. A few hours won't make any difference to this leg. Tonight, could we watch one of your *Mummy* movies. You've got my favorite. Maybe you'll scream and I can save you. Or call on Bren Black to save us both."

Katie shook her head. "I'm not going to keep you in bed, am I?" She'd seen AJ's reaction to that e-mail this morning. There was work to be done.

"I'm hoping for some quality time in that bed with you, but I really do need some different clothes, not to mention a different coat. Oh, and there's a family photo I want you to see."

Katie held out her hands as if defeated. "Okay, I suppose if I don't do what you want, you'll just pull your gun. Besides, I love that restaurant. We'll have a clear sky tonight, and it's the best place in town to see the moon come up. Come on, sweetie."

"Sweetie?" AJ repeated with a wide grin. "I don't think anyone's ever called me that."

"Get used to it," Katie said with a very deep breath. It was exactly what she'd wanted. To get used to everything about AJ. And it was spring, a perfect time for new beginnings.

About the Author

Born in Wisconsin and raised in Iowa, C. P. Rowlands attended college in Iowa and lived in the southwest and on the West Coast before returning to Wisconsin. She is an artist in addition to having worked in radio, sales, and various other jobs before retirement. She has two children, four grandchildren, a partner of twenty-three years, plus two huge cats. She loves to fish, camp, walk, and read but most of all, writing is where it all comes together.

Books Available From Bold Strokes Books

Month of Sundays by Yolanda Wallace. Love doesn't always happen overnight; sometimes it takes a month of Sundays. (978-1-60282-739-4)

Jacob's War by C.P. Rowlands. ATF Special Agent Allison Jacob's task force is in the middle of an all-out war, from the streets to the boardrooms of America. Small business owner Katie Blackburn is the latest victim who accidentally breaks it wide open but may break AJ's heart at the same time. (978-1-60282-740-0)

The Pyramid Waltz by Barbara Ann Wright. Princess Katya Nar Umbriel wants a perfect romance, but her Fiendish nature and duties to the crown mean she can never tell the truth-until she meets Starbride, a woman who gets to the heart of every secret, even if it will be the death of her. (978-1-60282-741-7)

The Secret of Othello by Sam Cameron. Florida teen detectives Steven and Denny risk their lives to search for a sunken NASA satellite-but under the waves, no one can hear you scream . . . (978-1-60282-742-4)

Dreaming of Her by Maggie Morton. Isa has begun to dream of the most amazing woman—a woman named Lilith with a gorgeous face, an amazing body, and the ability to turn Isa on like no other. But Lilith is just a dream...isn't she? (978-1-60282-847-6)

Andy Squared by Jennifer Lavoie. Andrew never thought anyone could come between him and his twin sister, Andrea...until Ryder rode into town. (978-1-60282-743-1)

Finding Bluefield by Elan Barnehama. Set in the backdrop of Virginia and New York and spanning the years 1960-1982, Finding Bluefield chronicles the lives of Nicky Stewart, Barbara Philips, and their son, Paul, as they struggle to define themselves as a family. (978-1-60282-744-8)

The Jetsetters by David-Matthew Barnes. As rock band The Jetsetters skyrocket from obscurity to super stardom, Justin Holt, a lonely barista, and Diego Delgado, the band's guitarist, fight with everything they have to stay together, despite the chaos and fame. (978-1-60282-745-5)

Strange Bedfellows by Rob Byrnes. Partners in life and crime, Grant Lambert and Chase LaMarca, are hired to make a politician's compromising photo disappear, but what should be an easy job quickly spins out of control. (978-1-60282-746-2)

Speed Demons by Gun Brooke. When NASCAR star Evangeline Marshall returns to the race track after a close brush with death, will famous photographer Blythe Pierce document her triumph and reciprocate her love—or will they succumb to their respective demons and fail? (978-1-60282-678-6)

Summoning Shadows: A Rosso Lussuria Vampire Novel by Winter Pennington. The Rosso Lussuria vampires face enemies both old and new, and to prevail they must call on even more strange alliances, unite as a clan, and draw on every weapon within their reach—but with a clan of vampires, that's easier said than done. (978-1-60282-679-3)

Sometime Yesterday by Yvonne Heidt. When Natalie Chambers learns her Victorian house is haunted by a pair of lovers and a Dark Man, can she and her lover Van Easton solve the mystery that will set the ghosts free and banish the evil presence in the house? Or will they have to run to survive as well? (978-1-60282-680-9)

Into the Flames by Mel Bossa. In order to save one of his patients, psychiatrist Jamie Scarborough will have to confront his own monsters—including those he unknowingly helped create. (978-1-60282-681-6)

Coming Attractions: Author's Edition by Bobbi Marolt. For Helen Townsend, chasing turns to caring, and caring turns to loving, but will love take five steps back and turn to leaving? (978-1-60282-732-5)

OMGqueer, edited by Radclyffe and Katherine E. Lynch. Through stories imagined and told by youth across America, this anthology provides a snapshot of queerness at the dawn of the new millennium. (978-1-60282-682-3)

Oath of Honor by Radclyffe. A First Responders novel. First do no harm…First Physician of the United States Wes Masters discovers that being the president's doctor demands more than brains and personal sacrifice—especially when politics is the order of the day. (978-1-60282-671-7)

A Question of Ghosts by Cate Culpepper. Becca Healy hopes Dr. Joanne Call can help her learn if her mother really committed suicide—but she's not sure she can handle her mother's ghost, a decades-old mystery, and lusting after the difficult Dr. Call without some serious chocolate consumption. (978-1-60282-672-4)

The Night Off by Meghan O'Brien. When Emily Parker pays for a taboo role-playing fantasy encounter from the Xtreme Encounters escort agency, she expects to surrender control—but never imagines losing her heart to dangerous butch Nat Swayne. (978-1-60282-673-1)

Sara by Greg Herren. A mysterious and beautiful new student at Southern Heights High School stirs things up when students start dying. (978-1-60282-674-8)

Fontana by Joshua Martino. Fame, obsession, and vengeance collide in a novel that asks: What if America's greatest hero was gay? (978-1-60282-675-5)

Lemon Reef by Robin Silverman. What would you risk for the memory of your first love? When Jenna Ross learns her high school love Del Soto died on Lemon Reef, she refuses to accept the medical examiner's report of a death from natural causes and risks everything to find the truth. (978-1-60282-676-2)

The Dirty Diner: Gay Erotica on the Menu, edited by Jerry L. Wheeler. Gay erotica set in restaurants, featuring food, sex, and men—could you really ask for anything more? (978-1-60282-677-9)

Sweat: Gay Jock Erotica by Todd Gregory. Sizzling tales of smoking hot sex with the athletic studs everyone fantasizes about. (978-1-60282-669-4)